DRAGON'S BREATH

by

Stephen T. Gerdel

Dragon's Breath

Book Three
The Oak Mountain Trilogy
Second Edition

By
Stephen T. Gerdel

Published by
Watershed Inc.
524 Olympus
Cedar Hill, TX 75104
www.watershedarts.com

Edited by Bethany Swoboda

Cover design by Katy Tapley

ISBN 978-0-9814541-4-6

DRAGON'S BREATH

BOOK THREE

The Oak Mountain Trilogy

by

Stephen T. Gerdel

List of Main Characters

Reggie Porter	Town drunk and future mayor of Lakeside, OR
Al Makin	President of the United States of America
Mike Trapper	Chief of Staff for the president
Elli Trapper	Mike's wife
Mark Strattmann	Lieutenant leading patrol in Los Angeles, CA
Aaron Stevens	Colonel in command of OCT Little Rock
Robert Hitchens	Former Navy Seal, volunteer in Oklahoma City
Jim Parker	Lieutenant sniper with Frisco national guard unit
Will Minks	Sergeant spotter with Frisco national guard unit
Gene Westrup	Brigadier general commanding Camp Pendleton
Perry Hitchens	Cleveland County, TX sheriff / Robert's father
Steven Granger	Special agent attached to the president
Samantha Long	State Department munitions expert
Rick Johnston	Secret Service agent Washington DC
George Raker	Secret Service agent Washington DC
Matt Kreiter	Special agent for emergency response, St. Louis
Jon Michaels	Sergeant major, security chief Camp Pendleton
Bob Prescott	Marine captain/ psychiatrist at Camp Pendleton
Caleb Hamza	Muslim Chaplin at Camp Pendleton
Zu Cheng	Colonel, 1st Paratrooper Brigade, People's Army
Wang Shang yi Ho	Lieutenant general of the People's Army
Woo Liang	Corporal in People's Army
Alvaro Herrera	Invading colonel East Los Angeles, CA
Tom Crawford	Lt colonel Army Rangers, Oklahoma City, OK
Bill Ketcham	Director of Secret Service, Washington DC
Wang Zhu	Chinese ambassador to the United States
Deng Hê	Lieutenant General of the People's Army

This book is dedicated
To my best friend
And beloved wife,

Jan

who is still my
best friend.

chapter 1

Marty Connors needed a smoke. His eyes were tired from the monitors at his workstation, and scanning a distant horizon would ease the strain. He stepped out of the building and closed the door, leaving the noise and activity behind him. He lit a cigarette and inhaled deeply.

Outside it was still cold. Marty loved the cold. As a kid, he would run and play in the snow wearing only a light jacket. His mother scolded him that he would catch his death of pneumonia. But he never did. He was simply built for the cold.

Then, there was darkness. He was a night person. Marty found himself the most productive and active during the night. When all around him was quiet, he was amazed at what he accomplished. His mind was focused and creative when there was little to distract him. Sleeping all day created problems only for the people at the school he was supposed to attend. It had never bothered Marty.

The job at Clear AFS, Alaska, had sounded to him like a dream come true. Alaska was cold most of the time and never hot. It was also dark for a good part of the year. When the sun came up and stayed up for five months, he could pull the curtains. It would be great. This particular night was both cold and dark. The frigid night air made his skin tingle. He felt refreshed, like jumping into a glacier-fed spring. It was exhilarating!

Marty took another drag on his cigarette and gazed across the tundra. The land stretched before him flat and desolate. A wilderness. He knew if he stood on that porch all night he would see very little wildlife, and not a single person. Perfection.

The buzzing was faint at first. He thought of the sound of lawnmowers on the next block when he was a kid in Illinois. But the buzzing grew louder . . . much louder. Something was coming at him, and it was coming fast. Marty turned around to look to the northwest, wondering if he could see it.

The plane was the biggest he'd ever seen. It roared straight at him, barely one hundred feet from the ground. Marty stood transfixed, slack-jawed and awestruck. The giant black plane swooshed past him with a thunderous roar. The concussion of air and sound almost knocked him over.

He clung to the handrail with a white-knuckled grip as the giant apparition fled southward from his sight. To the east, where the sky was slightly brighter, he saw the silhouettes of at least a dozen more aircraft. Marty quickly spun to the west and could make out the same black shapes moving through the darkness.

What the hell! he thought. *What the blinkin' hell!* Marty tossed his half-smoked cigarette to the ground and threw the door open. He rushed inside to a room filled with radar technicians who seemed oblivious to what he had just observed.

"Hey!" he yelled into the room. "Did you guys see that?" Conversation came to a sudden halt and everyone looked at Marty. "Did you see that?" he asked again.

"Well, Marty, what is it that we were supposed to see?" Tim, his supervisor asked. Marty was white as a sheet, bug-eyed, and looked totally spooked.

"You didn't see it?" he was incredulous. "I just watched the biggest plane I have ever seen fly not more than one hundred feet directly over this station, going what had to be nearly three hundred miles an hour, and you didn't see it?"

"Marty, nothing has showed up at all on the radar." As supervisor, Tim had seen it before. The isolation, the extended darkness, the bitter cold, took a toll on a man. Sometimes they cracked. He feared Marty was falling apart.

"Wait!" Marty said putting his hands up as if to ward off the doubts of the people in the room. "Just wait! I just saw, and *heard*, a huge plane fly over, and this fancy radar stuff didn't see a thing?"

"We did have that glitch a minute ago, chief." Penny came to Marty's aid.

"What do you mean 'glitch'?" Marty asked.

"Probably a sunrise anomaly we get now and then," Tim responded calmly. "You know about them, Marty. It looks like a crow flying a couple hundred miles-per-hour, and it turns out to be an echo from a satellite or the moon coming up."

"Okay, okay. Tell me then, was there more than one 'crow' flying over?" Marty asked looking a bit more wild-eyed.

"Yeah," Penny replied. "There were dozens. Why?"

"I'm telling you, they weren't *crows!*" Marty suddenly realized he sounded like a raving lunatic.

"Marty, just what are you telling us?" Tim asked, finally with sincere concern.

"Tim." Marty shook his head and swallowed hard. He turned and faced Tim square on. "Tim, an airplane just flew right over this building at close to three hundred miles per hour, not one hundred feet up. It was black, the wings had to stretch close to five hundred feet across, and the fuselage was like a long, square box. And on the underside of the wing . . ." Marty stopped and gasped. "Under the wing was a big gold star!"

Tim suddenly felt as crazy as Marty looked. He stumbled backward toward his desk and grabbed his phone. The numbers he punched in meant only one thing. DEFCON 2.

Lakeside, OR – 4:35 AM PST

His eyes simply refused to open. He wasn't sure if they were taped closed or if he had been drugged. The sounds around him were familiar but different from what he remembered before everything went black. His head felt horrible.

The first thing I need to do, he told himself, *is wake up.* But he didn't know where he was. He needed to know what had happened and why he couldn't remember anything. The pain in his head was blinding.

Maybe that's why my eyes won't open, he thought. *Maybe they've just given up on me, too.* But he still wasn't sure. He moved just a bit. His back disapproved. *What the he*—he thought. Everything hurt. *If I move again I'm gonna throw-up and die!*

He knew he couldn't stay, but wasn't sure why. He just knew he couldn't stay. They would be looking for him. He would have to be very careful because he knew they wouldn't approve. They would be on him like a duck on a June bug, and he was in no shape to deal with that.

Okay, just one eye. It was all he could manage. Through an excruciating process of incoherent thought, he selected his left eye. *Just a crack,* he thought. *Just enough to let a little light in.*

Then, he would know. It took all his effort and the small amount of concentration that was available. He forced it, and his left eyelid moved. Pain stabbed into his eye. The light was too bright.

Oh, don't do that again! He couldn't move enough to get away from the pain. His breath was shallow and labored. He clinched his teeth and the pain lessened. *Okay, I'll try it again,* he thought. *Just a little slower this time.*

Very slowly, he opened his left eye, just a bit. Between the eyelids and the lashes, he could make out the pinewood slats on the ceiling. The blades of the ceiling fan turned slowly overhead. *Oh, good. I'm not dead.* He let out a long breath and felt relief. He decided he would try both eyes, but very slowly. First, he had to make a decision. He resolved to never, absolutely never drink that much rum in such a brief time ever again. The risk was too great.

The new laws had come with the invasion. All the bars were closed and their owners shot. Anyone caught drinking, or with alcoholic beverages, was immediately shot. There were no questions asked. Drinking alcohol was no longer tolerated.

The churches were closed. No public assembly was allowed. Radio and television broadcasting was strictly controlled and only allowed during certain hours of the day. There was nothing on the broadcast that interested Americans, but TV sets were required to be on during broadcast hours. No exceptions.

Everyone worked their jobs unless they were told to go home. No reason was given; people were simply told to stop working and leave. The few incidents that had occurred were convincing enough. Everyone learned quickly to go home.

Curfews were established. No one was allowed outside after dark or before dawn. Anyone caught out during curfew was shot. Several made the attempt and paid the price.

The world had changed, and no one in Lakeside, Oregon understood why. When the invaders arrived, and killed everyone in the sheriff and police departments, the television and radio broadcasts stopped. Phones stopped working, and cell phones and internet communications were a thing of the past.

The local officials encouraged cooperation. There was no reason for anyone to be hurt or killed. Just mind your own business, they said. Leave well enough alone. In essence, shut-up and submit.

That was fine for the city officials, but several people around town resented the bars' being closed. A handful of homes held secret stashes of booze. Those who knew were the ones who cared, and they could keep a secret.

Reggie Porter found himself at risk of being caught. Not only was he too drunk to walk, he could barely open his eyes. Racked with pain, he considered staying right where he was and sleeping it off. He knew that wouldn't work. He'd stayed too late, and drank too much. He needed to be home by sunrise.

With considerable effort, and significant assistance from his friend John, Reggie made his way out the side-door of John Nelson's house. At that point, he was on his own.

It wasn't far, but Reggie felt he was taking two steps backwards or sideways for every three he went forward. He knew he was pathetic. He also knew if a patrol came by he would be finished.

He only had to make it through the town square, past the courthouse, and two blocks down North Lake Avenue to Sixth Street. Then, he was home free. He didn't remember walking ever being this difficult.

As he approached the courthouse, everything looked different. Of course, the lights were out. Street lights were no longer needed or allowed. Other than moonlight, it was dark. But it didn't look right.

As he walked, Reggie did his best to figure it out. The courthouse was there all right, but it was wavy. Then he saw the lines. He couldn't tell what they were. He got curious. Drunk and curious was a bad combination for Reggie Porter.

What the hell is that? he asked himself. The light was bad, he was drunk, and nothing made sense. As he looked at the line of objects, they seemed to be suspended in thin air. Every one of them hovered about head high. They didn't move. He could see beneath them, behind them, over and between each of them. But what the hell were they?

Reggie placed each foot firmly and deliberately on the ground, and set a course as straight as he could toward the floating objects. He didn't take his eyes off them.

"There," Reggie said out loud. "Shhhh!" he said holding his index finger to his pursed lips, and quieting everything around him with his other hand.

"There. That one," he whispered. He selected one of the objects, and pointed his finger so he would not lose it. He focused and plunged ahead.

He drew closer to the objects. They didn't move. They hung in the air motionless. Then suddenly, he was close enough to see it.

"Oh, my God!" Reggie said in a full voice. "Oh, my *God!*" He walked directly up to it. Reggie was only three inches from it.

Floating in mid-air, with nothing holding it up, just hanging there was the face of a man!

"Oh, my God!" he exclaimed a third time.

Suddenly the face looked back at him and spoke. "Good morning!" the face said with a broad smile.

Reggie Porter's knees buckled and he collapsed. He passed out on the spot.

White House – 7:37 AM EST

Even presidents are allowed time for a shower after a morning workout. Al Makin felt his insufficiency for the office of the president in many ways. He wasn't a Washington insider and didn't fit the mold of a professional politician. He knew he was selected as a running-mate for Harriett Marshall for that reason. His judicial acumen was sufficient, but his true strength was his ability to relate and understand everyday folks. He was at his best in a face-to-face discussion over a cup of coffee.

President Makin, wrapped in his robe, exited his private bath in the residence barefooted and drying his hair with a hand towel.

A knock rattled his bedroom door, and before he could respond, it flew open.

"Excuse me, Mr. President. We have a situation."

chapter 2

Trapper Home, Washington DC – 7:40 AM EST

Mike Trapper rolled to his side and looked at Elli sleeping quietly. The last five days had taken him to the limit and nearly cost him everything. The assassination of President Marshall on Sunday afternoon in St. Louis seemed eons ago. Distant history. But it wasn't, and Mike knew it.

As he watched Elli, she winced slightly. He didn't know if it was pain from the knife wound or a frightening memory of the night in the hills behind her childhood home. The wound from the attacker's knife was real and, fortunately, not as deep as Mike originally feared. The terrorist's initial attack struck a glancing blow with a knife just below Elli's left collarbone.

When Mike first saw her on the ground, he thought she was dead. She was knocked unconscious by the impact of the attack, but roused at her son's call. The medics gave her their best field-dressing, and the physicians at Andrews AFB finished the work. Elli would be fine, but for now she needed rest. He knew if he tried to comfort her, she would wake up. Mike did everything he could to be still.

Downstairs, Mike heard Elli's parents in the kitchen making coffee and talking softly. The idea for them to move into the guest room was an excellent one. He was able to rest with Elli, and the kids could feast on grandma's tender and tan pancakes drenched in melted butter and syrup. It would be months until their home was rebuilt, and a couple of weeks before Elli would be able to manage everything again. Her mom, her dad, and Mike were there to slow her down and make her rest. They had all determined this arrangement was their best option.

Elli stirred and opened her eyes. She looked directly at him and smiled. Just as quickly, her brow furrowed as pain shot through her shoulder.

"Ooo!" she said with a wince, "I forgot all about that." Then she smiled.

For the first few years of their marriage, Mike had been in Iraq. He completed three tours and returned a decorated hero. Elli's patience was almost more than he could believe. Her passion for him upon his return left him exhausted and, at the same time, in awe. He knew their love and friendship was unique. It was something special just for them.

"I was hoping you'd sleep a little longer," Mike said gently stroking her forehead.

"Yeah, but it isn't *your* mom about to tear through *your* kitchen," Elli replied with a sinister grin. She knew she wasn't the cook her mother was. Elli was a self-described hack, yet her mother was a magician when it came to food. "I need to get down there."

"You need to rest," Mike replied. "The doctor said it's important."

"Babe, I have given birth four times. This little cut is nothing, believe me. I've been asleep for over twenty-four hours. I *want* to get out of bed. I have all kinds of time to rest. Besides, *my* mom is in *my* kitchen, and if I'm not there, I will never find anything, ever again! I promise you, Mom and Dad will make me rest." Elli smiled and grimaced in pain at the same time. "You want me to learn from her, don't you?"

"I do just fine on your cooking," he paused, "or military cooking. They're both fine to me."

Elli swatted at him for that comment. Slowly, she pulled herself to a sitting position and sighed deeply. Mike helped her stand and put on her robe. He realized she wouldn't rest with her mom and the kids in the kitchen, but she wouldn't do anything but watch. To Elli the show that was about to unfold downstairs was worth the effort.

Whittier Blvd, East Los Angeles, CA – 4:45 AM PST

The patrol of Marines and Army National Guard drove slowly through what a week before was a bustling business district in East LA. The shops were closed, and only a few brave souls ventured out. Most of the time it simply wasn't safe enough for civilians to be out and about.

Lieutenant Mark Strattmann was frustrated. The street before them was absolutely barren. Not a soul was in sight. On rare occasions, he would catch a glimpse of someone ducking back through a window.

On an earlier patrol, a middle-aged man ran from his building toward the advancing vehicles. He never made it. A single burst of gunfire knocked him to the ground. The source, a hidden sniper, was never identified. The enemy stayed hidden.

Those who had invaded California and much of the Southwest learned quickly they were no match for the United States military. They lost every encounter. As quickly as the invasion had come, the challenges stopped.

When a military patrol left the area, the hoodlums would come out in full strength and terrorize the civilians. The deployment of troops in Afghanistan and Iraq limited the manpower necessary to liberate a city the size of Los Angeles, much less the rest of the state. Trying to fight an enemy who remained hidden made it all the more difficult.

Military strategists at Camp Pendleton decided that a regular show of force would be the best tactic. When the full assault could be executed, it would be swift, door-to-door, and room-by-room.

The very thought made Mark Strattmann nervous. Twice, he'd been deployed in Afghanistan on door-to-door searches. Those had been the most frightening experiences of his time in the Middle East. He either burst in on a terrified family or an angry terrorist. He hated the uncertainty.

For now, it was simply show up and be seen. That was all. Since the battle at the Main Gate at Pendleton, not a single shot had been fired at the Marines, but they knew the enemy was there. They were simply out of sight.

Office of Counter Terrorism, Little Rock, AR – 6:50 AM CST

Colonel Aaron Stevens always arrived early. This morning his day was scheduled to begin at seven o'clock on the dot. He arrived fifteen minutes early to straighten his desk and prepare for the day. After the last few days he was convinced he and his team could handle anything.

Thursday had given him the opportunity to sort through the piles of data and information that had helped uncover the assault at Oak Mountain. He linked the chain of events into a clear time line. It had begun to make sense.

The breakdown of the communication grid had contributed to the confusion as the enemy had intended. The invasion had been launched under a cloud of silence first noticed in the lack of DHS First Response log-ins. The mystery was resolved when Barry Goldstein was discovered working treachery from inside the White House. After his removal, channels for data and voice communication rapidly returned to near normal.

The report of the chain of events Aaron had gathered was nearly complete. A few more details would provide a clear outline for posterity. Aaron looked at the stack of papers, hoping those in his position in the future would learn to prevent anything like it again.

Keith Dillon poked his head into the open office door. One look at the expression on Keith's face, and Aaron's heart sank.

"No. You're not going to tell me . . ." Aaron's voice trailed off, but his eyes were locked on Keith's. "You don't have another phone call or something."

"Not a phone call, sir," Keith swallowed, "but it's something."

As he stood behind his desk, Aaron felt weakness in his knees. He followed Keith's long, loping strides toward the situation room. A small crowd had gathered, stone-faced and silent.

"Sir," Keith began as he turned to Colonel Stevens, "thirty minutes ago Clear AFS in Alaska sent a Defcon 2 alert into the system."

"Defcon 2! You've got to be kidding!" Stevens lowered himself into an available chair. His mouth hung open, his eyes darkened by deep furrows of dread. His knees buckled slightly advancing his descent to the chair.

"Just about everybody felt the same, like it was a cruel joke," Keith responded. "Nothing showed on radar until about five minutes ago." Keith turned to a technician. "Tom, will you run that loop again for the colonel?"

Tom spun to his desktop and quickly entered commands on his keyboard. As he finished, he turned toward the large screen on the wall. The room was silent as they watched.

The screen held a satellite view of the United States not unlike the radar maps used in weather reports on the evening news. But the radar, or more accurately, the spectrum of radar images employed, was much more sophisticated.

As the men watched, lightly colored dots began to trace the borders of the United States. Both the Canadian and Mexican borders were outlined, but the tracing didn't begin at the east or west end of the border. It started from hundreds of locations along each border and continued until it connected with the spray of dots ahead of it.

"They started at the same instant," Keith began, "all along both borders, at the same instant! And within forty-five seconds they all disappeared. What do you make of it, sir?"

Aaron Stevens could hardly believe his eyes. He knew he'd seen something like this before but couldn't place it.

"Tom, can you zoom in?" he asked. "Go in on one plume of dots. Make it full screen."

The room stood transfixed, and Tom typed furiously. The zoom effect was slightly dizzying as the view rushed to a single plume of dots.

"Try this," he announced with a final declarative tap to his keyboard.

The screen played what appeared to be a string of dots. Each dot blossomed into a rectangular shape, remained stationary, then faded from view. Several hundred of the shapes would appear followed by a larger cluster of rectangles. Every series was the same with hundreds of smaller images followed by a larger shape. Again and again, all along the border it was the same.

"Can you go in any closer?" Aaron asked. The ultra high-def screens used by the government carried six times the resolution of the commercial models. Still, any radar image from space presented a challenge.

"I'll take it to maximum resolution, sir," Tom replied as he turned to his keyboard. In a few keystrokes the image on the screen began to change. As the pixels blurred and cleared, no questions remained.

"Damn," Keith muttered. "They're parachutes!"

"But what are they coming from?" Aaron exclaimed. "There's nothing on radar for them to jump from!"

Keith was slack-jawed. He looked at Aaron with dawning revelation. "Sir, they're stealth." Keith stood and rummaged through a stack of papers. "Here it is. This report details one individual's observation of a very large, low-flying aircraft that swept right over Clear AFS in Alaska. The guy saw it with his own eyes, but the radar showed nothing. The only marking on the underside of the wing was a gold star."

Breathless words came from Aaron's lips as they formed in everyone's mind. "The Chinese!"

North Flynn Ave., Oklahoma City, OK – 6:55 AM CST

Robert Hitchens lay absolutely still in the tall grass of a vacant lot roughly two hundred yards from the Habana Place Hotel. He and three other retired Navy SEALs hugged the ground as dawn crept into the city. It was dark when they had arrived forty-five minutes earlier.

ALI maps and satellite reconnaissance photos were great intelligence, but eyes on the ground were the best. A team of well-trained recon SEALs could confirm what photographs would only suggest.

The target of their surveillance was the thirty-five-year-old hotel. It showed its age. Just like hundreds of other locations around the country, terrorists had commandeered the hotel. Who was actually in the building was unknown, but everyone was convinced they were unfriendly.

The blue-collar neighborhood to the south had been subject to random home invasions since the terrorists swept into town two days prior. The first house hit was on the north end of the street, the home of the Derlinger family.

A group of six invaders smashed their way through the front door of the old frame structure. Jerry Derlinger defended his home and family with the only weapon he owned, a double barrel, break-action shotgun he used for deer hunting. The first two marauders were stopped in their tracks by .45 caliber deer slugs exploding from the barrel of the shotgun. The problem for Jerry was re-loading.

The four remaining attackers charged ahead, firing automatic weapons, killing Jerry, his wife Brenda, and their two children. The thugs ransacked the house for the Derlingers' valuables before turning their attention to the bodies of their comrades. The family was left where they had fallen.

Under the cover of darkness, the neighborhood came to life. In silence, the neighbors made their way into the house, recovered the bodies of the family, wrapped them in bed sheets, and moved them to the basement storage room to wait until sanity returned to their hometown. The stealthy arrival of four Navy SEALs brought hope.

Robert Hitchens and the SEALs were in place to survey the hotel, to make an account of troop strength, and to prepare for a military strike. Wearing hunting camouflage, carrying no radios, wearing no helmets nor body armor, the men neither looked nor felt combat prepared. But then again, no one ever was.

chapter 3

National Guard Armory, Frisco, TX – 7:00 AM CST

Jim Parker sat gingerly behind the desk of his commanding officer. Though the desk chair was sufficiently cushioned, the wounds on his buttocks were still sensitive. Jim had moved a fraction of a second late to escape the grenade. Most of his body had found safety, but his rear end hadn't quite made it.

The eleven veterans who remained at the Armory continued commando raids both day and night. Sniper positions were taken near known command centers throughout the city, and one by one the invaders were shot. The random nature of the attacks was intended to demoralize the enemy and instill fear. The tactic was working.

The enemy's "barracks" were commandeered cheap hotels and easy targets. The invaders increased their security by placing armed guards on the rooftops of the buildings. Their forms, silhouetted against the sky, were clear shots. The darkness of night afforded the

American snipers the opportunity to launch a rocket-propelled grenade into a lighted room. Those who had invaded Texas to bring terror began to cower from an unseen threat that was killing them at random.

"Good to see you actually sitting."

Parker looked up as Doc, Captain Jerry Smith, flew into the room. He was fresh from morning rounds at the hospital and wanted to check Jim's wounds.

"Morning, Doc," Parker answered as he slowly stood and began unbuckling his pants. "I hope your visits at the hospital were more pleasant than this." He dropped his trousers exposing his backside for inspection.

"Hmm," Doc muttered as he gingerly probed the wounds, "no sign of infection, just a little swelling. How does it feel?"

"Like I sat on a cactus. What should it feel like?"

Doc smiled. "I think you have it about right. Cactus will do."

Three sniper teams entered the office and came to an abrupt halt. The sight of Doc examining Lieutenant Parker's rear end in the Colonel's office was too much to let pass without a comment.

"Can we get a room for you two?" Will Minks asked with a smile. Sergeant Minks, an expert spotter, worked with John Lewis, a marksman sniper. The Marines unloaded their weapons and gear and seated themselves in the chairs around the conference table at the end of the office. Every man was smiling.

"Purely professional, men," Doc responded with nonchalance. "Purely professional."

"What's to report?" Parker asked from his hunched position.

"We're more concerned about what Doc's found," Minks quipped with a grin.

"All's well that ends well," Doc replied.

"Come on, guys. What happened while you were out?" Jim's voice carried enough of an edge to bring more serious topics to the conversation.

"We took out thirteen," Minks reported. "Three down at the old Days Inn on North 75, six at the Hilton off Cedar Springs Road, and the rest at the Residence on I-35. But they're getting better at bein' careful."

"All the more reason we keep moving around a lot." Jim looked at them, fully aware of the danger these men faced. "Have the ALI maps shown more locations we might pursue?"

"Only three more," Minks answered. "They are pretty much clustered along major highways and interstates. Guess it helps them stay mobile."

"That would make sense. Seems they want to strike terror, slip away and show up again unannounced." Jim Parker knew his opponents were cunning and vicious. He also knew that he and his companions must be more cunning and willing to inflict punishment on them. He had hoped to leave that cunning behind in Afghanistan. But it had followed him home, and he knew it must be dealt with.

"Okay, I've got an idea that I think will shake things up a bit— Ouch!" Jim lurched against the table against the sharp pain.

"Sorry," Doc replied. "One stitch is a little loose."

"Better pull it tight, Doc," Minks said with feigned concern. "Can't have Jim's ass fallin' off in a firefight."

Jim buried his face in a towel. *It will never end!*

White House Basement – 8:05 AM EST

President Al Makin walked briskly into the ALI Map room. He'd been in the highly-classified room only once before. The experience had overwhelmed him. As he approached the small cluster of men at the console, he took a deep breath and settled himself.

"Good morning, Mr. President," said Ray Jergins as he turned from the group. Jergins was with the Department of Justice and a consultant to the president since the assassination. "You've met Alex Hodson, FBI, and Angela Crain, DHS."

"Of course, good morning," said the president. "What do you have that requires me to come so deep into the catacombs?"

"Mr. President," Jergins began, "our research team in Little Rock reviewed the satellite images we received after the Defcon 2 alert was sounded in Alaska. Mort, would you bring up the image, fully enhanced?"

Mort began furiously punching his keyboard. His fingers seemed a blur. But every stroke was exactly right. The huge screen before them came to life.

"Mr. President," Ray Jergins continued, "we're looking at the Canadian border with Montana and North Dakota. You can see what appear to be plumes spreading along the border area. Is that the highest resolution, Mort?"

"Nope," replied Mort as his fingers flew over the keys again. In only seconds the screen took a dizzying plunge to a lower altitude. The men standing behind him adjusted their stances for the visual sensation of falling. Mort was glad he was seated and enjoyed the ride.

"All right, thanks Mort." Jergins paused for a moment until the sensation passed, and then turned to the president. "Sir, what appeared as plumes along the border have been identified by the guys at OCT as parachutes, about two hundred at a time, followed by a larger object. We can only assume at this point, but the larger objects seem to be command or communication centers."

"And this is the Chinese army taking command of our borders?" asked the president.

"Uh, yes sir."

"Have there been any reports of confrontation or contact with our border guards?" he asked turning to Angela Crain.

"No, sir," she replied. "We've received four reports of visual contact, but considering their numbers, our guards have requested instructions from DHS as to their next move."

"So, we don't really know why they're here, do we?" The president's eyes angrily darted back and forth between his advisors. He had never been the one who wanted the responsibility of the job, particularly this job. "Here's what we'll do. I want our border guards to know as much as we do. Angela, dispatch a memo to all our border stations saying that we have visitors. But everyone stays put. No contact. Alex, who is on top of this at CIA? Who took Rachel Jones's position?"

"Thomas Davies, Mr. President. He's actually on his way over as we speak."

"Good," the president nodded. "I want State to summon the Chinese ambassador immediately. Ray, I want Mike in here ASAP and the whole team. Is that clear?"

"Yes, Mr. President."

"If we're gonna play a chess game with China, we need to set our strategy." The president glanced at the giant screen and turned back toward the elevator. He'd had enough of the catacombs.

Habana Place, Oklahoma City, OK – 7:12 AM CST

Robert counted thirty-five pickup trucks in the stalls along the side of the hotel. Several were heavily armored with large caliber weapons welded to their beds. The surveillance confirmed this wasn't an event created by happenstance. Much planning and preparation had gone into it.

"Okay, I counted thirty-five. That should be everybody," Robert said in a half-voice. "Must have everyone in for a morning briefing." The sarcasm was not lost on his companions.

"Did you say thirty-five?" one of the SEALs asked. "I thought the recon photos showed thirty-six."

"Close enough. We need to get back." Robert began backing away from their observation point. They moved slowly to avoid being noticed.

The vehicle they drove from the intersection of I-44 and I-240 was nearly two blocks away. They would be the only people on the street in what was now broad daylight. If they encountered the enemy, Robert knew they would be outgunned. Each of the men carried a hunting rifle, semi-automatic and very accurate, but the fully automatic weapons the enemy carried were far more dangerous in a standoff.

The four SEALs scooted to the curb and made a hunched trot into the neighborhood. Bushes and trees in the yards and in front of the houses provided a modicum of protection, but not much.

They passed the first house, weaving behind the hedge in a staggered advance. Three watched, one moved. It wasn't fast, but it was cautious. Regardless of their caution, what happened next surprised them.

"Hey, Gringo! What are you doing on my street?" The voice was gruff and sinister.

It was the thirty-sixth truck loaded with a dozen armed men.

The SEALs spun to the far side of the nearest trees for cover and leveled their weapons on the truck. It was all the time they had. The men in the truck opened fire on full automatic as they dismounted. They fanned out as they advanced.

There wasn't time for a staggered retreat. The four men were under full attack. Robert shouldered his Remington 750 and opened fire. He would have much preferred hand-to-hand combat.

The fury of incoming ordnance was terrifying. Bark and woodchips splintered on the far side of the tree. As the insurgents fanned out from their vehicle, Robert's wedge of safety behind the tree was narrowed, but it created an opportunity.

Robert slid to a sitting position. He motioned to his fellow SEALs who followed suit. Rolling to a prone position, he could peer around the base of the tree. And there he was. The attacker who had moved farthest to the right came into his sites.

Boom! The attacker was thrown backward to the ground. Boom! Boom! Two other SEALs opened up killing two more terrorists on the left. The odds improved. It was only nine against four.

The roaring buzz of automatic fire was constant. The insurgents were persistent and continued toward the SEALs' positions, but their short-barreled weapons held waist high were very inaccurate.

Boom! The Remington 750 claimed another hit. Robert rolled to his left side and shouldered the rifle left-handed. Boom! Another man hit.

Someone shouted in Spanish. The automatic firing let off, becoming a more staggered pattern. They were retreating.

Each of the SEALs sited a retreating insurgent. On Robert's command, they fired. Four terrorists fell to the ground in their retreat. One was able to get up and hobble out of sight.

"You guys all right?" Robert asked catching his breath.

"Yeah," one Seal answered without taking his eyes off the end of the street. All four men were relieved to have found the thirty-sixth pickup, but they knew those who fled had enough friends to fill another thirty-five trucks. Once again, the odds didn't look so hot.

"Hey!" A voice called to them from one of the houses. "Hey, over here!"

Robert saw the silhouette of a man waving at them from a front porch. The man looked down the street in the direction of the hotel, and then he cautiously made his way toward them.

"You know what's gonna happen, don't you?" the man said with a sharp edge to his voice. "You know they're gonna be back here in ten minutes with three hundred of those killers! You know that, don't ya! What the hell are you doing here?"

Suddenly, Robert was asking himself the same question. *What the hell am I doing here?*

Camp Pendleton, CA – 5:15 AM PST

Brigadier General Gene Westrup was up early. Sleeping had been difficult since a favored nephew, Barry Goldstein, was discovered to be part of the attacks on the Oak Mountain Power Plant and the invasion that had crossed the nation's borders. Barry's sensitive position in White House security made his treason all the more troubling. The general had recommended him for the position.

General Westrup stood at the large window in his office that overlooked the hub of Camp Pendleton, Mainside. His office was above the parade grounds and provided a view of the part of the camp most like a small town. At least, the presence of a Subway sandwich shop and Jack-in-the-box burgers brought a memory of small town America to mind. As peaceful as the scene was at dawn, he knew the day would bring anything but peace.

Westrup had already read the report from Alaska. Something was underway that would disrupt the serenity before him. Until the morning status reports arrived from Washington, there was little he could do. The Camp was on full alert. Security was at the highest level. Readiness was constantly reviewed to address any event.

But since the raids at the gates, the Camp remained quiet. The main focus of gathering information was in observing the insurgents captured and interrogating them. As enemy combatants, they were well trained to hold their tongues, but the emotional toll was wearing on them. The general knew he simply must wait. He didn't like it one bit.

chapter 4

North Flynn Ave., Oklahoma City, OK – 7:17 AM CST

Robert cleared his cell phone and shoved it into his pocket. Their surveillance mission had taken a very serious turn, and the rules were changing. He walked over to the small group of residents who had ventured into the daylight.

"How do you keep in contact with each other?" Robert asked.

"We've been texting to everyone along the street, and it seems to work pretty good," the man said. He was the one who had called to them from his porch. "We keep watch and tell everyone if they come into the street."

"How many are you talking about, with everyone?"

"There's more than fifty families right in this area," he paused and glanced at the ground, "but that don't count the Derlingers." He explained to Robert that he was the one who found his neighbor and family after the attack on their home. "I don't know why they're here messin' with us. We ain't got nothin' they'd want."

Bitterness seethed behind the man's confusion. No one understood why they were attacked, why they were threatened in their own homes. What had these people done to deserve such brutality?

"I know it doesn't make any sense. But, it's not just you. Just about the whole country has been hit in one way or another." He told them stories of the invasion and vicious treatment many had received at the hands of the terrorists.

The man's eyes softened as he learned of the widespread events of terror and savagery. The man's face darkened as he heard the stories from across the Southwest. His eyes reflected his resolve. For now, it would be up to them to defend their homes and families.

"Between us we got about two hundred rifles, if that helps," the man offered.

"For now, it most certainly does," Robert said, "especially if you have plenty of ammo."

"We got enough," he said as he reached into his pocket for his phone. He read the text and shook his head. "We'd better wrap this up 'cause they're comin'. Wendell says here there's a bunch straight up the block comin' 'round to the west on Youngs Boulevard. and another bunch comin' down Barnes. Heck, we're surrounded."

"Get back to your families and be ready for anything," Robert said loudly. "This time we're flyin' by the seat of our pants." He pulled out his phone and began to dial.

Exit 104, Interstate 35, Norman OK – 7:30 AM CST

Sheriff Perry Hitchens stood on the spot of the bridge over the interstate where he faced down the army of invaders only hours before. Half of a dozen sentries stood around the scene. Their job was to keep sightseers away, even though there were no sightseers.

The roadway below was littered with the burned remains of nearly one hundred cars and trucks that had carried the men and their weapons from Dallas to the city limits of Norman. Sheriff Hitchens was no fan of violence, but neither was he fearful of it. Brutish behavior is best dealt with by the use of overwhelming force. Such was the case. The three missiles from the F-22A Raptor had ended the matter.

Through the night, the coroner and medics from local ambulance services and hospitals helped to remove the dead from the twisted and burned vehicles. The process was tedious, and only a few had survived.

Those who had surrendered before the strike and moved away from the lines of cars and trucks were only slightly injured. They had been taken into custody. Sheriff Hitchens's jail was filled to capacity. Interrogations ran late into the night with several men providing information they'd overheard on plans to invade both Norman and Oklahoma City.

Sheriff Hitchens decided to leave the strategy planning to the officers of the local National Guard and Reserves. He was concentrating on overseeing the cleanup of the interstate and getting things back to normal as soon as possible.

Hitchens shuddered, looking at the smoldering wreckage. *So many lives wasted in a futile effort*, he thought. *Families missing fathers, brothers and sons.* It bothered him, but the stories told of the violence in Dallas held a more grave concern. How many more of these men were still in Dallas? How many had they killed?

"Sheriff Hitchens!" The voice came from below the overpass. It jarred the sheriff from his thoughts.

"Hey, Travis," the sheriff replied. "What's up?"

"I've got Pauline on the phone here. Says she needs to talk to you." Travis Temple served as colonel in the Army Reserve in Goldsby, a short distance down Highway 7. The sheriff made his way off the overpass and down the grassy slope to his cruiser below. Travis waited patiently, but he looked drawn.

"Thanks, Travis." Sheriff Hitchens took the phone. The haunted look in his old friend's eye caused him to pause. "Are you okay?"

Travis dropped his gaze to the ground at his feet and kicked a rock with the toe of his boot. When he looked up his eyes were moist. "Oh, I guess killin' them sons-a-bitches kinda getting' to me some."

"I know, Travis. It's nothin' we're used to, nor should it be. But it just *is*, and we gotta deal with it."

"Yeah, I know. A lot like Nam, just closer to home."

"We'll get some coffee in a bit, okay?"

"That'd be good, sheriff. I'd like that." Travis smiled slightly, he nodded in agreement and sauntered toward his truck.

Sheriff Hitchens watched him go. He drew in a deep breath and put his phone to his ear.

"Morning, Pauline. What's got you up this early?"

"Sheriff, I'm always up this early." Pauline's response was laced with a saucy attitude.

"You've got me there. What gives?" Perry replied smiling.

"We need you here at the office to authorize some weapons acquisitions. Can you get away from there and take care of this?"

"Now, Pauline. I know you just want me to chase all those soldiers out of your office."

"You are exactly right. But you'd do a better job of it by signing these papers. I think they'll be happy to leave. I know it's fine with me."

"Listen, the crew with the equipment to move all this junk off the interstate is due any minute," Sheriff Hitchens answered. "As soon as they get started, I'll head in. Soon enough for you?"

"That will be fine," she said. "Gotta keep you pullin' your weight."

"Thank you, Pauline." The sheriff closed his phone and turned back to the littered highway. *The generals need to take this by the horns. I'll get this started, and I'm outta here.* Perry Hitchens knew he was no military planner. Anytime, he would gladly step aside.

National Guard Armory, Frisco, TX – 7:40 AM CST

Jim Parker's cell phone buzzed on the desktop.

"Parker," he snapped into the receiver.

"Lieutenant Parker, this is Colonel Joseph Maris, Chief of Staff of III Phantom Corps, Fort Hood." Fort Hood is home to the 3rd Armored Cavalry Regiment (III ACR). The regiment deploys over 4,700 soldiers and acts as the primary contingency force for emergency situations. This was such a time, and they were on the move in their own backyard.

"Lieutenant General Caldwell and Brigadier General DiSosa have been ordered by the president of the United States to deploy and repel the invaders," Colonel Maris explained. "Over the last two days we have moved simultaneously toward Dallas and Austin, clearing smaller towns along the way. I need your immediate location."

"Uh . . . sir," Parker was taken by surprise. "Yes sir! We're located in the armory for the Marine Reserve unit in Frisco. Most of our unit evacuated north with their families. We stayed behind, I guess, sir, to wait for you."

"A brave decision for you. Have you seen combat?"

"Yes sir, I did my first tour in Iraq and another in Afghanistan. When this mess kicked up the other day, several of us decided we still had some fight in us. Especially for here at home, sir."

"Thank you for your service. Son, I need coordinates, so we can deliver some supplies."

"Yes sir!" Parker rustled books and maps, unfolding them, and laying them across the desk. "Sir, our location is 33°08'06.14"N, 96°49'16.15"W."

"Okay. We're on our way, soldier. Are any of your troops in the field?"

"No sir. They got back a few minutes ago. Everyone's here."

"Good. I want all of you to stay where you are until you receive orders from me. You are now under my command and will coordinate your activities with our efforts. Do you understand?"

"Yes sir!"

"I have an Apache AH-64 en route, about sixteen klicks out. Its approach will be from the north. They have supplies, ammunition, and some special equipment. We don't want to shoot you by accident. Do you have any questions, lieutenant?"

"Uh, no sir!" Parker was dazed by the rapid-fire instructions. He looked at the map. *Sixteen klicks?* "Thank you, sir!"

"Thank you, young man. Thank you for taking a stand." The colonel's words brought a flush to Jim Parker's face. As he closed his phone, Doc walked back into the office.

"Jim, you look flush. Are you all right?" the doctor asked.

"Yeah. Yeah, of course," he replied slowly. "But it looks like someone just called in the cavalry."

Streets of Washington DC – 8:45 AM EST

Mike Trapper felt relaxed as he drove through the streets of Washington DC. He couldn't help thinking about the frantic trip he'd made to the White House only a couple of days earlier.

In the middle of the night, he was called in to receive an encrypted document from the OCT in Little Rock. His nerves were frazzled that night which had allowed his imagination to run wild. In the end, his worst fears were realized, and the action had ratcheted to new heights.

On this morning his thoughts were drawn back. He relived each thought, every event or turn that was threatening on that dark night. Still, as he drove in broad daylight, the hairs on the back of his neck prickled with each passing memory. The threat had come too close that night.

As a decorated Marine, Mike served his country through three tours in the Iraq conflict with distinction. His bravery in the face of the enemy awarded him the Silver Star. The closeness of the combat brought him two Purple Hearts and the gratitude of a member of the Iraqi Parliament for saving his life.

Trapper had served the former president, Harriet Marshall, as the head of her Secret Service detail. He was with her when she was assassinated in St. Louis on opening day of the baseball season, that distant day only five days past. During her short term as president, he had become friends with Harriet Marshall and her husband

Preston. His experience, professionalism, and personable nature made him a valuable companion to the first family.

Mike was rightfully assigned the lead position investigating the assassination since he was on the site of the murder in St. Louis. He had worked around the clock with a team of professionals in pursuit of the killer.

Of course, the assassination of Harriet Marshall was not the ultimate goal of the evil minds behind it all. It was only a decoy to divert attention from the true objective. The decoy plan had included the explosion of the Oak Mountain Nuclear Power Plant. The intended blast would have contaminated the atmosphere around Washington DC with tons of radioactive particles. The dust particles would have settled over Washington, creating the worst nuclear disaster in history.

The destruction of Oak Mountain had been narrowly avoided. The efforts of Mike, his best friend Steve Granger, Samantha Long of the State Department, Sam's boss Phil Stearns, and a small team of Marines had averted the disaster. But all the planning they had uncovered was not the whole story. The next morning, as the nation mourned and watched the funeral of the slain president, the invasion began.

Thousands of mid-eastern insurgents led hordes of Mexican and African Americans in a revolt against law enforcement and every authority along their way. Taking advantage of the porous southern border, thousands of men and women made their way across the boundary and into several states in the Midwest and West.

The assassination was their call-to-arms, the funeral their signal for attack. After a day of confusion, terror, and bloodshed, a significant part of the western United States had been held by hostile mobs. The invasion was an effort of epic proportion that brought horrific loss to American citizens.

Trapper sighed as he entered the reserved parking lot behind the White House. An underlying tension accompanied him. Alex Hodson's call less than an hour earlier held an implied urgency for him to get to work. Something was up.

The walk to the West Wing wasn't long, yet Mike couldn't shake the feeling he was entering the White House for another very long day. The days blended together in a fog of information and activity. *When was the last time I had a weekend?* he wondered as he opened the door. He knew he wouldn't have time to even think about it.

West Haven Arms, Apt 3B, Washington, DC – 8:50 AM EST

The fight wasn't the first time Sam and Steve disagreed. But it was the first time this week. And for whatever reason, this time it seemed to matter.

"You can't just walk away, say nothing and leave me hanging like that!" Sam said, her voice lifting into a falsetto.

"I didn't! This is ridiculous!" Steve said, dragging his fingers through his hair. "All I did was go into the shoe store for a second. I came right back!"

"Ridiculous! Now I'm ridiculous!" Sam was steaming. "Mr. Granger, you do not come in here and tell me I'm ridiculous!"

"Sammy, no, you are not that. I didn't say *you* were ridiculous. This . . . us yelling at each other like this, is . . . or could be considered . . . not the best." Steve looked at Sam. She could have been auditioning for *Taming of the Shrew*. He was wise enough not to mention it.

"I know! It's me!" Sam switched to an instant pout. Steve's eyes widened watching the change. "I just don't want anything to happen!" She threw her arms around his neck and sobbed, leaning on his chest.

Steve held her tight. He had no idea what he should do next. So he did nothing, and that was the right choice. Sam lifted her head and sniffed. Actually, she snorted, but one does not tell a beautiful woman in an emotional snit she just snorted.

"Just remember, I waited and wanted to be with you for a long time," she said calmly. "I watched you get shot, and it terrified me. I don't know on which side of *panic* I'll find myself next."

Steve realized why and how much he loved her. She was an amalgam of passion and strength, a ping-pong ball in a bedpan. Again, not something to mention at that moment. But she was fiery and sweet. Barbed wire and teddy bears. Could he ever get it right? "I know. And I marvel at you. The fight in you. The way you live," he said drawing her face toward his. "I love you. That won't change. It's never going anywhere." *Score one, Steve-o.*

She melted into his embrace and kissed him. It was a long kiss. She pulled back. She was smiling.

"Okay, I love you, too," she said softly. "Give me a minute to freshen up. We've gotta get going." She spun and almost skipped from the room.

He was still breathless from her kiss.

chapter 5

Oval Office, White House – 9:00 AM EST

Mike Trapper walked into the White House. He was the newly appointed personal advisor to the president of the United States of America. That was his technical title. In reality, he was the president's closest confidant.

"Hey, Mike! Good to see you!" Rick Johnston said with a grin and outstretched hand. George Raker was with him. George was a giant of a man whose years of experience in the Marines, Special Forces and the Secret Service granted him high regard.

Rick, about twenty-five years younger than George, was smart and capable, and current with the technology of his generation. The two were a great team and had held key roles in stopping the effort to destroy the Oak Mountain Nuclear Power Station.

"You too," Trapper replied taking his hand. He then greeted George, again amazed by his size and gentle demeanor. "What's the scoop this morning, guys?"

"We just got here, Mike. Not sure," George replied.

The three men walked briskly down the hall to the Oval Office and were quickly ushered in by Sharon Fair, the President's secretary. As they entered, Mike saw Steven Granger, his best friend and fellow warrior, and the newest member of the White House Presidential Security Team.

He greeted the president. Then Samantha Long, a long-time friend, munitions expert, acting Assistant Secretary of Verification, Compliance and Implementation at the State Department, and a drop-dead gorgeous woman. The former Assistant Secretary of VCI was Phil Stearns, Sam's boss. He had perished in the attack at the Oak Mountain Power Plant.

"Agent Trapper," the president began, taking Mike by the elbow, "I want to introduce you to Matt Kreiter, Special Agent-in-Charge of the Emergency Response Team in the St. Louis Field Office. I don't suppose you two met in all the confusion last Sunday?"

"No sir, Mr. President," Kreiter said shaking Mike's hand. "I wasn't far behind Agent Trapper, but then again, he's a hard guy to keep up with." Matt Kreiter was not a large man, but he was extremely fit, sculpted muscles, and handsome. His eyes darted from Mike to the president, relaying his sharp intelligence and focused attention.

Mike smiled and replied, "When we're around *him*," nodding toward the president, "you can call me Agent Trapper, but please, call me Mike the rest of the time." The smiles and chuckles were brief. Mike knew instantly he would like Matt Kreiter. He could see he was quick and confident. He would be a great addition to the team.

"Good morning," President Makin began, "you're here for some serious business. I have requested Agent Kreiter to join this team because of the background work they have completed in the St. Louis field office. The people that initiated the planning of the disaster reach far beyond our borders and far beyond our wildest imaginations. Agent Kreiter?"

"Thank you, Mr. President," Agent Kreiter said as he stepped toward a video screen by the fireplace. "Our initial investigations took us into a handful of small organizations that managed to stay in the background, hidden, for over forty years. During that time, literally hundreds of sleeper agents were moved into our government. Not as lawmakers, judges or political leaders, but as assistants at just about every level of government. They were listening ears and a real force of influence on our officials.

"When the assassination occurred in St. Louis, they all fled. Within hours, federal employees and their families were on flights to Europe and the Middle East, or across the Canadian and Mexican borders. Although we can find out who every one of these people is, tracking them internationally will prove very difficult."

"Exactly how many people are involved in this?" Samantha Long asked from across the room.

"Exactly? Other than those who left we can't be certain," Kreiter replied. "The overall total could be more than sixteen hundred."

The discussion continued, detailing the participation of different cults and organizations in the Middle East, the Far East, and Europe. All relatively unknown groups to the West, but obviously very well known to each other. The video screen displayed the links of suspected travel routes. Windows opened to show payments made from group to group, and continent to continent.

"Although we had suspicions about the source of funding for all this, we didn't have any proof," Kreiter continued, "until yesterday. You'll remember earlier this week the police in Singapore picked up a man named Renee Broussard."

"His day-timer was a treasure trove of intelligence," Mike acknowledged.

"Right," Kreiter nodded. "But that was just the beginning of the information that was gathered. Our brothers-in-arms in Singapore don't fool around and can get down to business in very short order. When they went through Broussard's hotel room on Monday, things went ballistic!"

"If I may interrupt here," President Makin broke in, "most of the rest of this is very sensitive. This is the kind of thing that can start a world war. We have enough to deal with along our borders right now without getting strung out across the globe."

"That's exactly right," added Agent Kreiter. "The primary source of funding that has armed the invaders, paid them, and provided transportation is someone in China. Whoever that is also selected the person to pull the trigger in St. Louis."

"Have you been able to determine if this is the Chinese government?" Steve Granger asked.

"No, not yet," Kreiter replied. "There seems to be a deaf ear, a blind spot, or a total lack of knowledge from the contacts we've made in just the last few days."

"But you're sure its China. Somehow . . ." Mike said.

"Positive," Kreiter interrupted. "Broussard's room was filled with Chinese Yuan."

"Now, something none of you know." President Makin stood and walked to the video screen. He clicked the remote and a radar map of the United States appeared. "This is satellite video taken at exactly 7:20 this morning."

Astonished, the group watched the plumes appear on radar along the Mexican and Canadian borders simultaneously. Within seconds the plumes disappeared.

"Those plumes you saw," the president said, "were parachutes. We've estimated that somewhere between one-hundred-twenty and one-hundred-thirty thousand Chinese soldiers were deployed on our borders in less than one minute."

North Flynn Ave., Oklahoma City, OK – 8:05 AM CST

No one is ever eager to start a gunfight. This day was no different. The neighborhood on North Flynn was armed, dug in, and waiting for the inevitable. The inevitable was at the door.

The SEALs divided themselves among families along the street. The neighbors gathered in the brick homes that provided more protection than those of wood frames. Three or four families combined food, weapons and ammunition to a single location. Three sets of parents bearing weapons increased their confidence. Standing alone as a family had not gone well for the Derlingers. No one wanted to see that repeated.

Robert went with the Marcinks. After the initial firefight, David Marcink was the first to call to the SEALs. His wife Pamela was a mom-turned-hunter when the season was right. Their fourteen-year-old son Jonathan was a licensed hunter as well. They were hosts to the Williams family from next door and the Kendells from across the street. That made four armed men, a mom, and a fourteen-year-old boy to stand watch while six children and two wives huddled in the basement rec room.

Robert sized up their position. An assault through the front door could be contained. Six semi-automatic hunting rifles provided a significant deterrent, especially in the confined area of the front entrance. The rear of the home was less secure and more difficult to defend. A double-pronged attack would mean disaster for everyone on both sides.

Pamela was given the task of watching the back of the house and the alley. She scoped the end of the block, watching for movement. Robert noticed beads of perspiration on her forehead. This wasn't a job a mom expected to fill. She faced it with the courage of a pioneer woman awaiting a counterattack. She would protect her children with her life if needed. Robert's hope was to avoid that.

As men and women settled into defensive positions, the neighborhood was silent. The street appeared deserted, but it wasn't. More than two hundred angry terrorists were about to make a house-to-house search for those who gunned down their comrades.

National Guard Armory, Frisco, TX – 8:10 AM CST

The Apache helicopter had thundered over the roof of the armory only minutes earlier. It dropped into the parking lot like a rock, stopping inches above the paved surface before settling to the ground. The airman leaped to the ground and started pulling bundles of rations and munitions from the chopper.

Lieutenant Jim Parker and ten other veteran soldiers ran to the helicopter and began lugging the supplies back to the armory. Parker extended his hand in gratitude knowing that talking though the roar of the copper was useless. The airman gripped his hand, snapped to attention, and standing fully upright directly beneath the churning props, saluted him. Jim Parker returned the salute. Immediately, the airman was back in the Apache, and it lifted swiftly into the air.

Simultaneously, three other Apache AH-64s lifted from positions scattered within a half mile of the armory. Their deployment was intended to mask a singular mission. From a distance an enemy could watch a single helicopter land and depart and possibly reveal an important location. But four landings and departures would leave an enemy confused. It was standard operations for the 3rd Armored Cavalry Phantoms. Always focus first, "focus down." Be aware of your immediate surroundings, "know the environment." Then, never let the enemy see what you're really up to.

Parker and the troops quickly moved the bundles into the Armory. They were glad to see the additional munitions, but every man groaned when they opened the cases of Meals Ready to Eat (MREs). It didn't seem right. Here they were in the middle of America, and not a thickburger in sight.

"Hefty tools, man," commented Sergeant Minks as he admired the new helmets and body armor. "Lookie at the electro-gizmos!"

The most important items included new modular integrated communications helmets (MICH), popular with SWAT teams and dozens of militaries around the world. The MICH was originally designed for US Army Special Operations units, but quickly became useful in avoiding friendly fire incidents like the ones that occurred in the early hours of the invasion in Iraq.

"Hey, Doc," Minks mused holding a MICH in each hand, "we've got a couple extra!" He then stood and placed a helmet on each cheek of his buttocks and wagged his rear-end like a showgirl. "Whatcha think, lieutenant?" he said with a mocking grin.

The helmets, coupled with new modular tactical vests (MTV), assured the individual soldier's identification on command-video images and protected him from accidental injury. In close-quarter conflict that identification was vital.

"Careful, Will," Doc looked up from his medical bag, turned toward Minks and grinned. "That sort of action could get you assigned to stage duty down at the Dusty Dollar Strip Club."

The room roared with laughter as Will Minks blushed, embarrassed by his own folly. It was time to turn the other cheek, and Doc made sure he did.

Mainside Observation Room, Camp Pendleton – 6:15 AM PST

Sergeant Major John Michaels walked briskly into the room and began peering into the monitors along the wall.

"How did our boys do last night, Bob?" he asked in a soft voice.

"Slept pretty soundly, sir." Captain Bob Prescott was more than a Marine captain. He was a psychiatrist who spent the majority of his time with wounded warriors home from the Middle East. Over the years, he'd developed a unique understanding of the soldiers with whom he spoke, as well as the enemy they had fought.

But in spite of the knowledge gained through the years and the recognition for degrees earned, articles published, or books written, he refused to be Robert. His mother called him that, and he hated it. He was Bob. Not "doctor," not even "sir." Just Bob.

"The evening prayers were a little timid, especially from those we've *talked* with, but otherwise pretty quiet," he explained.

The Acoustic Phased Array used in the battle at the Main Gate a few days earlier also possessed the ability to focus a beam of sound to a very fine point. One person could be selected in a crowd of hundreds. By focusing the beam directly on that person, a sound could be projected only to him. In close quarters, such as a holding cell, the effect creates the illusion that the sound is coming from inside the subject's head.

Several of the insurgent warriors had been subjected to the treatment. That evening in an adjoining room, a Marine lieutenant repeated the evening prayers along with the subject, leaving the impression someone, possibly Allah himself, was speaking the prayers with him. Then, at a precise point in the prayer, as the subject asked for forgiveness, the Marine would stop and say, "No!" Forgiveness would not be granted for the shedding of innocent blood.

The enhanced technique was successful with each participant. The leaders were not chosen for this procedure but rather the younger men of lower rank. They were idealistic in their devotion, not tempered by their military training.

"There was one strange thing we noted about three this morning, sergeant major," Captain Prescott said softly, tipping his head, remembering. "As we scanned the rooms, all of the prisoners were asleep, except this one guy. He was kneeling on the floor, and it looked like he was talking to someone. But he was alone."

"That is odd," Michaels said. "Do you have any idea who he was talking to?"

"The name he used several times wasn't a traditional Muslim name and didn't match any that we had on the manifest," the captain replied.

"What was the name?" the sergeant major asked.

"*Isa*. Over and over he said the name *Isa*."

"Why don't you bring the base cleric in. See what he thinks," Michaels recommended as he leaned on the desk peering into the screens.

"Good idea, sergeant major. I'll get right on it."

chapter 6

Oval Office, White House – 9:25 AM EST

Mike Trapper and President Al Makin stood in front of the video screen with the others as they began a video conference with Colonel Aaron Stevens, Director of the Mid-West Office of Counter Terrorism (OCT) in Little Rock, Arkansas. The staff at OCT had gathered as much information as possible to pose different scenarios of Chinese intentions.

"Mr. President," Colonel Stevens began, "it took a matter of minutes from the troops' departing the aircraft to establishing a communications network. Pretty amazing stuff actually."

"When you say *aircraft*, colonel, exactly what do you mean? Nothing shows up on radar," the president asked.

"Mr. President, from the eye witness accounts, the aircraft are very similar to the Pelican program we abandoned a few years ago. The craft is designed to fly only a few dozen feet off the surface, whether that surface is land or water using what we call it *ground effect lift*. The compression of the air against the surface, the ocean or ground, tends to increase the air pressure under the wing. That means the greater pressure under the wing makes the lifting pressure above the wing a greater contrast, thus increasing lift.

"The planes were designed with a wingspan of a couple hundred feet and could move at about 300 miles per hour with an immense payload. The massive hull could carry large equipment like tanks or up to 1,500 troops. From what we saw on the video, each plane was loaded with maybe a thousand soldiers and other large objects, possibly command and control centers.

"And, of course, the biggest difference, these planes were aided with stealth technology," Colonel Stevens concluded.

"Which, of course, is why our radar couldn't see them," the president added.

"Sir, none of our radars, plural, could see them." Colonel Stevens's comment brought a sobering realization to the room. *If we can't see their planes, what else are we missing?*

"Aaron, has there been any report of contact between our border security and the Chinese?" Mike asked.

"Only observations at this point," Stevens replied. "The Defcon 2 brought all our military to full alert."

"And those who aren't focused on the action inside the borders are on stand-by for tactical moves when I give the word," the president said as he turned toward his desk. "A delegation from the Chinese embassy is due at the top of the hour."

"We are currently tasking satellites to monitor the Canadian border," Stevens said. "We also have border guards in contact with us at OCT. If anything else surfaces, we'll notify you immediately."

"Thank you, Colonel Stevens," The president clicked the monitor off and turned to the group around him. "Okay folks, I want you storming this thing in the Roosevelt Room for the rest of the day. Coordinate with the joint chiefs and put all, and I do mean *all*, of our resources to work. Mike, I want you back in here when the Chinese delegation arrives."

So many ends to tie together, and the time to do it had passed.

North Flynn Ave., Oklahoma City, OK – 8:30 AM CST

Tension rose to an unbearable level. Everyone froze in silence as the teams of terrorists entered the first two houses at the south end of the block. They burst into the home. Guns blazed into an empty house.

Sixteen families were secured in the four houses in the middle of the block. The homes faced each other, two on each side of the street and each made of brick.

In the basement rec room, one of the mothers almost screamed as the firestorm began three houses north. Everyone realized they were trapped between two small armies seeking to destroy every living soul they found. And they were closing in from both sides.

Robert leaned toward the back, peering down the alley to the south. He could only risk a peek. A quick count estimated about ten men in the backyard of the house two doors down. The men milled around the yard in an odd manner. They seemed too casual for killers.

Robert turned and looked quickly to the north. More men stood with their weapons thrown over their shoulders. He wondered if they were that confident or simply poorly trained. Now he was sure the dreaded two-pronged attack was the most likely scenario. Perhaps a certainty.

He opened his phone and called one of the SEALs across the street. He answered immediately.

"Whatcha got, Robert?"

"They're coming up the alley in back, as well as the street. Have you seen that?" Robert asked.

"Hang on," was the reply. The pause was laced with tension. Again, Robert checked out the back. The men had not moved.

"Yeah, we've got men to the rear as well," the SEAL reported.

"Okay. Pass it on and adjust your position to deal with it." He clicked his phone off. At that moment, gunfire erupted again to the south. It was deafening. The terrorists were entering the second house.

Lakeside, OR, City Hall – 6:35 AM PST

Reggie Porter was fully awake and huddled in the corner of the large room. He was surrounded by Chinese soldiers. With their invisibility cloaks removed, Reggie saw that they were mere human beings, although from the other side of the planet. He felt he was on another planet altogether.

"Mr. Porter, would you care for hot tea?" the soldier asked with passable English. He smiled gently. That made Reggie more comfortable. They weren't treating him as a prisoner, and seemed nothing like the beasts who had stormed the town earlier in the week. He felt good. He felt safe.

"Sure," Reggie replied. He unwrapped himself from the warm blanket and took the tea. It tasted very good to him. It also made him realize he was hungry. "Uh, do you have sumptin' I could eat?"

The young soldier was confused for a moment but finally deciphered Reggie's dialect. He smiled and nodded. "Yes, yes, one moment please." The young soldier bowed and backed away from him, smiling.

Reggie looked around the large room. It was bustling with dozens of soldiers, some studying area maps, others conferring with commanders through a video screen. He didn't understand anything that was going on, but it didn't bother him.

Suddenly, the young soldier was back, grinning broadly. "You eat!" he said rather emphatically.

Reggie looked at the food the soldier held gently in a towel. A look of confusion and disapproval crossed his face. He glanced back at the soldier.

"You eat. You like!" the soldier said gesturing to him with the food. "Yes!" he said with a broader grin.

Reggie took the towel from the soldier. He was suspicious that maybe these guys weren't so friendly. Maybe they were going to actually poison him! *What the heck is that stuff anyway? This Chinese guy sure seems eager for me to eat it. It has to be poison!*

But Reggie was very hungry. He made up his mind. If he was going to die for his country, it wasn't going to be with an empty stomach. He took a bite.

"You like?" the young grinning soldier asked. "Very good. *Ziao long bao*," the young soldier said pointing to the food. "*Ziao long bao*. You like? Yes?"

The warm meat inside the roll tasted wonderful. A warm sauce, more like a thick soup, trailed down Reggie's chin. *Man, this is better than booze!* he thought as he chewed. He looked at the young soldier and nodded. His eyes sparkled with approval as he wolfed down the steamed bun.

The soldier stood quickly to attention and proclaimed, "Excellent!" and marched back the way he'd come. Reggie watched him go. Maybe they weren't going to poison him after all.

Roosevelt Room, White House – 9:40 AM EST

The work on the assassination was near complete, as was the investigation of the attempt to destroy Oak Mountain. The investigating team believed a Muslim sect had instigated the plan in the early 1970s.

"It just doesn't make sense that a single small sect, or even a handful of small sects, could engineer such a massive plan," Matt Kreiter said walking to the head of the conference table. "I know that's what the evidence indicates. There simply has to be some outside help on this early on. Remember, the Persians invented the game of chess. Their minds think on a variety of levels, and for that matter, several plays ahead."

"So, do we need to be trying to think ahead of them? Like what their next move is?" Rick asked.

"Before we can go there, we need to know what we face right now," Trapper said quickly, tapping his stack of notes. "We have more than one-hundred thousand Chinese soldiers on our borders and an unknown number of angry citizens and non-citizens occupying a major portion of several states. I think we need to know how they all connect. What string pulls whom, and what response it might create."

Kreiter nodded. "I agree, Mike."

"Is there any chance these things aren't all that closely tied?" George Raker asked. "I mean, maybe we've been a target for both the Arabs and the Chinese and they just happened to move at the same time. Maybe it isn't all that coordinated."

"I think that's exactly where we'd be if we didn't have so much intelligence from Renee Broussard," Sam countered. "Seems there should be more we can get from him about the weapons transfers, like who initiated the buys and where the deliveries were made. That might give us a better picture of what is really going on."

Everyone in the room agreed. Clearly, much of their information was still scattered and disconnected. They began the long process of identifying each *end*, following the string as far back as possible, then moving to the next known *end*.

Mike's original evaluation was correct. Discovering how it all came to pass was important, but that could be given to other agents and assets of the FBI, CIA, and Secret Service.

The team determined the background work that needed to be done and dispatched assignments to the different agencies. Their stated purpose, in the meantime, was to find the right strings to pull while moving forward. And much to their surprise, it wouldn't be long until they did.

National Guard Armory, Frisco, TX – 8:45 AM CST

Lieutenant Jim Parker's cell phone buzzed on the desktop.

"Parker," he answered.

"Lieutenant, this is Colonel Maris, III ACR Phantoms. Are your troops rested and equipped for some action?"

Parker was a little surprised at how soon the colonel called. The guys had been out most of the night and had rested for just over an hour. He also knew the amount of rest they were able to catch had little to do with readiness.

"Yes sir. The supplies you sent are distributed, and we're ready to deploy." It was then Jim realized he hadn't prepared his own equipment. "What do you need, sir?"

"I want you to get your gear up and on," Colonel Maris continued. "Our forward contingent is working through the southern outskirts, moving toward some known hotspots. I want you to position yourselves so we can sandwich these bastards and pin 'em down. Do you copy?"

"Yes sir!"

"In about four minutes you will receive instructions through those new fancy helmets we sent ya. We just need you to be ready."

"Yes sir! Ready in four minutes, sir!" Parker felt like he was back in boot camp snapping responses to his drill sergeant. He grabbed his helmet and examined it looking for the ON switch.

"You will be called the Patriots squad. The Phantom Patriots!" the colonel said.

"Yes sir. Phantom Patriots at the ready, sir!"

Jim closed his phone and turned to call his troops together. He didn't need to say a word. Every man on the squad was standing in the office in full field dress, armed to the hilt, and ready for action.

"So, we're the Phantom Patriots, huh?" Will Minks said with a half grin on his face.

"That's us. But I still have to get my gear together!" Jim responded.

"No, you don't, lieutenant," Minks said with a broadening smile. "It's right here."

Each man held out a piece of Parker's field equipment. They always gave him a hard time, but when things got real, they were there to stand with their junior officer and proudly be with him.

Jim dressed quickly. Then the call came.

chapter 7

Mike Trapper was getting comfortable working in the White House, but he groaned under his breath at the mountain of reports from embassies all over the world. *Accounting didn't prepare me for this.*

Sometimes what appeared to be a genuine clue, something that looked like it should be important turned out to be a restaurant or pharmacy on one of Renee Broussard's lists. It was like a giant jigsaw puzzle of a photo of a million pennies. Every piece was a picture of a copper penny. They were all the same. Each piece fit in a particular place. Finding that place was tedious, maybe impossible.

"Hey, guys," Sam called from across the table, "look here. This is what I was talking about." Mike, Steve, and Kreiter moved quickly to her point of interest.

"Look," Sam continued, "the shipping manifest number on one of the crates in Iraq is a number in Broussard's phone list. Right here."

Sure enough and incredibly, the crates that Steven Granger and a unit of Marines and Rangers had discovered in the small garage in Abd al Baqi, Iraq, bore the exact numeric sequence as a "telephone number" in one of Broussard's contact lists.

Kreiter leaned toward the lists of numbers. "Has anyone done much work on the rest of these numbers?"

"Yeah." Sam pointed up the page. "Here, these are the coordinates for the containment domes at the Oak Mountain Power Plant."

"What about the rest?" Kreiter asked.

"Every number prior to those two are legit. Somebody he knew," Sam answered. "We sorta got busy and didn't take it any further, to my knowledge."

"Wasn't Tucker the one who brought that to your attention?" Mike asked. "Check with him and see what else they found."

"Got it," Sam replied as she reached for her phone.

"Matt, why don't you and Steve go over the phone list and see if any other manifest numbers match," Mike said, checking the time on his phone. It was getting close to the time the Chinese were set to arrive for a meeting with President Makin.

The phone in his pocket vibrated.

"Trapper."

"Hey, Trapper," Elli's voice cooed into his ear. She'd done it again. Her voice and the smile he could imagine accompanying it took him to an entirely different place, much like a fresh breeze or a cool splash of water. "Got a minute?"

"Just," Mike answered. "Big meeting in a minute. What's up?"

"Wanted to let you know I survived Mom's cooking breakfast in my kitchen," Elli snickered. It made Mike smile.

"Thanks, babe. I'll let the president know. I'm sure he's concerned," Mike teased.

"I knew he would be," Elli said with firm confidence. "Really, I just wanted to hear your voice. I think we're headed to the park later, so call my cell."

"Are you up to that?" Mike asked. "How's your shoulder?"

Two nights before, Mike had almost lost her in the hay field about a mile north of her parent's home. That was the night that terror came too close. From then on, every word, smile, touch or look was new and significant to him.

"I have to get out of the house," Elli replied. "Dad will drive and Mom will watch the kids. I just need some air."

Elli and Mike shared a unique friendship. She was a solid rock he could always count on. To her, he was the shield and protector she'd always dreamed about. They were perfect complements to each other.

"Okay. Sounds like an adventure. And hearing your voice makes my day." In the few seconds of their conversation, he felt his tension unwind. "I'll call you later, babe. I've gotta go."

They said goodbye. The president was waiting.

North Flynn Ave., Oklahoma City, OK – 8:55 AM CST

The fight would begin in a matter of seconds. The terrorist mob was trashing the house next door. Their laughter carried the threat of immediate danger. Robert watched his companions.

Pamela eyed the back, counting the men in her neighbor's backyard. Ten heavily armed men speaking Spanish. She understood what she could hear. What she could not comprehend was the cavalier attitude these men seemed to have about breaking into someone's home to kill them.

Then, everything grew quiet. Robert could not see the street from his position. Leaning out to see the back would reveal his hiding spot. Everyone was still. *The first shots fired at the assailants will draw the entire band of marauders to us.* He felt their odds of survival dropping quickly.

The front door burst open. Automatic weapons fire raked the living room and stopped suddenly. More men entered the room. As they came into the house they lowered their weapons and stood staring at the wall.

Why did they stop? Robert wondered. He could wait, but a second or two was more than enough.

"Now!" he whispered. Six rifles responded immediately. Each weapon held seven cartridges in a clip, and every shot had to count. The men in the living room scrambled to raise their guns but were cut down. The last man to enter turned to run and dropped dead on the porch.

"In back! In back!" Pamela shouted as she began firing. Robert spun and fired three times, dropping three men.

Pamela stopped to change her clip. Robert fired again. Then, *click!* He was out of ammunition. A lone man stood five feet from the screen door in back. He roared like a wild beast and charged the house.

Robert bolted toward the door. The bright morning sun prevented the attacker from seeing inside the shaded house, so Robert held the element of surprise if he could get to the door first.

The clash of wood, screen, weapons, and human flesh was unmistakable as Robert flew through the screen door, knocking the man backward and down the porch steps. They tumbled into the backyard.

Robert rolled to his right, tossed the screen door aside, and sprang to his feet. The man he flattened was disoriented but not ready to give up. He struggled to regain his footing. Robert dove into him, punching his face and bloodying his nose and lip. He then stomped on the man's abdomen, forcing the air from his lungs, grabbed his head and twisted it sharply to the right. He heard it snap.

Robert let him drop to the ground. BOOM! Pamela's rifle exploded just over his shoulder. He looked at her. The weapon was at her hip, and the smoke from the fired cartridge wafted around her. Robert spun to see another man crumple to the ground.

Quickly, they grabbed the weapons from the two fallen men and as much ammunition as they could find. Their position was known. The next few moments would be decisive. Robert was certain the next wave would be overwhelming.

Meanwhile, the men inside stripped the fallen terrorists of their weapons and moved to the front of the house. A large number of men gathered in front of the home. No question the enemy would be planning to bring an all-out assault.

Robert entered from the back of the house to survey the situation. To his surprise, the house-to-house search the terrorists had begun seemed to have fallen apart.

Armed fanatics ran from every direction and congregated directly in front of the house. A great discussion raged among the angry throng. The mob came to a decision and stormed the house.

Robert and the four others opened fire with the automatic weapons taken from the fallen thugs. In addition, the armed neighbors in the three other houses began firing. The group of terrorists was caught in the open.

Their retreat was without ceremony. They ran up the street toward the hotel with the hope of regrouping. The men and women of the neighborhood flooded into their front yards and continued firing until the insurgents were out of sight. The street was littered with dead and wounded.

Robert stood in the living room where the invaders had come to a stop. He turned to look at the wall at which the men had stared. He smiled. A painting of the Virgin Mary on black velvet hung on the wall. Something must have stirred in the men's memories. Something important enough to make them take a pause, a fatal pause.

From nowhere, three Apache attack helicopters swooped overhead. They were mere moments late, but the thunder of their fly-by provided a final display of force. A burst of .50 caliber machine gun fire echoed from the hotel. Two fireballs erupted into view. Robert presumed they were exploding fuel tanks, possibly on vehicles seeking escape.

The choppers wheeled back toward Flynn Ave. and set down on the south end of the street. A man in a flight suit hopped from the first Apache and jogged toward Robert.

"You guys are supposed to come back with us," he yelled over the thumping of the turning props. Robert acknowledged and turned to the men he'd fought alongside.

"You should probably plan a visit with family or friends a good ways away from here," Robert said to David Marcink and his neighbors, "and do it right now." No one needed a second recommendation. They all nodded and headed to their trucks and cars still parked along the street.

Robert and the three SEALs jogged toward the Apaches. The strike back at the invaders had begun. He knew they would be back to finish it. And they would be back soon.

Oval Office, White House – 10:00 AM EST

Mike stepped into the Oval Office. President Makin was on the phone and waved for him to come on in. He entered and sat on one of the couches by the Presidential Seal in the carpeting.

"No, no, that's fine," the president said into the phone. "I'm glad you found that. Just get it here as soon as you can, all right? Fine. Thank you." He hung up the phone and with a serious stare looked at Mike. "It seems there has been significant chatter from the Chinese on all this. Not all of it's friendly."

"I guess one might consider invading a sovereign nation without cause or warning as unfriendly chatter," Mike said.

"No, I mean between the Chinese! Several NORAD units have picked up some very heated discussions. It's all going through OCT Little Rock for verification." The president leaned back in his chair and stared across his desk. "Mike, we haven't heard a word down official channels. There is nothing through diplomats, courier, envoys, nothing. Anything new from you?"

"A thousand leads to something or other," Mike answered.

"I mobilized the military," the president offered. "The bases are communicating with each other, and the joint chiefs are making sure the plans don't conflict. We can't leave an open door for anyone to get away."

"It's going to be difficult for an army of troops to go after a mob."

"The ALI maps are a great tool." The president stood and walked toward the couch. "We have the advantage of advanced communications and surprise. We know where they are, and they don't know we're coming."

The door to the Oval Office opened swiftly. Steve Granger and Matt Kreiter entered, then Rick Johnston and George Raker. No one smiled.

"Mr. President," Granger began, "please excuse the intrusion. We have reason to believe there is a threat to the White House."

The president stood beside the couch across from Mike, then he sat. "You'd better fill me in on what you think it is then."

"Colonel Stevens at OCT Little Rock sent us this recording just a minute ago," Kreiter explained. "It's in Chinese, of course, but their interpretation is spot-on, and I agree with the translation. Here's the text."

The president scanned the report. "Okay, what does it mean?"

"Mr. President, we believe the code name for the deployment of soldiers along the borders is 'DRAGON.' Several initial transmissions have referred to the *foot of the Dragon*, leading us to believe the foot is that band of several thousand troops."

"All right, that makes sense. What about the White House?" the president asked.

"Sir, there have been references to the eye, tail, wings, breath and teeth of the dragon. The only other part we've identified is the *wing of the dragon*," Kreiter continued. "We believe the wings are the planes that were spotted flying over Alaska."

"In the last few minutes," Granger said, "several of those planes have landed at airports all along both borders and outside several major cities. We assume they're out of fuel. Some have landed in open country. Others glided into airports like an arriving flight. The crews simply deplaned and sat down on the ground."

"How many planes?" the president asked.

"Right at eleven hundred, Mr. President," Kreiter said.

"And one of them landed near here. Am I correct?"

"Yes, Mr. President," Granger answered, "One glided into Reagan National a few minutes ago. They rolled to a stop on the tarmac; the crew climbed down and sat on the pavement. No weapons. No other troops. The plane is empty."

"Didn't they get picked up on radar, or make radio contact?" the president stood in surprise and moved to his desk.

"The planes are stealth, and no, we didn't see them. No fighters were scrambled," Kreiter said. "The only radio contact was consistent with any approaching aircraft. The tower had no idea what was coming at them."

"Mr. President, these planes have a five-hundred-foot wingspan and are as long as a football field. The planes are so large there's barely room for one to park on the tarmac," Granger added.

The room was silent. The planes had circumnavigated the globe spotted by only one individual. Over one hundred thousand troops were deployed on the borders, and now giant planes were silently drifting into airports all over the country.

"It's as if they aren't even there. Like a breath," the president said.

"Yes, Mr. President," Kreiter replied. "Like a *dragon's breath*."

Los Angeles, CA – 7:15 AM PST

Lieutenant Mark Strattmann rode in the passenger seat of the lead car in a six-vehicle convoy through the streets of Los Angeles. The enemy never showed until after the Marines were gone. Even when the convoy looped back, somehow the enemy knew they were coming and vanished. The lieutenant and his detail felt they were being tricked, made fun of. None of it sat well. Everyone was on edge.

Their morning excursion had taken them through the city streets paralleling the Santa Monica Freeway, then the Rosa Parks Freeway. Always the same, no one in sight. They looped north past Wilshire Boulevard and headed east on Sixth Street through New Downtown. As they passed under the Golden State Freeway, they saw a large crowd in Hollenbeck Park. It looked like an army.

The convoy pulled to the curb at the north end of the park. The American soldiers looked at the crowd in amazement. It *was* an army. At that moment, at least a dozen armed soldiers began jogging toward the convoy.

"Weapons up!" Lieutenant Strattmann commanded through his headset. Sixty-two Marines shouldered their rifles and every nerve in their bodies ran hot. "Hold your fire and position," he commanded.

The soldiers stopped twenty-five feet from the convoy in a spread formation. The barrels of their weapons were pointed toward the sky. They were sober and well-disciplined soldiers, strictly commanded by their officer. And there was one more thing that was beyond question. There was no doubt. They were Chinese.

Dallas North Tollway, Addison, TX – 9:15 AM CST

Parker thought how strange it was to see this highway deserted. The Tollway was always busy in rush hour. Today, it was deserted. But it made getting somewhere easy, and limited both travel time and exposure. The latter being the more important.

The two Bradley personnel carriers screamed down the roadway, each loaded with a half dozen heavily armed Marines. They were Marine Reserves each with a minimum of two Mid-Eastern tours. Remembering how to fight was never a problem, a skill that returned automatically. Forgetting the firefights of the past was another matter.

Their target was the Courtyard on Belt Line Road less than a block off the Tollway. Parker's orders were to get his men in place along the east side of the hotel. The east side of the building provided great cover according to the satellite pictures Parker reviewed. Their deployment would be simple and unseen from the east, but to the north was an open field. How does one deploy covertly in broad daylight in an open field? He decided to leave that to Colonel Maris and the III ACR Phantoms.

Parker would simply play it by ear the same way they had all week. Watch, wait, and then make their move. Their small patrol was only back-up for the regular Army. The Phantoms would arrive on the scene with overwhelming force without warning. If they were lucky, the regulars would eliminate or contain the enemy force with little resistance and a minimal contribution from the Phantom Patriots. If they were lucky.

Their exit came up fast. Minks rode the brakes hard to slow the massive Bradley and make the turn onto Spectrum Drive. He steered into the first parking lot and came to a hard stop beneath the trees along the east side curb.

"Minks," Parker complained, "this is a tow-away zone, you idiot!"

Minks grinned at the ribbing and looked at Jim as he opened the cab door. "So," he said, "I've got a great big gun. Nobody gonna fuss with me, Lieutenant." Minks laughed and pulled the chinstrap tight on his helmet. "Let's go get some target practice!"

"Hold on!" Parker called as the soldiers exited the vehicles. "Circle up!" The men circled around their young officer for directions to their positions. Jim felt they were in a good spot, out of direct sight from the Courtyard Hotel, and they had plenty of time. He gave them the specifics for their positions before they headed west across Spectrum Drive.

Parker estimated they were just over two hundred yards from the hotel where the high command of the invaders had established their headquarters. The hotel was plush in comparison to the ones Parker and his small army had sacked earlier in the week. The Courtyard was less than a mile from what remained of the Addison Police Department where the terror had begun. To be part of the mission to finish off this bunch was an honor.

The small group, the Phantom Patriots, walked steadily toward the hedgerow now only yards away. As they drew near, they crept to their positions. Parker studied their deployment and adjusted their locations with hand signals.

Suddenly, Parker's earpiece crackled.

"Phantom Patriots, this is III ACR Phantoms, Eagle Three. Do you copy? Over."

Jim pulled the mouthpiece to position. "Eagle Three, this is Phantom Patriots, Viper Six. We do copy. Over."

"Viper Six, this is Eagle Three, confirm your grid. Over."

"Eagle Three, Phantom Patriots are on grid and set. Over." Jim Parker had not a clue who Eagle Three was, but he knew the 3rd Armored Cavalry Regiment was on the way.

"Affirmative. Eagle Three out." Things were about to get very busy.

chapter 8

I-35 and I-240, Oklahoma City, OK – 9:12 AM CST

The Apache helicopters carrying Robert and the SEALs wheeled to a landing in the median of the interstate. The location was designated as the point of rendezvous for the volunteers from Norman, Oklahoma City and the 2nd and 3rd Air Defense Artillery Regiments from Fort Sill, OK.

A small group of retired soldiers stood at the roadside. As the giant props of the helicopters silently swung toward a stop, Robert and the SEALs greeted their fellow retirees. They shared the morning's events and discussed the troop strength and weaponry they were up against.

Until the main battle group arrived from Fort Sill there was little more to do than keep their eyes open and wait. Waiting was something every recruit learns early in their military career, though it was never easy. Waiting was simply part of the plan.

Oval Office, White House – 10:20 AM EST

President Al Makin was not known for being a strong man, but he wasn't a coward. In his short term as president, he'd faced difficult decisions and frightening events, and handled them well. The news of a threat to Washington DC and the White House didn't send him scurrying to a secure location. He would stand his ground until there was a visible threat, then decide about leaving the premises.

The large Chinese airplane was indeed on the ground and empty. The location of the troops and equipment the plane carried halfway around the world was unknown. But then again, there were lots of unknowns at the moment. One more wouldn't change very much.

The president concluded the discussion of immediate options with the five Secret Service agents standing around his desk asking him to relocate for his safety. He would not be running away from this. He was commander-in-chief, and he would stay in command. The agents surrendered to his wish.

"I know you're thinking about the country and protecting the office of the president, but we have no immediate threat. No need to relocate." The president was firm. The intercom beeped on his desk.

"Yes, Sharon, what is it?" he asked.

"Mr. President, the gentleman from the Chinese Embassy is here to see you."

"Thank you, Sharon. Give us a minute, please." President Makin turned to the men around his desk. "Normally, I'd ask you to leave. This time I want all of you in here for this meeting, especially you, Kreiter. Your Chinese might come in handy. Besides, I like having my team around me."

"Yes, Mr. President," each man responded respectfully. If there was an actionable threat on the White House, at least they would be at the center of it.

"Mr. President," Mike Trapper said quietly leaning close to his ear, "does it strike you odd that the ambassador himself is not here?"

"It does, Mike. We'll just have to see who this is, and what he has to offer us." The president shrugged. Then he spoke to the intercom. "Sharon, please bring the gentleman in."

The door opened, but before entering the Oval Office, a very smartly dressed man adjusted his tie and jacket using the mirror just outside the door.

Mike watched the man adjust his tie, thinking it a strange moment for vanity, then his vision blurred, just for a second. He blinked and rubbed his eyes. *I must be more tired than I thought,* he said to himself. Then, it happened again! And, a third time! *What's going on?*

Mike inwardly feared the stress of the week was finally crashing on him. His vision never blurred. He had perfect eyesight. He checked his pulse by covering his ear with his index finger. His normal whooshing pulse echoed in his eardrum. He didn't feel dizzy or nauseous. The oddity in his vision was not normal, but he felt fine.

The Chinese representative, a man in his early forties who had a slight build and engaging smile, walked to the front of the president's desk, bowed respectfully and extended his hand. "Good morning, Mr. President. I am the special envoy to the ambassador, Chen Bai Lan," he said without breaking his smile.

President Makin shook his hand and replied, "Very pleased to meet you Mr. Chen. I was hoping the ambassador would come personally."

"Please, Mr. President, do excuse my superior's absence from this meeting. We understand your surprise regarding the events of the past few hours. Ambassador Wang has been in constant contact with our State Council seeking clarification. He asked that I meet with you at this time."

"Mr. Chen," the president said without wavering, "with all due respect, and I appreciate your coming to meet with me this morning, but the relationship between our countries is at a dangerous juncture. I must have some explanation of your Party's intent and justification for your actions. I mean, one country just doesn't occupy the borders of another nation on a whim."

"Of course, Mr. President," Chen replied and bowed slightly, showing respect. Chen's eyes shifted downward and across the Resolute Desk that served many past presidents. The Resolute Desk that was born of history, and witness to much more. This day was to be another of those days of history. Chen raised his eyes to look directly into the eyes of the president of the United States of America.

"Mr. President," Chen said firmly and without a smile, "for decades we have worked together to build our nations, both as adversaries and friends. But the strength of our nations can only be measured by action and determination, not in mere words. As we witnessed the assassination of President Marshall a few days ago, the People's Republic of China realized you have not taken the measures of strength necessary to protect yourselves. Your borders are open and have allowed an enemy to invade your lands, ravish your citizens, and threaten your national treasure! Such weakness and lack of resolve is dangerous and cannot be permitted.

"As we watched the confusion, we knew we must take action that you would not take yourselves. We mobilized nearly two hundred thousand soldiers to deploy in your country for your protection. Using our superior technology, we have compromised your highest security and taken command of the borders of your nation. Our stealth transport planes were developed from technology you discarded. Our troops deployed without detection, enabled by concepts your military deemed childish. Toy-like. But we are not working with toys, Mr. President. Behold! *Xian ming!*"

At Chen's command, the Oval Office became host to six Chinese soldiers. Trapper and the others stood in stunned silence.

How is that possible? Mike thought. *Where'd they come . . . the blurs! The blurs in my vision! Wrinkles in light from the bent rays in the visual spectrum. Meta-black material! Ultra-black cloth that absorbs all visible light while allowing reflected light from other sources to pass through the shrouded object. Invisibility cloaks!*

Trapper's eyes shifted wildly from soldier to soldier, looking for an indication of threat or danger to the president. The soldiers stood at attention, perfectly still. They didn't move. No one raised a weapon. Their presence in the office of the president was more than enough.

"Mr. President, gentlemen," Chen finally said, "we mean you no harm. We mean only to demonstrate to you our capabilities, so you might understand the power we have."

"Very effective. Very impressive," The president's voice cracked, obviously stressed by the shocking revelation. Soldiers of a foreign army had never stood in the Oval Office. "You have demonstrated a very unique," he paused, "advantage over us."

As he spoke, Al Makin leaned forward with both hands on the Desk. He appeared shaken, weak and on the verge of collapse. As he rested his hands on the edge of that old desk, his left thumb pressed firmly into the carved inlay trimming the top.

At the same instant, a small blue light flashed on his secretary's computer screen. It meant "threat to the president," *lese majeste,* violation of a sovereign. Sharon Fair had never rehearsed for this alert, but she knew exactly what to do. She pushed the small button on the left pedestal of her desk, picked up her purse, and walked directly out of the office.

Throughout the White House small obscure blue lights flashed. The earpieces of the Secret Service Agents on every floor and at every station in the complex sounded the warning. As civilian employees abandoned their workstations, agents converged to assigned positions.

"Mr. President," Chen said, "my nation fears the weakness we have observed in this country may affect our financial interest in the United States. The action we have taken is to preserve and help protect our interests."

As Chen spoke, George Raker slowly took the president's arm and moved him behind his own large frame. The president did not resist. Steve Granger and Rick Johnston inched closer to the president's side. Trapper and Kreiter stood at each end of the Resolute Desk, watching for movement from anyone. The Chinese soldiers remained frozen at attention.

"We wish to bring—" Chen began.

A loud POP came from a peculiar object in the hand of the Chinese soldier immediately behind Chen. The diplomat dropped to the floor, blood oozing from a wound behind his right ear.

"Imperialist!" the soldier shouted loudly, still holding the strange weapon he used to kill the Chinese envoy.

Boom! Kreiter's .40 caliber Smith & Wesson blasted the head of the assassin, throwing him across the room. The next second was filled with the metallic rustle of weapons being drawn and hammers cocked. Five armed American agents surrounded the president, facing the five Chinese soldiers who now held the same strangely shaped weapons. Two Chinese nationals lay dead on the floor of the Oval Office. It was a standoff.

"Your weapons are no good," Kreiter said in flawless Mandarin. "They are made of plastic and will explode in your hand if they fire at all." The Chinese looked at their guns then at each other. "Your dead friend was lucky his gun did not explode. You are not lucky right now. Our weapons are proven and deadly. You may choose."

As Kreiter spoke, George Raker backed the president toward the bookshelf to his left. They moved very slowly, their eyes never leaving the Chinese. George reached out with his left hand and pushed on the three end volumes on the fourth shelf. With a soft whishing sound the panel slid back revealing an opening, an avenue of escape.

President Makin was thrust into the opening quickly, followed by George Raker, Rick Johnston, and Steve Granger. Trapper and Kreiter backed their way to the doorway with their weapons at ready, then slipped through the narrow opening just as the panel slammed shut.

Mainside Observation Room, Camp Pendleton – 7:25 AM PST

Sergeant Major John Michaels sat at the observation console with Captain Bob Prescott. The monitors before them flicked from one cell to another. Some of the men in the cells slept, some prayed, others simply sat on their sleeping mats.

The interrogations of the prisoners were hard, but not enhanced. Newer technology allowed prisoners to be probed for emotional responses, for keys in how to direct the questioning. It was very effective and revealed a great deal. None of the men held in the cells possessed documentation that brought them into the country by legal channels. All of them participated in the attack of a US Military base. Every one of them was a foreign national from the Middle East and Muslim. Each man embraced jihad against the West, a jihad that failed.

"What else have you learned from these guys, captain?" asked Michaels. John Michaels knew the value as well as the risks of enhanced or unusual methods of interrogations. From his experience in the evacuation of Vietnam, dealing with prisoners from Central America, Iraq and Afghanistan, and the ongoing campaigns at Gitmo, he knew interrogation can be a slippery slope. Today, the utmost care and professionalism was required.

"Other than the five guys who talked about this *Isa*, pretty much what we expected," Captain Prescott replied. "We've determined who the ringleaders are and given them special attention. They provided information on the larger plan. That's the stuff we sent to Washington last night. Most of these guys, they're just troops. Generally, nice people who want to see us dead."

Prescott smiled, and both men chuckled slightly. It wasn't a funny matter, but they were glad the tables were turned for these insurgents. The world was much safer with them locked in a room.

The door to the observation room opened partway, and a man in his thirties poked his head in. "Captain Prescott?"

"Lieutenant Hamza, please come in," Prescott said as he stood and extended his hand.

Caleb Hamza, Muslim cleric at Camp Pendleton, smiled and entered the room. Sergeant Major Michaels stood and greeted the cleric. Lieutenant Hamza was born in Iran, but his parents managed to escape and come to the States by way of a handful of European countries.

Hamza remembered little of the journey in his childhood and grew up on Chicago's Southside. His father often joked that the rough neighborhood of Chicago was heaven on earth compared to the insanity he witnessed in their hometown, Eslam Shahr, on the outskirts of Tehran. The family continued as devoted Muslims, hard-working business people, and a loving family. The disaster of the World Trade Center towers in 2001 inspired young Caleb Hamza to serve his adopted country. His father and mother were proud of him and how his personal faith had led him to study and serve Muslim members of the military. His desire was to promote understanding and tolerance among the American soldiers.

"I am sorry for you to have waited so long for me. I worked late last night and was sleeping when the call came," Hamza explained.

"Chaplain Hamza, no explanation required," Michaels replied. "Thank you for coming."

"Very well, then," the chaplain said. "What can I do for you?"

"We have several of the prisoners demonstrating unusual behavior. We were hoping you could help us," Captain Prescott said. "We're not sure if it is a Muslim thing or not."

"Captain, I am very well versed in Muslim *things*, as you call them," Hamza countered with a smile. "What's happening?"

"We've monitored all the prisoners for the last several days, as well as interrogated them. But there is one event we've encountered we can't figure out." Captain Prescott was not a religious man and displayed his discomfort by glancing away from the chaplain, then down at the desk top.

"And this event you speak of is . . .? Can you be more specific?"

"Five of the men have been observed standing or kneeling in their cells, as if . . . well, they're having a conversation with a person, but no one else is there. I mean, we hear the prisoner talk . . . they even ask questions. Then respond saying they understand. But nobody said anything." Prescott fumbled his words, glancing away and back at Humza. He was clearly out of his element. "It . . . it just doesn't make sense. Is there some Muslim tradition, mystic ritual or something we don't understand?"

"Do the men have a name for this *person* with whom they are speaking?" Hamza asked.

"Yeah, they all say the same thing," Prescott responded. "They all call him *Isa*."

Caleb Hamza's eyes fell to the floor. His response was clearly emotional. He was silent.

"Lieutenant Hamza," Michaels inquired, "are you all right?"

"Yes. Yes, I am fine," Hamza answered without raising his head. "I am sorry, sergeant major. I am fine." Chaplin Hamza raised his head and looked at the two men; his eyes were moist.

"Gentlemen," he said, "this man, *Isa*, I know him."

chapter 9

White House Basement – 10:27 AM EST

The descent was rapid, almost freefall. The stop at the bottom was jarring, but not to the point of breaking a bone. Mike had no idea how deep into the earth they were, but he'd never moved down as far and as fast as in this elevator in a few seconds. When the door opened the room before them was dark.

George was the first out of the elevator. He turned immediately to his left, and the lights flickered on. Before them was a sterile environment of grey carpets and institutionally colored walls from the sixties. Oddly enough, the hallway was very clean. Old, unused, but surprisingly clean.

"How long has this been here?" asked a slightly disturbed president.

"Since Kennedy, sir," George replied. "In the early days of the Cold War, surprise attack was expected. This went in after the standoff with Cuba, shortly before Kennedy was assassinated."

"And it's never been used?" Granger asked.

"Not to my knowledge," George replied. "Let's see what we have down here."

Trapper and Granger moved down the hallway to the right, which was lined by six closed but unlocked doors. As they opened each door, the lights automatically illuminated the room. The first two rooms looked about thirty feet square and held up-to-date computers, video screens and communications equipment. The next four rooms were filled with bunk beds, made up and ready for use.

Kreiter stayed at the elevator with the president as George and Rick checked the four doors to the left. The first door opened to a larger conference room, again loaded with the latest hardware. A door on the far side toward the corner appeared to be a closet. The other three rooms contained a kitchen fitted with every possible convenience, another communications room, and a workshop equipped with every imaginable machining tool.

"Hey, guys!" Kreiter called down the hall to Trapper and Granger. "There's a conference room down here with phones." He escorted the president into the room as the others joined them. President Makin sat at the head of the table and reached for a phone. Before he said anything into the receiver, he heard a voice.

"Yes, Mr. President." It was Larry Brewer, a Secret Service agent who participated in the arrest and interrogation of Ron Wallis.

"Agent Brewer?" The president was baffled by everything around him. It seemed everyone else knew what was going on while he felt lost. "Uh, where are you at the moment?" he asked sheepishly.

"Mr. President, my team and I are in Pod Four. You and the men with you are in Pod One."

Pod One? Pod Four? The president's head was spinning. "Do you have any questions, Mr. President?"

Well, that was the understatement of the month. Al Makin didn't quite know where to begin. He had a thousand questions.

"First," he began, "tell me what's going on. Wait, I want this on speaker."

Agent Brewer told the president and the men with him the events of the last ten minutes in the White House and the surrounding grounds. More than five hundred Chinese soldiers, equipped with the invisibility cloaks, suddenly appeared moments after the shots were fired in the Oval Office.

The Secret Service agents at the mansion were overwhelmed. The odds were two invisible soldiers from the Peoples Republic of China to each agent. No additional shots were fired.

Most of the civilian employees made it out of the building but not off the White House grounds. An undetermined number were being detained. According to Brewer, four of the six rapid-descent elevators had been activated and on the lower level, but no contact with the occupants was established.

"All right, thank you Agent Brewer. We need to get a count of everyone, and then we need to get out of here," the president said.

"Yes, Mr. President," Brewer replied. "As we speak, agents are bringing the remaining two elevators down. That seals the openings in the White House and denies access from above."

"Very go—"

Before the president's words escaped his mouth, the metal "closet" door in the corner swung open. Five holstered weapons were whipped out simultaneously and aimed at the intruder.

It was Sam.

Sheriff's Office, Norman, OK – 9:30 AM CST

Sheriff Perry Hitchens sat at the head of the conference room table. Captain Richard Turner was mapping a strategy to deal with the known locations of terrorists in Oklahoma City. Everyone at the table wanted a key role in the assault, and employing the best assets of every team demanded some very serious strategizing.

"I got a text message from Fort Sill," the captain began. "They are fully mobilized and will depart their base within the hour. It'll take them an hour or so to cover the seventy miles between Fort Sill and Oklahoma City, so there's not a lot of time to spare. We're gonna meet up at I-240 and the H. E. Bailey. McConnell has promised some more air support as soon as we get the new ALI maps from Washington. Get as many of the guys from your units as you can and report back here by 1100 hours. We'll have the deployments for the regulars ready before they arrive. Any questions?"

As the men left the conference room, Sheriff Hitchens approached the captain.

"Richard, I did have one question, if you don't mind?" the sheriff asked.

"Not at all, Perry, what can I do for you?"

"My son, Robert. I know he went into the city for some surveillance. Have you heard anything?" The look in Perry Hitchens's eye conveyed dark concern. He wasn't a fatalistic man, but he understood the odds, and that soldiers were sometimes expendable.

"I haven't. I'll let you know first thing I hear." Captain Turner took a breath. "He's a very skilled fighter, Perry."

Sheriff Hitchens knew he was right. Still his eyes fell to the floor as he nodded agreement. The sheriff looked up at the younger officer. He knew they were doing everything possible to find Robert.

"You're right," Perry said. "He's strong. He can handle himself."

National Zoological Park, Washington DC – 10:33 AM EST

The arrival at the zoo was as one might expect. The children burst from the car and ran into the parking lot, unaware there might be approaching traffic. Quick responses from the grandparents corralled the extra energy.

Elli slowly eased herself from the vehicle. She was white as a sheet and a little wobbly on her feet. She didn't know if it was the drugs or the shock of the attack hanging on, but she wasn't well.

"Honey, are you feeling all right?" Granddad asked as they walked toward the gate. "You look like you're about to faint."

"Oh, Dad, I think I'm going insane," she replied.

"You've been through an awful lot," he said, comforting her. "Give yourself a little space. It's gonna take some time before you're one-hundred percent."

"I'm not sure one-hundred percent is possible," she moaned. "I hate to be a drag on such a wonderful day, but I just don't know. I think I'm hallucinating."

"You're gonna be fine," he said. "The great outdoors will help."

Elli was so focused on how she felt that she had ignored the bright sun and wonderful fresh air. She stopped and breathed deeply. It did help. The spring air washed through her, making her tingle. She looked at her dad and smiled.

"I think you're right," she said. "I'll be fine."

As they drew nearer to the gate, Elli suddenly gasped and stopped. She was looking at the bushes beside the entrance.

"Elli?" Grandma asked. "Sweetheart, are you okay?"

Elli looked at the ground and stiffened her internal resolve.

"Yes, Mom," she said looking straight ahead. "I'm fine. The pain pills are making me a little crazy today, but I'm fine." Elli looked directly ahead and made a beeline for the gate. *Nope, I don't believe it. I'm not going to be crazy today*, she said to herself.

Hollenbeck Park, Los Angeles, CA – 7:35 AM PST

Lieutenant Strattmann spent half an hour waiting for a response from Camp Pendleton command. The Chinese officer remained standing about twenty-five feet away from the Marine vehicles. He just looked at them. He didn't move. He didn't speak. None of the Chinese spoke or moved. Finally, the radio squawked.

"Rover Six, this is Central Six, do you read me? Over." It was the voice of Brigadier General Gene Westrup. Strattmann knew his voice well.

"Central Six, this is Rover Six. We copy. Over." Strattmann fidgeted in his seat.

"Rover Six, I've been advised of your situation. Is there any change? Over."

"Central Six, conditions are static. Awaiting your recommendation, sir. Over."

"Rover Six, why don't you just go over to the man and ask him what he wants? Over." Strattmann couldn't quite believe what he heard, but it made sense. No one wanted a gunfight, but it was obvious these men had flown around the globe for a reason.

"Affirmative, Central Six. I'll be right back. Over." Strattmann handed the mike to the sergeant, leaned his rifle against the Bradley, and walked toward the Chinese officer. He came to a stop only a few feet from the man.

"Lieutenant Mark Strattmann, US Marine Corp. How may I help you?" Strattmann kept his tone moderated. He didn't want to sound threatening, nor did he want to appear timid. He extended his right hand.

The Chinese officer reached out and took his hand and broke into a broad smile. "I am very pleased to meet you, Lieutenant Strattmann. I am Colonel Zu Cheng of the 1st Paratrooper Brigade of the Army of the People's Republic of China."

His grip was firm and his English impeccable. Strattmann was surprised, and it registered on his face.

"Colonel, you speak very well. I mean, well, I was—"

"I understand, Lieutenant Strattmann. I attended four years of college a couple of miles west of here. This is like coming home for me. I am very excited!" The officer was grinning broadly.

Strattmann was shocked. Of course, he knew about foreign exchange programs, even from China, but he never imagined a Chinese army in Los Angeles led by one. He was speechless.

"Lieutenant," Zu Cheng began, "Our High Command in Beijing was greatly alarmed with the assassination of your President Marshall. We were mobilized that very night. We didn't know if your nation could or *would* hold itself together under the strain. When our leaders witnessed the invasion of your borders, we were immediately deployed. Lieutenant, we have come to aid you in repelling the vermin that has overrun your country."

Lieutenant Strattmann was certain his mouth was hanging open. He blinked, moistened his lips, and, raising his index finger, said, "Colonel, please wait right here for just one minute. Okay?"

"Most certainly, lieutenant," Zu Cheng replied smiling.

He wasn't sure if he staggered, stumbled, or ran back to the Bradley and the sergeant holding the mike. But he was pretty sure his retreat wasn't graceful.

"Uh, general, sir," he stammered, "I mean, Central Six, this is Rover Six. Do you copy? Over."

"Yes, we do, son. What did you find out?" The general's voice was soothing.

"Well, uh, sir, you're just not going to believe this."

chapter 10

Courtyard Hotel, Dallas, TX – 9:40 AM CST

Lieutenant Jim Parker and ten Marines, now known as the Phantom Patriots, were deployed in the brush lining the east edge of the parking lot for the Courtyard Hotel. Parker knew his men were patient. His biggest concern was not their lack of discipline. It was fire ants.

Parker hated fire ants. Their sting was painful and usually covered a large area of the victim's body. He really hated fire ants, but they seemed to love him. Even a casual outing like a picnic would draw the nasty critters to Jim Parker before anyone else. It never failed. And here he was lying flat on his belly in the brush. It was a perfect place to find fire ants. Rather, for them to find Jim Parker.

The earpiece in Parker's helmet crackled to life.

"Phantom Patriots, this is III ACR Phantoms, Eagle Three. Do you copy? Over."

Jim lowered the mouthpiece and said, "Eagle Three, this is Phantom Patriots, Viper Six. Copy. Over."

"Viper Six, this is Eagle Three, we have you on grid. Be advised we are proceeding to engage. Over."

"Roger, Eagle Three. On your command. Over."

"Eagle Three out." The abrupt end of the transmission struck Parker as a little odd. He wondered if something was wrong, or if Eagle Three was just busy. He didn't have to wait very long.

The air around him was filled with what sounded like a thousand choppers arriving at a motorcycle convention. He didn't duck but strained through the brush to see what was going on. All he could make out through the tall grass was a cloud of dust and smoke.

As the dust settled, Jim could see the shapes of large military vehicles. They were Cougars and RG-33Ls like he'd ridden in Iraq. The MRAPs were practically bomb-shelters on wheels. Their huge diesel engines were able to propel the vehicle over or through any blockade or embankment. He didn't miss the ride, but they sure were impressive to watch.

Parker counted eight MRAPs in the south parking lot and could see nine more on the north. Possibly an additional three or four were to the west of the Courtyard, but he wasn't sure. What impressed him most was their arrival. A quiet morning was interrupted without warning by the roar of the engines of the MRAPs. When the dust settled, they were there. Like Phantoms, true to their name.

Then, a voice broke the silence. Parker recognized it was the same voice he'd heard in his earpiece. It was Eagle Three.

"Attention!" Eagle Three's voice boomed from speakers on every vehicle surrounding the building. "Attention, those inhabiting the Courtyard Hotel. This is the 3rd Armored Cavalry Regiment of the United States Army. You are guilty of unlawful seizure of private property, bearing arms against the citizens of the United States, and unlawful entry to this country. You will throw down your arms and surrender immediately."

More than a minute passed. The announcement was repeated in Spanish. *"Atención, los que habitan el Hotel Courtyard. Este es el Tercer Regimiento de Caballería del Ejército de los Estados Unidos.*

Ustedes son culpables de violar la propiedad privada, portación de armas contra los ciudadanos de los Estados Unidos, y el allanamiento de este país. ¡Tiren al suelo sus armas y se rindan inmediatamente!"

Again, it was quiet. The only sound was the rustling of the wind in the trees and the occasional cry of a bird in flight. Parker fidgeted in the grass. He knew the fire ants were searching him out. Suddenly, another voice repeated the instructions. This time, it was in Arabic.

Again, no response. The intelligence was good. The only people in the hotel were hostiles. The tenants had been run out or killed days ago. Infrared scans of the building assured those in command that insurgents were hiding in the building. Their time was running out.

"Attention, those on the third floor. Throw down your weapons and surrender immediately!" The command was repeated in Spanish and Arabic. No response.

Parker's earpiece crackled, "SMAW-NE, commence firing at your discretion." The controversial Shoulder Mounted Assault Weapon (SMAW) fires a thermobaric warhead designated as a Novel Explosive (NE.) A single round is capable of demolishing a structure upon impact. The ordnance explodes igniting the air within the structure, incinerating the inhabitants, and producing a shockwave of unparalleled destructive power.

A solitary soldier targeted the SMAW-NE at the third floor. The warhead made a whooshing sound as it streaked toward the hotel that lasted only a second. Within milliseconds the entire top-floor of the hotel was vaporized in a ball of flame. Everything and anyone on that floor was instantly turned to ash. There was no question it was a disproportionate display of force. But it was decisive.

All was silent as the smoke cleared. Suddenly, the silence broke.

"Attention, those on the second floor." It was the same announcement in Spanish and Arabic. *Oh, brother. These guys are going to wait it out!* Parker thought. The silence spoke volumes. Neither side was backing down.

White House Basement – 10:50 AM EST

Mike Trapper's hands were still shaking. Steve Granger hustled Sam to one corner of the room. They were in a very serious discussion, both greatly shaken by the varieties of outcomes her sudden entrance to Pod One had presented. The only man who appeared calm was President Makin. Of course, he hadn't aimed a loaded weapon at a close friend and valuable State Department employee.

George Raker found a file drawer containing a diagram of the six underground Pods. The only access from above was by the high-speed elevators. The original design would have enabled dozens of valued elected officials and staff an escape route from a sudden and undetected nuclear attack, as was feared in the Sixties. Technology had circumvented the reasoning of fear but didn't account for an unexpected arrival of a non-nuclear force in the form of invisible soldiers.

"Have you figured out the diagram?" Trapper asked over George's shoulder. Seeing over the large man was only possible because he rested his elbows on the conference table. The diagram illustrated the locations of the Pods and the elevators leading to them.

"Here's the one we came down in," George said pointing to the overlay of the Oval Office. He then moved his finger across the sheet to the Cabinet Room where the second hidden elevator was found. It hadn't been used.

Sam joined the group at the table. "We came down through the vice president's office. Who would have thought?" Trapper looked at her, wondering if the thought was that of saving the vice president in an emergency or that she was just surprised at the location of the elevator.

A fourth escape elevator was located in the president's study on the other side of the kitchen next to the Oval Office. That one was also unused. The last two escape elevators that were activated had their origin in the White House Residence and the conference room recently used by the Joint Chiefs.

"Sam, did you or anyone on your team make contact with anyone else?" Mike asked.

"Our situation was a little different," she began. "When we heard the shots, the Secret Service guys hustled us out of the Roosevelt Room and into the elevator. Next thing I knew, we were walking into a dark room with lots of doors. We split up and went down several hallways. I stumbled in here and . . . well," Sam shrugged her shoulders, "I know I came very close to being shot."

"I'm glad they were a little slow on the trigger this time. At least they know we're here," the president said.

"That's right. Here's what we're going to do," Mike said taking the lead. "Agent Kreiter, you remain here with the president. Sir, there is no need for you to be running around down here. The rest of us will go back the way Sam came, find everyone, and reassemble here. George, you stay with the diagrams and see if there's a way out."

"Fair enough, Mike," George replied. "I don't care much to be running through dark tunnels hundreds of feet underground. Not appealing."

Mike led Steve, Sam and Rick through the door and down the hallway. The door closed with a heavy thud as they left. The three men remaining in the room were struck by the absolute silence surrounding them. They immediately began poring over the diagrams for a clue to an escape route.

Mainside Observation Room, Camp Pendleton – 8:00 AM PST

The Muslim chaplain, Lieutenant Hamza requested a meeting with the prisoner immediately. Sergeant Major John Michaels was a patient man, but his patience was wearing thin at the moment. The two senior officers agreed to wait, yielding to the importance of the pastoral care of a like-minded believer. They both looked up as the chaplain returned.

"Gentlemen," Hamza began, "thank you so much for your patience. This is a very difficult matter. Sergeant major, captain, what these men are seeing and experiencing is very real. They are well-trained soldiers who have traveled halfway around the world for their faith. This is as much a part of their belief as it is a battle. In Islam, and especially to these men, faith and warfare are difficult to separate.

"American Christians don't understand this alliance of war and faith. Certain believers acknowledge a spiritual warfare between good and evil, darkness and light. Is this not true?"

"Yes," Michaels replied, nodding in agreement. "I think that's close enough."

"Well, a Muslim fights against evil in the same way. But in their case, the *evil* they fight is non-Muslims, other people, especially Americans and Europeans." The young chaplain looked at the two officers, hoping they understood.

Michaels leaned back in his chair with his arms folded across his chest. His face was pensive, but it looked downright scary to the chaplain. Captain Prescott sat stiffly in the straight-backed chair, showing little emotion.

"So, we find these men far from home," Hamza continued, "facing death or a lifetime in prison for the belief they have held all their lives in Islam. Sirs, they are more than fanatical. They are certain of the righteousness of their cause, beyond any shadow or question.

"Suddenly, in their captivity, a man in a glowing white robe appears in their locked cell and speaks to them in their own language. Some in their specific dialect," Hamza said measuring the response on the officers' faces. "This man, this *Isa*, tells them he loves them and understands what they are doing. But he explains to them their devotion is misplaced. He makes it very clear they have followed a dangerous path, and that over time, *Isa* will show them a different path of life. How men can find peace."

"You say, *over time*. What do you mean? These men have only been here a few days," Michaels said, leaning forward on his elbows.

Chaplain Caleb Hamza, man of devotion, a decorated warrior, sat straight in his chair. He looked at each officer. His eyes were unsteady.

"Chaplain?" Captain Prescott asked.

"Sirs, four years ago I served in Afghanistan," Hamza's words were measured and difficult for him to say. "I watched my Muslim brothers fight viciously against my fellow countrymen. I watched them murder and blowup innocent women and children. I couldn't understand what madness had taken hold of Islam. How could these men as Muslims be so brutal to other Muslims? It was driving me insane. Even our American Muslim soldiers lived in terrible turmoil.

"One day, I had more than I could bear. That day, I watched a seven-year-old boy run toward us carrying a small box. He was smiling. Forty or fifty feet from us, the box exploded. He didn't run fast enough to get to us. He was coming to kill us with a smile on his face. I watched him burst into pieces in the explosion.

"After that, I was finished. I took a grenade and walked away from my fellow soldiers. I wanted to die. I was going to pull the pin, curl myself around it, and let it explode. As I knelt to pull the pin, I heard him. I looked up, and a man was standing before me with his hands outstretched to me.

"He said, *'This is not what I have planned for you. This is not the path you are to walk.'* I didn't know who he was, or how he arrived, but the peace that flooded me made me lay the grenade on the ground and listen to him. I don't know, he could have spoken to me for only a minute, or it could have been hours, I do not know.

"I asked him, *'Who are you, and why did you come to me?'* He looked at me with a kindness I have never known. He said, *'I am the one you call Isa al Masih.'*

"I was stunned. I had heard of such a man, but only in legends, stories told by grandfathers to their grandchildren. He is a great prophet of peace and everlasting kindness."

"This *Isa*, you say you saw him too?" Michaels asked.

"Yes sir. I saw him and spoke with him several times," Hamza affirmed.

"Well then, chaplain," Captain Prescott inquired, "who is this *Isa* person?"

"Captain, you would call him Jesus." The young cleric's words fell like boulders of granite in the small office. "I met with him many times in Afghanistan. He explained things to me, and his words changed me. I became a follower of Isa."

"You became a Christian?" Michaels was in shock.

"You can't do that!" Prescott boomed. "Hell, you're the damn Muslim cleric!" Prescott paused and reflected on his words. "Well, what I mean is, how can you be a Muslim chaplain and at the same time follow this man, *Isa*? Jesus!"

Sergeant Major Michaels looked at Captain Prescott with amazement. The conversation had not taken the path he expected. He said, "Yes, chaplain, how do you do that?"

"Yes sir," Hamza replied, "it is a bit of a problem."

chapter 11

Reggie Porter felt great. He didn't know how or why, but the blinding headache was gone. He felt energy he hadn't experienced in over ten years. Whatever was in that *ziao long bao* he'd eaten was amazing. Reggie was determined that once he was on his feet *financially*, he would open a restaurant and sell those things. They were a modern miracle!

In reality, the ancient recipe was a powerful source of protein and herbs that refreshes one's system. Still, Reggie was convinced the wonder-food was the reason those Oriental soldiers could run through the bamboo forest and treetops like he'd seen in movies.

As he pondered his newly realized future, a group of very distinguished Chinese officers escorted by the smiling young soldier approached. He stood, fully aware he smelled like a still, hadn't shaved in a couple of days, and looked like a genuine homeless wino.

"Mr. Porter," the young soldier began, smiling, always smiling, "I am most pleased to introduce you to our esteemed commander.

This is Lieutenant General Wang Shang yi Ho, of the People's Liberation Army."

"Pleased to meet you, General Ho," Reggie stammered extending his hand.

The young soldier's face suddenly blanched as he stepped forward and lowered Reggie's hand. He came close to Reggie's ear and whispered, "No! No, his name is General Wang! *Ho* is first name. And do not shake hands! Bow slightly at waist!"

From the young soldier's near frantic description and his sample bow, Reggie saw the error in his approach. He placed his hands to his side, glanced at the young soldier, and bowed awkwardly toward the general.

"It is quite fine. Thank you, Liang," the general said smiling. "I understand not everyone in America is familiar with our customs and traditions. I am happy to make your acquaintance, Mr. Porter."

The general stepped forward to Reggie and extended his hand. Reggie wasn't accustomed to making anyone's *acquaintance,* much less with Chinese tradition, but he knew a friendly handshake.

"Likewise, I'm sure, general," Reggie replied, this time smiling as well. If everyone around him was smiling, he was going to smile.

"I trust you are feeling better?"

"Oh, yes sir. I don't know what was in that thing, *Liang*, is that your name? Liang?" he asked turning to the young soldier. Liang blushed when Reggie spoke directly to him, rather than to his superior. His furtive glances at the general informed Reggie that he'd blown it again. "What I mean, sir, is that Liang was very helpful, and I feel much better. Thank you," he added hastily.

"Mr. Porter," General Wang took a step away and looked over the activity of troops swirling around them. "You can be very valuable to us in finding the invaders, so we might deal with them quickly. Do you know where we might find them?"

"Oh, yes, sir!" Reggie replied. Although he wasn't sure of their exact location, he was confident he could find them with an army backing him up. "Yes sir. They've been all over the place, but finding them will not be a problem, sir."

"Very well," Wang said. "Corporal Woo Liang will escort you, and you will lead us to them." He barked some commands in Chinese, and soldiers began scurrying in all directions. The general turned and walked away.

"Please, Mr. Porter, you will come with me," Corporal Woo said waving Reggie outside, toward a large troop transport. He ushered him to the front and helped him climb into the roofless cab. The cab of the truck contained two rows of seats, the back row slightly elevated from the driver's seat. The corporal indicated Reggie should get in the back.

Reggie plopped himself into the seat. It dawned on him that he was someone of importance. Suddenly, he was a vital component of the liberation of Lakeside, OR, his hometown.

"No! Mr. Porter, you must not sit!" Corporal Woo said in near panic. "You lead! You must stand! Hold here, so you not fall." He was emphatic that Reggie was the leader and that he should look like one. So, he stood.

Reggie Porter, the town drunk, was thrown into a position of responsibility. He stood, stuck his whiskered chin out, and imagined himself looking like General MacArthur on his return to the Philippines during WWII. He had no idea where MacArthur had gone or what he'd done, but Reggie had seen pictures, and that's what ran through his mind.

He held his right hand over his head and thrust it forward. The huge truck lurched ahead, followed by a dozen just like it.

The second thought that ran through Reggie's mind was, *"Where the hell am I taking these guys?"*

Courtyard Hotel, Dallas, TX – 10:15 AM CST

The top two floors of the Courtyard Hotel were destroyed. The blackened concrete pillars framed what only a short time before had been guest rooms. The RPGs launched against the invaders in the hotel effectively left a smoking, charred pile of rubble. Not a word of response, not a single gunshot was returned to the regiment surrounding the building.

Lieutenant Jim Parker and his small band of soldiers lay in prone positions along the east side of the smoldering hotel. Parker felt the tension rising. He didn't believe the enemy occupying the Courtyard would go down without a fight. He was puzzled by their lack of response. His other concern, and the one causing more angst than a firefight, was fire ants. They were coming without question. The guys in the hotel were another matter.

For the third time the loud speakers broke the silence, demanding those inside surrender their weapons and come out. For the third time it was given in English, Spanish, and Arabic. For the third time there was no response.

Parker's earpiece crackled to life. "SMAW-NE prepare to open fire. Fire!" The earth shook with the concussion of the ordnance striking the ground floor. Glass, stone, wood, and plaster shattered to dust, fogging the lower floor from view.

Suddenly, the ground floor door on the east end of the building burst open. More than three-dozen men ran from the building toward the trees and brush shielding the Phantom Patriots from view. As they ran, the men fired their weapons at the vehicles to the north and south of the building.

"Open fire!" Parker yelled into his mouthpiece. The woods exploded with a blaze of automatic weapons fire that took the fleeing insurgents by surprise. Rather than surrender, the trapped invaders turned the barrels of their guns toward the brush and trees. It was their only hope of escape.

Bullets shredded the foliage over the heads of the Phantom Patriots. The soil beneath the band of citizen soldiers skipped and popped all around, but the entrenched, well-trained marksmen reservists performed their task with swift professionalism. Those seeking escape were completely exposed to the Phantom Patriots' deadly battering. The invaders' guns fell silent.

White House Basement – 11:25 AM CST

Mike Trapper felt he had figured out the labyrinth of hallways and rooms on this deep level under the White House, but it wasn't easy. It wasn't intended to be simple. The fact that everything was painted the same color didn't help. Institutional beige was nearly blinding after a while.

As they left the conference room, he marked the door. It gave him a central reference point. After several minutes, he, along with Sam, Steve, and Rick, rounded up the other White House staffers and security that had made the trip down. They converged in the conference room with the president.

"George, what did you find with the floor plans?" Trapper asked while the last individuals filed into the room.

"Mike, there might be another way out," George replied leaning over the drawing. "We're right here. If we go down the hall and take the second right, about thirty-five feet down that hallway, there's an exit."

"And if we take that route, where do we come out on the surface?" Trapper asked.

"I don't know. The chart doesn't show the end, just where there might be a passage." George knew it wasn't a good answer, but it was all he had.

Mike Trapper raised his voice over the murmurs around him. "All right, everyone please give me your attention. We have a route that might get us out of here and the president to safety. I want a three-man team to come with me. We'll survey the area and see if it's our way out. In the meantime, Cliff, can you monitor what's happening in the White House from here?"

"Probably, Mike. I'll get on it." The conference room was equipped with a control station. Cliff began working to bring up the cameras in the White House.

"Rick, Steve," but before Mike could say another word, Sam stepped forward, "and Sam. Come with me."

The team of four left, and those remaining gathered around the monitors to see what was happening on the floors far above. Every man and woman secured in the Pod had friends now held by the small Chinese army.

Trapper led the way down the hall and took the second right. He paced off thirty-five feet, but there was no door. Steve Granger ran back and paced the thirty-five feet again. The walls were solid. The only cracks in the surface were between the panels composing the walls.

Mike stepped back then leaned forward, looking at the joint between the ceiling and the wall panel. "Maybe, if we . . ." he said as he pressed firmly against the panel. He heard a click. As Mike released pressure against the panel, it popped out about an inch.

Sliding the panel to the right cleared the opening. It was a cave. The walls were dark, jagged solid rock. The pathway, about five feet high and four feet across, led upward. Granger pulled a small flashlight from his pocket and peered into the tunnel.

"My guess is this heads west," Steve said looking into the dark passage.

"Toward the Old Executive Office building." Mike stepped to Steve's side. "Let's go." The foursome ducked into the opening and moved quickly over the craggy cave floor. Mike counted his paces as best he could on uneven terrain.

The darkness kept the small group close together. Mike touched each side of the tunnel as they made their way up the dimly lit passage. Suddenly the wall of rough stone was smooth.

"Stop!" he commanded. "Steve, put your light here." As Steve swung the small beam toward Mike's hand, they saw the fibrous, white surface he was touching.

"It's fiberglass," Rick said touching the rough surface. The other three looked at him blankly. "It's the swimming pool. Two years ago they replaced the old pool with a fiberglass insert. Remember?"

No, no one remembered. Everyone knew the White House had a swimming pool. The fact was that no one working in the White House would ever have the time or opportunity to enjoy the pool.

The First Family rarely swam, and certainly none of the staff. It was never a consideration.

"It was my first week assigned to DC. I watched them lower the liner in place. The workmen said they found a small opening and asked if they should fill it in, but the uppity-ups said no. The whole thing was dropped. Now, we know why."

The White House swimming pool, Mike nodded, *now I know where we are.*

East Los Angeles, CA – 8:23 AM PST

Colonel Alvaro Herrera and his three closest confidants stood at the back of four trucks loaded with looted treasure. The total of the value of the plunder was unknown, but probably enough to provide a wealthy lifestyle for a long time. The colonel was very pleased, yet no pleasure registered on his face. Ferocious was the only word to match his demeanor. It was reflected in his speech, his eyes, and in the manner he led his army. One step out of line, and the punishment was swift and permanent.

"Here is where we will take the gold," he said loud enough for the guards standing nearby to hear. "It will be safe there. Far from the American Army we see driving around the streets of Los Angeles."

The men laughed loudly. The guards smiled and risked a chuckle. The American Marines looked weak to the colonel. They never stopped to engage his army of liberators. Every day they simply drove down the street. Herrera convinced his men the Marines were afraid of the people's uprising.

And the new "location" for the gold was a ruse. The guards were loyal to the colonel. He held no loyalty to them, however. They were simply pawns in his plan. He needed the people to think he was a hero of the revolution and that he would do as he promised. They believed he would protect the wealth of the New Republic of California, The People's Republic.

Herrera spread a map on the floor of the truck he had chosen to drive. He called his henchmen, Cero, Esteban, and Jubal to his side.

"This is where we will go," he said softly. His finger traced the line of Interstate 10 going east toward Palm Springs. "Then we will go south through the desert to the border. Once we are in Mexico, the Gringo Marines will not dare follow us!"

The men laughed again. This was a very good plan. They all loved it. Soon they would all be very rich. Rich with Gringo money and gold.

chapter 12

Hollenbeck Park, Los Angeles, CA – 8:25 AM PST

Less than an hour had passed since the US military patrol met the forces from the People's Republic of China. General Westrup's phone conversation with the Chinese colonel was cordial and lengthy. Why did the Chinese think we needed their help? What was the extent of their involvement in confronting US citizens in their homeland? What was the long-term goal of the deployment?

Westrup immediately asked the colonel to wait while he contacted the joint chiefs in Washington. The chiefs in DC were beginning their second day in the Bunker, the military command center underneath the White House.

The Bunker had been sealed with all personnel on duty at the time the shots were fired in the Oval Office. Communications with the surface had been established, but exactly what was going on directly overhead a little sketchy.

"Colonel Zu," General Westrup began, "how are you proposing to assist us in Los Angeles? We have combat troops committed to regular patrols. Where do you fit in our operation?"

"General Westrup, sir," the colonel replied, "your forces are minimal at the moment, and your enemy specifically avoids them. We have committed twenty-five thousand troops to the city for a door-to-door search. We are prepared to begin immediately."

"That's a big undertaking," Westrup said. "How do you plan executing such a maneuver?"

"Sir, during our eleven-hour flight we found ample time to place our troops strategically. At present, we have contingents of soldiers in thirty locations throughout the city. We have been ordered to provide the search in coordination with your plans and deployable units. In essence, General Westrup, we are at your disposal and command."

For two days manpower had been the missing component for an effective response. Simple patrols were all that had been available. The new recruits were just beginning their training, and Westrup preferred they remain at Camp Pendleton. Eight thousand Marines on base were experienced and in shape for combat. Most of the 1st, 11th, and 15th Expeditionary forces maintained positions in Afghanistan and other points around the world.

General Westrup knew it was his call. Washington was hip-deep in its own problems, much less the rest of the country. The west coast was his territory. He had the authority to proceed.

"Colonel Zu, on behalf of the United States of America, we accept your assistance. I will direct my communications staff to establish a link with your forces to coordinate our efforts. Never before has a foreign army, intent on waging battle, set foot on US soil. Then again, never in our history have we faced an unmarked army of brutes and thugs numbering in the tens, perhaps hundreds of thousands. Please understand, colonel, this is a difficult and dangerous path we are on, and once we have concluded this operation, we will assist you in a prompt return to your homeland." General Gene Westrup hoped the chiefs in Washington knew what they were up against. This made him very uncomfortable.

"General, we await contact and instructions in how we may assist," Colonel Zu replied.

He then turned to Lieutenant Strattmann and said, "Please allow me to introduce you to my officers and communications staff. You will find them ready to go to work."

Strattmann was still taken aback by the idea of Chinese soldiers in LA. But his commander made the decision, and he would soon receive his orders to move forward. This was a different day in America.

The Courtyard Hotel, Dallas TX – 10:30 AM CST

The smoke and dust of the firefight slowly cleared. Nearly forty men lay still on the blacktop on the east side of the hotel. The regular Army on the west end of the building began the sweep. Units on the north and south of the building held their positions, weapons trained on the smoldering structure.

After only three minutes the all-clear was sounded. No survivors were found in the hotel.

At the same moment, a colony of fire ants found Lieutenant Jim Parker. The adrenal rush numbed the initial stings, but seconds after the all-clear, a cry of agony was heard from the trees. Sergeant Will Minks recognized the voice and sprang from his position. He knew his lieutenant was in trouble. *But no one fired at us!* he thought as he ran down the line. Heads popped out of the brush.

"Who got hit?" John Lewis asked.

"The lieutenant! Call a medic!" Minks replied as he ran. He flew around the end of the hedgerow and came to a dead stop. He couldn't believe the sight before him.

Lieutenant Jim Parker was standing with his helmet off, rifle tossed to the side and his pants at his ankles. Parker was feverishly brushing the insides of his thighs and knees.

"Where are you hit, Jim! Where are you hit?" Minks called running toward him.

"Hit? I'm not hit!" Parker shrieked.

A medic ran around the end of the row of trees with a wild look in his eyes. "Who got hit?" he yelled as he slid to a stop. He did a double-take, seeing an officer in his BVDs with his pants around his ankles. "Where are you hit, sir?"

"Not hit. Bit!" Parker snarled at the medic. "Ants!" he yelled. "Damn fire ants! Are you gonna help or just stand there?" Fire ants loved Lieutenant Jim Parker.

The medic ran to the lieutenant's aid. Both Minks and the medic worked madly with Parker to brush the swarm of ants from his legs and clothing.

"Who got h—What the hell?" It was another voice. The voice Parker had heard in his headset and over the loud speakers. It was Eagle Three, Colonel Herman Maris, commander of the III ACR Phantoms.

This is never going to end! Jim Parker said to himself, brushing vigorously to remove ants from his legs. *This is never going to end!*

Mainside Brig Observation Room, Camp Pendleton, CA
8:33 AM PST

General Westrup finished talking on the phone with the Chinese colonel and turned to Chaplain Caleb Hamza. The two men were alone. The general was dealing with a day filled with cultural conflicts. Westrup looked at the young Muslim chaplain and shook his head.

"Chaplain, I'm not sure what I should do with you. Here you are, the spiritual leader and guide to our Muslim soldiers, and you confide in me that you have become a Christian. How do I deal with that in the middle of this bigger mess?"

"Sir, I am the last person to tell you what to do," Hamza began softly, "but if I may, I would like to be permitted to present my thoughts for your consideration."

"Please, I'm all ears," Westrup leaned against a table behind him and folded his arms across his chest.

"General, my American Muslim brothers find themselves in deep conflict between their love of country and many elements of their faith. Our captives, who have chosen to fight against us, and especially those who have encountered Isa, are equally confused. They believed Allah would deliver victory into their hands. It has not happened.

"I am no one special, General Westrup," the chaplain continued, "but I have enjoyed similar experiences and conflicts with some resolution. Sir, I know how to speak to these men. I know how to help resolve their conflicts. And who knows, perhaps they will ultimately be helpful in solving the mystery of this entire attack?" Hamza looked hopefully at Westrup. "Then, sir, after we see our way through this, you may proceed to deal with me however you wish."

Chaplain Hamza's humility and sincerity impressed General Westrup. He looked at the young man and felt he could believe him. This wasn't as big a problem as those he faced elsewhere, and maybe it could be turned into an asset.

"All right, Chaplain," Westrup stood. "You've made a compelling point. I believe you can help these men and our intelligence gathering as well. I'll let Captain Prescott know how this is going to be handled. You've got a mountain to climb with that one, you know."

Both men smiled. Prescott would be a problem, but he was a good officer and would follow orders. The two men stood and shook hands.

"Chaplain, you do what you need to do, keep Prescott in the loop, and we'll speak again later. Now, I've got to go deal with the Chinese." The general stood and left the room, leaving Hamza with his jaw dropped wide open in confusion.

White House Basement – 11:40 AM EST

Mike Trapper moved carefully through the tunnel leading away from the Pods under the White House. After passing the swimming pool, the walls were again solid, jagged rock. Keeping one's feet on level ground was as challenging as avoiding stones projecting from the low ceiling. Progress was slow.

The four rounded a corner and came to concrete steps leading to a metal door. Mike turned and cautioned the others to be quiet. Slowly and carefully they advanced to the door. He put his ear against the cold metal, hoping to hear something on the other side. The only sounds Mike heard was the blood rushing through his eardrum and the rapid pounding of his heart.

"I'm going to open it very slowly," he whispered to those behind him. He grasped the knob and gently turned it. Carefully, he pulled the door toward him. Dim light flooded the tunnel. Mike could make out panels that looked like electrical boxes. He opened the door a little farther. More panels. More breaker boxes.

"Some kind of utility room," he whispered over his shoulder.

Slowly, Mike stuck his head into the room. The dim lighting made the adjustment easy on his eyes. Now he could see the cinderblock walls. He reached around the door only to find there was no knob on that side of the door. *One-way access*, he thought. At the far end of the small room was another door.

Mike entered the room and motioned the others to follow. Once inside, he showed the rest there was no knob on this side of the door. Sam quietly slid her backpack off and placed it against the doorframe to prevent the door from closing.

As quietly as possible, Mike moved toward the far end of the room and the second door. Again, he paused and listened. This time it was not quiet on the other side. He brought his finger to his lips. Slowly, he opened the door.

Mike peered through the quarter-inch crack. His breath stopped. A large military truck was only a few feet away. He heard voices. The people outside were speaking Chinese.

H. E. Bailey Turnpike & I-240, Oklahoma City, OK
10:45 AM CST

The arrival of hundreds of soldiers at the intersection of the two highways was no small matter. Elements from Fort Sill of the 2nd and 3rd Air Defense Artillery Regiments, the 13th and 18th Field

Artillery Regiments, and the 26th Field Artillery Regiment specializing in target acquisition, threw up a dust cloud visible for miles.

Overhead the percussive whacks from the rotors of CH-47HL Chinooks from the 159th Aviation Regiment pounded those on the ground. The giant choppers carried the lighter weapons that were not deployed on flatbed trucks over the turnpike. More than thirty-five Chinooks fanned across the southern half of the city, lowering M109A6 Paladin howitzers to the ground. The range of the M109s allowed 155mm ordnance to be dropped on targets as far as eleven miles away. While the .50 caliber M2 machine guns effectively dealt with closer encounters

The artillery of the United States Army was no longer an entrenched line of heavy weapons firing at distant targets. It had grown to an aggressor that, while on approach to an enemy position, could engage and even destroy the enemy before its eminent arrival. American artillery brigades could now chase down and crush the enemy.

Captain Robert Hitchens, US Navy SEAL, stood in the front line of a group of thirty-two veteran SEALs, Rangers, and Special Forces. As a unit, they possessed special and much needed skills in advanced surveillance and target confirmation, in addition to hand-to-hand combat training. They would be the first to move into the targeted areas.

Captain Richard Turner of the Oklahoma City National Guard walked toward Hitchens with a small group of officers. The dust was still settling as they approached.

"Captain Hitchens, this is Lieutenant Colonel Crawford from Fort Sill," Turner said as the men shook hands. "These are his boys," he said gesturing to the massive artillery surrounding them.

"Pleased to have you men join us," Colonel Crawford clasped his hands behind his back. "You're gonna be our eyes and ears, right up front. You understand, captain?"

"Yes, sir, and thank you for your help up north. Every man here has friends and family caught up in this mess. We intend to be there to clean it up, sir."

"You're welcome, Captain. I couldn't see it happening any other way." Crawford's smile was grim. "You all have your instructions and assigned positions?"

"Yes, sir," echoed through the ranks of volunteers. The men were sober and determined. They had all fought against the aggressor in Iraq and Afghanistan, but this was home. They knew the city, the neighborhoods, and the people. Liberation had a new meaning to these men, a new and personal meaning.

"All right, then," the colonel said as he looked over the soldiers. "Stay alert. Every moment, every movement is crucial. We have a message to deliver to these bastards, and we're going to do it today. Gentlemen, God speed and let's roll!"

chapter 13

White House Basement – 11:50 AM EST

Mike Trapper entered the door to Pod One followed by Steve, Sam, and Rick. Every head looked in their direction, and each face registered relief none of those coming in were Chinese.

"What did you find?" asked the president walking toward them.

"Well, there is a passage," Trapper replied, "but it isn't one we'll be using anytime soon."

"What do you mean?" George asked. He stood at the long conference table that was littered with the plans he had been studying.

"The tunnel behind that panel took us up and alongside the swimming pool," Mike began. "After another sixty or seventy feet, we found a metal door that opened into a utility room off the parking garage of the Old Executive Building. The garage is filled with troop carriers and Chinese soldiers. At the moment, we're trapped. Until we find another way out."

"Have you been able to monitor what's going on in the White House?" Steve asked.

"Well, yes, to a degree," Cliff replied turning to the bank of monitors. "We can't see everything, but," he paused for a flurry of key strokes, "we can see what we need to see."

Six flat-screen monitors came to life, showing different views inside the West Wing. With the exception of two bodies on the floor, the Oval office was empty. The bodies remained where they had fallen just an hour earlier.

In the hallway outside the Office, two guards stood holding automatic rifles. The Roosevelt Room was empty, but maps, files, and papers were thrown everywhere.

"Sam," Mike asked, "is this how you left the room when you evacuated?"

"No," she shook her head. "It looks like they tore the place up."

"Any ideas what they're looking for?"

"None whatsoever." Her response was a combination of curiosity and disgust. Cleaning up the mess was one thing, but connecting all the dots again was something else.

"Mike, watch this," Cliff said peering into the Oval Office monitor. "Right here in front of the President's desk."

Everyone watched the monitor. Cliff slowly adjusted the contrast and then the various color gradients. As he reduced the level of blue in the monitor, one small area on the floor appeared to have a yellowish tinge. He reduced the red hues on the screen, and the object was better defined.

"It's one of the cloaks," Mike said. "Try it with the monitor in the hall."

Cliff turned his attention to the next monitor. He reduced the gain on the blue and slightly on the red in the monitor. To the right of each soldier, a patch of yellow tinge appeared. Every mouth in the Pod was hanging open. The invisibility cloaks weren't entirely invisible!

"That gives me an idea," Mike said moving toward the elevator.

"Wait! You can't go up there alone," Matt Kreiter said grabbing Mike's arm.

"I will just this one time," Mike replied grinning. "I want those capes. Two can play this little invisibility game."

He tapped the button, and the door on the elevator slid open. The trip up was much slower than the descent. Finally, he reached the ground level. Mike took a deep breath. He wished he'd thought about bringing a radio. The elevator door opened.

The Oval Office was empty and silent. Mike peeked around the opening just to make sure. Quickly, he moved across the room to the Resolute Desk and knelt beside the dead man on the floor.

He extended his hand to where he remembered seeing the yellowish form. He touched it! He couldn't see it, but he felt something. It was a cloak. Carefully he lifted and unfolded it. It was made of the meta-material.

I wonder what kind of madness this looks like on the monitor, he said to himself. Then, he slid it over his head.

Lakeside, OR – 8:55 AM PST

For nearly an hour Reggie Porter had led the Chinese Army through the neighborhoods and business district of Lakeside without spotting a single enemy soldier. Corporal Woo looked worried and repeatedly glanced over his shoulder at the general sitting in the vehicle immediately behind them. Even Reggie was beginning to worry.

Where did the bad guys go? he asked himself repeatedly. On any other day Reggie would have been stopped a half of a dozen times just walking across town. Today felt more like a Sunday drive than a search-and-destroy mission.

As the convoy made its way along the north side of the park, Reggie's luck changed. The rag-tag army of very mean, brutal men stretched across the south end of the park, right next to the see-saws and jungle-gym. Every man was armed to the teeth.

Reggie breathed a sigh of relief. However, he feared that very soon bullets would be flying in every direction. That was when he began to sweat.

"Very wise plan, Mr. Porter," the general said as he walked to the side of Reggie's vehicle. "You knew, of course, these cowards would be in hiding, so you led us all through the town to challenge them. Well done, Mr. Porter." Lieutenant General Wang looked up at Reggie and smiled at him admiringly.

Reggie could only nod his head, confirming he was glad the general discerned his intent. His confidence perked enough that he looked directly at General Wang, pursed his lips, and said, "They're a lazy and stupid bunch, general. Lazy and stupid."

Reggie gazed across the park, grimaced, and shook his head in displeasure and contempt at his enemy. Slowly he climbed down the far side of the large vehicle. Once out of sight, he began to tremble. He was terrified.

General Wang shouted orders in Mandarin, and three hundred soldiers scrambled out of the troop carriers. They looked like an army of ninja robots. Every man was equipped with black body armor, helmets with visors covering their faces, and the biggest rifles Reggie had ever seen.

General Wang shouted more orders. Soldiers scurried into lines facing their opponent. They arranged themselves in two rows, one kneeling, another standing. One more command and three hundred weapons came to firing position.

The ragged group of men across the park looked at each other. Some of them chuckled others shouldered their weapons and took aim. Every one of them was surprised that this group of little men would challenge them.

"*She ji!*" The only sound was a loud hum accompanied by a bright, red flash. The army of rugged, mean men dropped to the ground. Only one man was left standing, the apparent commander of the group. He stood frozen in the bed of a pickup.

"*Yi hou!*" the general commanded. The Chinese soldiers broke rank and ran toward the fallen invaders.

When he slowly peeked from his hiding place behind the vehicle, Reggie Porter was amazed. He walked to the general's side with caution. General Wang stood erect, obviously proud of his fighting men.

"Uh, general, sir," Reggie stammered, "well, that was hardly fair."

"We didn't come here to be fair," the general replied smiling. "We came to fight. They too slow on trigger!" He strode across the park to accept the surrender of the lone man standing in stunned silence in the pickup bed.

I-44 & I-240, Oklahoma City, OK – 11:00 AM CST

Since he had left active duty, Robert Hitchens had never considered going back into combat. That part of his life was over, and he was moving on to whatever was next. That is until this morning. What surprised him was how easily it came back to him. Loading magazines with rounds of ammunition was almost automatic. Cleaning and checking his M-16 accomplished without so much as a thought. However, looking at an army of several hundred men and walking away alive with a group of only four required a second thought.

Their biggest problem was that they could be seen from a mile away. It was broad daylight. That couldn't be helped. The time to move was now.

Robert and three retired Navy SEALs headed north through the southern neighborhoods of Oklahoma City. Their objective was Habana Place Hotel, just off Highway 66 on the north side. They avoided the larger highways, a preferred route of the terrorist bands. The neighborhood streets were bare.

*   *   *   *   *

Two teams of Marine Reservists were en route from Tinker Air Force Base to known locations of enemy command centers on the east side of the city. The ALI maps from Washington clearly showed where the invaders congregated. Boots on the ground would need to confirm it.

The 552d Air Control Wing had been dispatched as dawn broke over the Oklahoma plains. The E-3 Sentry AWACS roared from the runway, two at a time. The planes fanned across the southwest to enable communications, command and control, as well as lend a high-tech ear to action on the ground.

The 327th Aircraft Sustainment Wing was on full alert. Their mission reached farther than refueling the Army vehicles from Fort Sill. The Wing's C/KC 135 tankers would provide fuel to AWACS that were tasked to monitor all activity from the Gulf to the Baja Peninsula. The 327th ASW would keep them flying.

*   *   *   *   *

Robert Hitchens and the three SEALs were the advance team to observe activity at the hotel. The equipment they carried was designed to pinpoint the artillery fired from eight miles to the south. If the timing was right, if the invaders behaved as they had for the last two days, if nothing went wrong, it was a dangerous assignment. That was a lot of 'ifs.'

Robert marveled to himself how the sudden assault of terror gripped the city into a silent stalemate. Normally peaceful streets of family homes and small businesses were now abandoned. As in most of the west and southwest, radio and television stations were off the air. Cable services stopped at the distribution centers, and Internet connections displayed blank screens.

Outraged citizens had taken to the streets only once. The confrontation with the terrorists from the south had been brief. Many Americans did not return home that night. Their bodies remained where they had fallen as a reminder. The word spread rapidly. It was best to stay home and out of sight.

If they were successful, the three teams moving to their assigned destinations would aid in the elimination of sixty-percent of the invading horde with a single artillery assault. As the firing commenced, squads of combat troops would move rapidly through the city to the scene of the attack for a final cleanup. It all depended on the spotters' success.

Oval Office, White House – 12:05 PM EST

Mike Trapper stood to his full height covered by the meta-metal cloak. As he crept down the hallway past the Cabinet Room, his heart pounded in his chest. The fear of being discovered was a constant threat. Did the Chinese have a method of *seeing* their cloaked soldiers? Did they know about the limited invisibility?

He heard voices coming toward him. Mike ducked into the Press Secretary's office and hid behind the open door. The men came closer. They were speaking Mandarin in a very animated conversation. They almost sounded like they were arguing.

Suddenly, the cell phone in Mike's pocket rang. Under the cloak, he pulled the phone from his pocket and glanced at the screen. It was Elli. He muted the ring. The conversation in the hallway stopped. Mike froze.

He knew he could not be seen under normal conditions. But he was unsure what those conditions really were. The ringing stopped, but the two men moved quietly to the doorway. They slowly entered the room.

Mike stood motionless behind the open door, afraid to breathe. The two Chinese officers scanned the room. One walked to the desk and picked up a cell phone left behind in the panic. He said something Mike could not understand.

The second officer broke into a laugh and replied to the man by the desk. That caused the first man to laugh as well. He replaced the phone on the desk, and the two left the office resuming their conversation.

Mike silently scolded himself for being so careless. He had no communication with the people below in the Pod. He was too far out on a limb, depending on his own wits, and that almost got him caught. It was time to go back.

He eased himself into the hallway and headed back toward the Oval Office. As he moved easily down the hall, Mike remembered the two soldiers by the south door to the Roosevelt Room. He came to the corner and hazarded a peek.

The two soldiers stood casually at their posts. The radios on their belts squawked to life, and both men took off at a jog toward the stairs leading to the second floor.

Mike wasn't certain, but he played his hunch. Carefully he crept along the hall, hugging the wall until he came to the soldiers' former positions. He didn't see it, but he felt it with his foot. The soldier's cloak! The second one was two feet away. Cautiously, Mike knelt to the floor and slid the two cloaks under the one he wore and gripped them tightly to his chest.

He ran for the Oval Office and the elevator.

chapter 14

Lieutenant Jim Parker returned to the Armory humiliated a second time. The deployment ended with no casualties. The enemy was successfully routed and their command post neutralized, but the attack of the fire ants had ruined the day.

His gait was awkward, and he winced with pain. His fellow soldiers swaggered along unable to suppress their snickers. Their comments were minimal and intended to be respectful.

"Doin' better, lieutenant?" "Man! That bites!" Jim Parker took it in stride. His battle stories would live on in infamy. He really didn't care anymore. It felt like his legs were on fire, and he wanted to put it out.

Doc was standing just inside the door of the armory. His arms were folded across his chest, and a mildly sour scowl covered his face. He shook his head in feigned disbelief.

"How in the world does this stuff keep happening to you, Jim? I'll bet you kept your mom busy fixing home remedies when you were a kid, right?"

Jim muttered something that included the words "my mother," but no one asked for clarification. Doc took him by the arm and led him to the kitchen for treatment. The progress had been slow, but now that he was "home," Jim didn't complain.

Doc gave Jim a powerful antihistamine and opened a tube of hydrocortisone to apply to his skin as the pustules developed. He was most concerned about infection, and the possibility of shock setting in if the infection spread.

The building began to shake under the pounding of a helicopter's approach. A few moments later Colonel Herman Maris, Eagle Three, walked into the room.

"Atten-hut!" echoed in the hallway, and the snapping of heels together followed. The colonel strode into the kitchen without hesitation.

"As you were!" the colonel snapped. "Lieutenant, don't even try. Good to see you have some doctorin' for those blasted bites." He greeted Doc, and the necessary introductions were made. "I understand you have a link for these ALI maps that have been so valuable to you."

"Yes, sir," Jim said struggling to get up.

"Just point, lieutenant. I can find my way."

Jim obliged the officer and pointed to the computer in the corner. The setup looked anything but high-tech. It was patched together at the height of a national emergency, and though the equipment was good enough, making it work required creativity.

"This is it?" Colonel Maris asked astonished. He turned to Jim with widened eyes, his jaw hung slack. "*This* is how you get those amazing maps from Washington?"

"Yes sir. That's our National Security hook-up," Parker said from the table.

"Okay, lieutenant, let's see where the bad guys are. Fire it up." The colonel pulled up a chair as Corporal Meeks brought the patched together up-link to life.

Visitor Center, National Zoo, Washington DC – 12:12 PM EST

The first loop of the park was complete. After the Kid's Farm, where granddad was as interested as the kids, they made their way through the cats and the ape exhibit. Sara loved cats and thought having a leopard for a pet was a wonderful idea. Elli and her mom sat on a bench in the shade and waited patiently for their return.

"That's such a five-year-old thing!" Robbie taunted with all his six-year-old wisdom.

"Mom!" Sara whined back.

"Don't start it!" Elli warned. She still felt stressed, sore, tired, and as if she were in a dream. She saw things she knew were not there. Things like drug-induced flashes of light. She was nauseated, and she was pretty sure she wasn't pregnant. It simply was not one of her best days.

Grandma and Granddad settled the kids for lunch while Robbie and Sara spat, poked, and pinched at each other. Three-year-old Jackson rocked from cheek to cheek in his seat in anticipation of the midday meal. Fourteen-month-old Riley clung to Grandma, buzzing his lips and drooling.

Elli dropped into a seat in the covered picnic area and took off her sunglasses. The shade was good. She rubbed her forehead and face with her hands and let out a long breath. She was really ready for a nap, one that wouldn't come for at least a few more hours.

Granddad distributed the hamburgers and hotdogs while the children chattered endlessly about their favorite parts of the zoo so far. Their energy was unlimited, almost annoying. Then he said grace.

"Mom, Jackson had his eyes open during the prayer!" Sara blurted immediately after Granddad's amen.

"Did not!" Jackson instantly retorted.

"You two stop it this instant," Elli demanded. "Any more of that kind of behavior, and we'll all go straight home and right to bed."

The idea sounded like an excellent option to Elli, even though she was loving the fresh air and sunshine. She looked at her mom, sighed, and shook her head.

"Are you feeling any better, Elli?" her mom asked. "Should I be concerned about anything?"

"No, Mom," Elli replied. "Actually, sitting here in the shade is very nice. I hope this wasn't the wrong thing to do today."

"Anytime you want to leave, sweetheart, we can pack-up and scoot home," her dad offered.

"No, I'll be okay. I feel better just sitting here for a little while," Elli said. "I cannot *wait* to get off these pain pills! It's not so bad now, but I've been seeing things. I feel like I'm about to throw up. Ugh! Not the best day."

"You're not, well—" her mom began.

"No, Mom, I'm not!" Elli snapped. She sighed. "Sorry, it's the drugs talking."

"Well, eat some lunch and I'll take the kids through the Bird House," her dad suggested. "Then we can go." He looked at Grandma who shook her head and rolled her eyes. Elli was acting like an out-of-sorts teenager or a person on pain-killers. It would pass.

At least half of the kids' lunches were eaten. The other half had fallen to the floor unobserved. Stories and jokes mumbled through mouths packed full of food made the midday meal both repulsive and hilarious. Elli did her best to eat something. The children's antics brightened her mood.

Two more hours, she said to herself. *I can handle two more hours.*

Hollenbeck Park, Los Angeles, CA – 9:14 AM PST

Lieutenant Mark Strattmann stood beside his Humvee watching the Chinese soldiers prepare for a sweep maneuver. As they spread across the park, the soldiers ran in a remarkably tight formation.

Officers were shouting orders that were repeated through bullhorns. Troops responded to the commands as a single unit.

With the same precision, several hundred soldiers came to a simultaneous halt. It was like a dance with all the dancers ending on the same beat. Strattmann was amazed.

Next to him stood Corporal Sun Huang, who watched the preparations and noticed Strattmann's reaction. "China much different than America. Chinese see things in different way." Strattmann looked at the small soldier who was smiling back at him with pride.

"What are they going to do next?" he asked.

"All soldiers will break into platoons of one hundred men and go into buildings for door-to-door inspection," Sun replied. "It will be very fast."

"What if someone shoots at them?"

"Very simple. We shoot back until shooting stop. Then, go on." The logic was indeed simplistic. Definitely not the way American soldiers could treat Iraqis. In the field, they were required to see the sniper's weapon fired at them before returning fire.

The stillness in the park was shattered by a single command.

"Téng!" Instantly, each unit began to move. The sweep entered buildings along the east side of the park. The officer commanding the units stood in his lead vehicle and moved down the street as scores of soldiers scurried from building to building.

What Mark Strattmann could not see or know was that the exact same process was underway in every Chinese encampment across Los Angeles. During the long flight military strategists in Beijing had divided the city and coordinated the units for greatest efficiency.

The plan to sweep through the city like the unfolding of a fan had been made before the troops left their aircraft. They would first clear and secure the areas known to have few insurgent fighters. Then, as they approached the known locations of the invaders, the armies would move toward each other surrounding them from all sides.

As the soldiers entered the first building, loud speakers began the announcement.

"Citizens of Los Angeles, your attention please! Your building is being inspected for members of the invading army of terrorists. The United States Marines and the Army of the People's Republic of China are coming to your door to assist in your liberation. Please welcome them for a short and courteous visit."

The plan was complete. Lieutenant Strattmann stared in astonishment. His American soldiers ran alongside the leaders of each platoon. A smiling Chinese soldier and an American Marine in full battle dress would greet every American. It was a sight to behold.

White House Basement – 12:17 PM EST

The elevator door to Pod One opened. It was empty. Steve Granger looked into the carriage with surprise. The entire group had watched the ghostly yellowish form they assumed to be Mike Trapper run into the elevator in the Oval Office.

"So, where are you Trapper?" he asked.

"Over here," Steve heard to his left. Mike whisked the cloak off. His appearance was dramatic. Light gasps came from everyone in the room.

"There is something I'm curious about," Matt Kreiter said stepping forward. He pulled a pair of sunglasses from his breast pocket. "These are blue-blockers, you know, for cutting down glare from the sun."

He slipped the sunglasses on.

"Well, I'll be." A smile crossed his face. "They work." Matt held the glasses out to Steve who confirmed the fact.

"Is this why Secret Service guys always wear sunglasses?" he asked passing the glasses on. Each person shared the experiment and confirmed their observation.

"The glasses wouldn't make any difference on the monitors because the blue hues are already removed. But now, under florescent lighting anyway, we know it works," Steve said.

"What about regular sunlight?" Sam asked touching the edge of the fabric. "Would there be a different effect?"

"Possibly," Cliff said. "Florescent lighting is a bluer light. Sunlight contains many more colors, some seen, some not. Chances are, if you were outside with these glasses on, the differences could be more defined. One might be seen more easily in brighter light."

"So, the best lighting for being the *most* invisible is either in shade, indoors, or twilight—even nighttime, right?" Mike postulated while cleaning the lenses of the blue-blockers.

"Can't know for certain. It's a guess, but I'd say less sunlight is better than more," Cliff replied holding the fabric close to his face, alternating the angle.

"What sort of communication equipment do we have with us?" Mike asked.

"Regular service issue comms," Steve said.

"And any agent who still has one would have switched to VLF by now," Cliff said.

The Very Low Frequency (VLF) units were upgrades to the long-used Extremely Low Frequency (ELF) devices in submarines. They were made even more functional by new technology, allowing for smaller antennas. The larger antennas allowed successful communication from KI Sawyer AFB in Michigan to link with submarines in the Pacific, and later in the Mediterranean Sea and Northern Polar Ice Cap. Smaller systems, like the one in the White House, made communication possible in the deep, underground regions of the complex, as in the Pods.

"If we had someone on ground level, we could talk to them, right?" Sam asked.

"That's what the VLF is designed to do." Cliff sat at the keyboard. "Our only problem is whether the system is activated or not."

"It's not on all the time?" Kreiter stood and walked behind him.

"No. Most of the time it isn't, for security reasons," Cliff added. "If someone monitors all the active frequencies, they might pick it up. Then when something really bad happens they might be able to listen to us."

"Do you know how to activate the system?" Steve asked.

"Nope. That would be the guys in the third or fourth basement, I think," Cliff said.

"Someone like Barry Goldstein?" Sam said contemptuously sitting at the conference table. She shuddered.

"Let's hope someone in the ALI Maps room does," Mike added glancing at Sam, then Steve.

Barry Goldstein had been a vital part of White House security for many years. His act of treason was warning the insurgent terrorists at the Oak Mountain Nuclear Power Plant that the Marines were approaching in helicopters from the north. Hours later, he had told the terrorists where Mike's family was. The terrorists had immediately selected the Trappers as a target. The thought of anyone else in the White House working with the enemy was very plausible . . . and terrifying.

"Let's gather the comm. units we have here and set all but three of them on VLF," Mike said. "Then I'm going back up to the ALI Maps room, or wherever this thing is activated. I'll need you here to help me through the building to avoid running into any Chinese."

"I'm going with you," Steve said without hesitation. He made a hasty glance toward Sam. Sam nodded.

"Do we know where the Chinese are holding the hostages?" Rick asked.

"I'll check the other floors of the West Wing and the Residence and see what I can find," Cliff answered.

The group of agents and politicians gathered around the conference table for a strategy session. The ability to move around the enemy camp while invisible was intriguing, but exactly *how* invisible the cloaks made a person remained a mystery. The risk was tremendous.

chapter 15

City Park, Lakeside, OR – 9:25 AM PST

Reggie Porter was thoroughly amazed at the weapons used by the Chinese. He had intentionally hidden behind the trucks to avoid the gunfire that never started. But he couldn't help peeking around the backend of the truck to watch the soldiers fire the weapons. It was something right out of Flash Gordon.

He cautiously sidled over to Corporal Woo, whose face was furrowed and intent on the large rifles.

"Corporal," he began warily, "just what kind of weapons are those . . . those things?"

"The very best!" Woo replied smiling broadly.

"No, I mean what *kind* are they? What do they shoot?" Reggie braced himself for a highly technical answer, so he pursed his lips and stroked his chin to convey his intelligence and understanding.

"They shoot electricity!" Corporal Woo seemed to have a permanent smile. Nothing changed his visage. "We got idea from America university."

"You got the idea from one of our American universities?" Reggie's eyes were flooded with shock. "Why in the world would a university of higher learning be working on a ray-gun?"

"How should I know? Maybe General Wang help you understand. Want me get him?" Reggie really liked Corporal Woo. He was very willing to be helpful. He was always smiling. The smiling part was beginning to bother Reggie.

"No, that won't be—" But before he could finish the sentence, Woo was halfway across the park, jogging up to the general. Corporal Woo spoke briefly, and they both turned and marched smartly toward Reggie.

"I understand you have some questions about our weaponry, Mr. Porter," the general asked. He was grinning from ear to ear. Reggie was starting to think he should just go home and let the Chinese have the whole town.

"Well, yes general. I've just never seen anything like that before."

"I understand, Mr. Porter," the general began. "Many of our young students come to the United States for their technical education. They are very well trained in the manner Americans think and act. The students we send are our very brightest, and they excel in your universities.

"We began to notice that many projects the students studied were of a military nature. And some of the projects were discarded, never coming to completion. We thought some of those projects held merit. When our students returned to their homeland we put them to work to finish the project. Simple."

"So, things like the ray-gun . . ." Reggie stammered.

"Yes, plasma-pulse weapons are very effective," the general said. "Your government, aided by research grants for our students, developed the weapon. But it wasn't very powerful. So, they gave up. They quit."

It was by accident the Chinese had discovered the plasma-echo effect when several plasma-pulse weapons were fired simultaneously. The trigger had to be precise, and the blasts needed to fire thirty times a second. One rifle provided a minor burst. Two fired simultaneously multiplied the effect to six times the power, three, the impact of eighteen, and so on. Although the math was still being analyzed, the effect of three hundred weapons amplified by the pulse-echo was decisive.

"And, the . . ." Reggie moved his hands and arms around himself.

"Yes, the ultra-black meta-material cloaks allow ninety-seven percent of all light to pass through an object making it virtually invisible. Both discarded as impractical. But as you have seen, both are very useful."

The general was beaming with pride. Every enemy soldier was rendered incapable of fighting yet unhurt. A perfect weapon, disable without killing.

Reggie nodded agreement. They were very useful and very effective. He began to wonder what other things the Chinese had learned in American universities. It was then the hair stood up on the back of Reggie's neck.

Mainside Brig, Camp Pendleton, CA – 9:27 AM PST

Cleric Caleb Hamza spent his morning visiting with prisoners. Most were greatly relieved to speak with a cleric. Some were very suspicious of a Muslim in the uniform of a US Marine. A few were outright belligerent.

But Caleb Hamza was most interested in the few men who had experienced visions of the man in a bright white robe speaking of peace. He felt anxious about his next encounter. It was with the man he had watched on video a few hours earlier.

The cell held Mustafa al Nubi. Hamza stood outside the door for nearly a minute gathering his thoughts. Every encounter brought a new challenge; some encounters were just plain risky. He was a trained soldier and could defend himself, but he still had to summon his courage before gently knocking on the cell door.

"Brother Mustafa, it is Cleric Hamza to visit you," he said softly. When no one responded, he slowly turned the knob and opened the door. Peering into the room, he saw the man Mustafa calmly sitting on his bed. Hamza nodded to the guard accompanying him and entered the cell.

"I am Caleb Hamza," he said.

"Allahu akbar," he said softly in Arabic. "Peace be with you." The young man's eyes were red, yet soft and unafraid.

Hamza knew the stress and confusion of combined fear and rage the young man held within. Still, he was calm.

"And with you," Hamza completed the customary greeting also in Arabic. Introductions were brief. "Is there anything you need that has not been provided to you?" Hamza asked softly.

"No," Mustafa replied. He smiled warmly. "Everything is fine. To me it is unusual to speak with a cleric in a military uniform. It seems funny to me. I should be upset or afraid, but I am not. Very funny this, is it not?"

"Under the circumstances," Hamza began, returning his smile, "it is very unusual. Not many of your comrades share your peace and calm demeanor."

"I am not surprised," Mustafa replied.

"Is it because of the man in white? Isa?" Hamza asked.

His question might well have been an electric shock. Mustafa winced and pulled back.

"What is this? How can you know this thing? I have told no one! How do you know?" His eyes were wide and filled with surprise more than fear. The question itself violated the man's most private thoughts, and he was alarmed by it.

"No, please," Hamza replied, "no one has spoken to me about you. None of your fellow warriors know you have seen the man in white."

"Then, how do *you* know?" Mustafa's eyes were wide with wonder.

Hamza told him about the surveillance videos of him in his cell and how the guards had heard his conversations when he was alone in the room. Hamza explained he had been called to the brig to help the Marines understand what had happened with this man.
Hamza paused. Suddenly, he understood. It was for this time, these men, that he was still a Muslim Chaplain. He began to tell his story. As he spoke, his confidence grew, and warmth filled the tiny, concrete cell. Mustafa listened intently, not moving a muscle.
When Hamza finished, Mustafa was quiet for a moment before he spoke. "You know Him."
"Yes, and I have come to know Him very well these last few months." Caleb Hamza felt complete at last. He understood his purpose for this time was a small group of fighters from his homeland who had encountered the man in white. It was finally very clear.

South of I-66, Oklahoma City, OK – 11:30 AM CST

Robert Hitchens parked the Humvee on 37th Street a couple blocks from the Habana Place. The side streets were eerily abandoned and lined with the cars and trucks of owners unwilling to venture out. It was too quiet.
Robert and the SEALs approached the building through a wooded lot about three hundred feet to the west. From the edge of the foliage, they could see the building clearly. More than a dozen pickups were parked in the slots that had been reserved for hotel guests in past days. Several were heavily armed with .50 caliber machine guns mounted in the beds. Swarthy, unshaven men smoked cigarettes and visited casually.
The SEALs set up their equipment quickly. One SEAL pulled the optoelectronic infrared sensor from his pack and unfolded it. It would "paint" the target. Another SEAL carried the battery unit to power the sensor. Robert and the fourth SEAL flanked the two hooking up the equipment and established a perimeter. They kept their M-16s trained on the building and the men around it.

Similar teams were in place at five other locations around the city. At the proper moment, when everything was ready, a single signal would bring an end to the occupation of Oklahoma City. A single drone aircraft circled high overhead, waiting.

National Guard Armory, Frisco, TX – 11:35 AM CST

Colonel Herman Maris bent over the ALI maps spread across the metal table in the kitchen. Lieutenant Jim Parker and Sergeant Minks were at his side. The men were deep in serious discussion. Several of the locations marked as enemy positions had suffered the terrifying attacks of the Dallas Phantom Patriots over the past few days.

The dots on the maps were fewer than before, attributing to the success of the Patriots, but enough of them remained to be a concern to the III ACR. With a thoughtful eye, Colonel Maris reviewed the estimated troop strength of the enemy.

"There's a mess of them, isn't there?" He rubbed his chin and mentally measured his forces against the enemy. He wasn't a general who entered a conflict with even ranks. As a young officer, Desert Storm had taught him that overwhelming force and firepower was the common denominator in victory.

"We can take each location one at a time quite easily," he said thinking out loud. "Men, the south side of the metropolitan area from Mesquite on the east, Waxahachie to the south, and Joe Pool Lake on the west have been cleaned out. Saber Squadron is working through Arlington and into Irving and making good progress. We still got a bunch to deal with right here in Dallas."

"Sir, what about Fort Sill? Can they come in from the north and put pressure from that side?" Parker asked.

"They're ready to engage the combatants in Oklahoma City, son. We might need to dig in and do the dirty work all on our own."

"Excuse me, General Maris? I have a call for you from Major Williams with Saber."

"Fine. I'll be right back, boys. Look this over real good for me," General Maris said as he walked briskly from the room to his Apache.

"This is Eagle Three. Bring it. Over."

"Sir, Saber One here. Sir, we advanced through Arlington and are on the west perimeter of DFW. A bit of a situation here, sir. Over."

"Saber One, that's why I said *bring it*. You are US Army. We expect situations. Over."

"Yes sir. On the tarmac at DFW are four of the biggest aircraft any of us have ever seen. We estimate the wingspan at about five hundred feet, sir. They're just sitting there, sir. Over."

General Maris drew a long breath. He knew he'd never seen an airplane with a five-hundred-foot wingspan. Who had such a plane? Where did it come from? Who or what was in it?

"Sir? This is Saber One. Do you read me, Eagle Three? Over."

"Yes! Yes, I read you." Again, he lowered his head and closed his eyes as if imagining what had been described to him. "I want you to advance on those aircraft and seal them off. Don't fire unless you're fired upon. I'm on my way. Out." The general tossed the mike into the seat and turned back to the armory.

"Lieutenant Parker!" he bellowed, entering the building.

"Sir!" Parker responded as he hobbled to his feet.

"You and your Patriots are gonna need to keep a sharp eye out until we can get some reinforcements free to help you up here. As we move north, you might see more activity around you. But I gotta get out to DFW, so you're in charge." The general spun and left as quickly as he came.

"Well, boss," Minks said through a grin, "looks like you're in charge. The burden of responsibility has once again bit you in the butt!"

Everyone in the room grinned except Lieutenant Parker.

chapter 16

Neighborhood Sweep, Los Angeles, CA – 9:45 AM PST

Lieutenant Strattmann watched as US Marines and soldiers of the Chinese People's Republic maneuvered through buildings six blocks from the park where he first met the Chinese. He wasn't sure if it looked like a swarm of ants or an amazing ballet. It reminded him of the opening ceremony of the Olympics in China a few years earlier. Hundreds of men ran from building to building. *Simply amazing*, he thought.

"Lieutenant Strattmann!" a voice called from behind him. He turned to see Colonel Zu waving from his vehicle. "Come! Ride with me!"

He took the invitation as a chance to get off his feet and learn more about the colonel. Strattmann pulled himself onto the large troop transport and swung into the seat beside the Chinese officer.

"You will see the technique we use better from here," the colonel said.

"Thank you very much, colonel," Strattmann replied.

"You see, one hundred soldiers enter a building," the colonel began. "Different platoons move up front and rear stairways while the elevator is guarded below. They will cover a floor in only a few minutes, each moving in rapid succession."

"How did you develop, or where did you perfect this technique?" Strattmann asked.

"In our own country. You must understand China is very large with a diverse population and many cultures. We frequently deal with dissidents to maintain order and, as far as the Party goes, stay in control."

"Then isn't that pretty much a police state?" Strattmann risked the potentially offensive question and was pleased when the colonel smiled.

"Yes, it is. And it will be until our present leaders change or die," Colonel Zu's smile did not fade. "China is politically divided much like your own government. You see the contest between progressive and conservative ideologies. Our struggle is between the old totalitarian state and one of people who have seen the value of free markets, independent of State control."

"People like you? Chinese nationals, who have come here to work or study?" The large vehicle crept along the street while scores of Chinese soldiers passed on either side, breaking stride only to politely enter a building.

"Exactly. While I was studying here in LA, I enjoyed the benefits of your free markets. The variety is endless! I saw and tasted many things I could only read about in China. It was all here and available!"

"But you have new technologies and businesses in China, don't you?" Strattmann asked.

"They are coming slowly, but there is great resistance to change . . . in both directions." Zu stood and spoke softly to the driver. Then he turned back to the lieutenant. "The old guard resists the unquestionable benefits of people owning their own businesses, and the new businessmen and women resist the regulation and control of the Central Committee. It's a very complicated process."

"I can imagine," Strattmann replied, scanning the field of soldiers crossing before them. The truck came to a stop.

"Early on, this search operation was used for identifying people who made problems for the government, and even though it was criticized by the West, it was highly effective," Zu said. "We don't use this maneuver very much anymore at home. But this is the perfect situation."

"I must admit, I never expected to see the Red Chinese Army running through the streets of Los Angeles," Strattmann said shaking his head. Zu laughed.

"As a student, I couldn't have imagined it either!"

"So, where did you go to school?" Strattmann asked.

"Harvest Bible College on Burlington Avenue," Zu replied casually.

"What?" the lieutenant spun in his seat to face the general. "You're a Chinese Communist officer in the People's Republic Army?"

"Oh, I'm definitely Chinese, but who said I'm a communist?"

"You're not a communist?"

"Well, not a very good one. I must confess I'm a much better follower of Christ than of Chairman Mao." Zu was clearly amused at Strattmann's consternation and confusion. "For China, the army provides a good paying job. And I told you China is a very difficult and diverse country. There are a lot of communists there. But there are millions of believers, and we are growing in number and influence every day."

"Well, I never . . ." Strattmann's jaw dropped.

"Don't be too surprised, Lieutenant Strattmann. One of your presidents once said you could learn a lot from China," Zu said. "It could be, whether he meant it or not, it could be Christianity is one of them!"

Pod One, White House Basement – 12:55 PM EST

Steve Granger was busy doing a final check of the communication equipment before they made their departure from the Pod. Both Steve and Mike were wired to keep in contact through regular channels while moving through the White House and into the Residence. Communications would be spotty and unreliable until the VLF was initiated.

Each man took turns donning one of the cloaks and moving about the room while others listened for their movements. A shuffle of feet or rustling of the cloak against a piece of furniture was a dead giveaway. Mike felt as clumsy as an ox at first. But with practice he was able to move without detection. Steve had it down from the very first try.

Finally, their equipment was on and working. The cloaks were placed over their heads with only the facemask down.

"Don't know that I'm very comfortable with your two faces floating around the room," Cliff said. He ran a final check of the security cameras, making notes of Chinese soldiers' positions. "We need to be particularly careful with the sentries around the White House."

Together with Mike and Steve he designed a pathway through the building avoiding the sentries. Everything would be fine as long as no one changed their position or happened to walk by at the wrong moment. Unpredictable events only raised the risk.

The time had come to make their move. Mike and Steve closed the face coverings on their cloaks and did a final radio check.

"Radio check, do you copy? Raider One, over," Mike said.

"You know we can hear you when you talk that loud, don't you?" Sam said dryly.

"Is it clearly audible or muddled?" he asked her.

"It's not clear, but I can hear someone talking," Sam replied. "I'm going with you." Sam quickly grabbed the third cloak and slid it over her head.

"Hold on, Sam!" Mike said opening his face cover. "I'm not sure three will make this any easier."

"Nothing is easy about any of this," Sam replied adjusting the facemask. "Your voices rumble even when you talk softly. Mine doesn't. I'm a girl. I have a softer voice. And I'm not going to just sit here and wait for you to get back, captured or . . . or anything else. I'm going."

Mike knew there was no argument he could make that would stand. Sam hadn't stayed behind when they went to the Oak Mountain Power Station. She hadn't stayed behind when Elli and the kids were threatened. And she wasn't going to sit this one out, either. That was clear.

Sam's communication gear checked out. She glared a challenge at Mike. He shrugged and closed his face cover. Sam closed hers with just the hint of a smile on her lips.

"Let's hope that you guys down here will be doing most of the talking," Mike said. "You keep us posted with what's in front of us and we'll be as quiet as possible."

He turned to where he thought Steve would be standing. "Copy that?"

"Raider Two copies, and out." Steve was invisible and quiet. Mike only hoped he wouldn't be the one to knock something over as they maneuvered room to room.

"Raider Three copies. Out," Sam replied softly. Her response was short and clipped, and full of excitement.

He walked to the elevator door, slid it open, and entered. Steve and Sam were right behind him. Radios were on, and their face coverings in place. Mike pushed the button to close the door and return to the Oval Office.

North Flynn Ave., Oklahoma City, OK – 12:00 Noon CST

Robert watched the men outside the hotel through his scope. They were very nonchalant. It bothered him. *Why are they standing in the open two hours after a gun battle?* It didn't make sense. *And where are the other trucks?* Earlier his team had counted thirty-six pickups at the hotel. Now, there were fewer than twenty.

He glanced at the men who had been preparing the optoelectronic infrared sensor. They were ready. The system was hot. *We probably got to our destination first. The other teams had a longer trip. They should be up soon.*

His comm. device came to life.

"SEALs Up One, this is Big Barker Six. Do you copy?"

"Big Barker Six, this is SEALs Up One. Copy," Robert replied.

"Stand-by."

He listened as the other teams responded.

"This is Big Barker Six. On my count, paint your targets and cover up." This was it. After a brief pause, then, "On my count, five, four, three, two, one, paint." Robert saw the SEAL flip the switch fifty feet away. The target was marked.

Overhead, the drone instantly registered the targets and relayed the information to five separate batteries of artillery. In seconds the rumble of the big guns eight miles south sounded like thunder.

Wait! We're only a few hundred yards from the point of impact. Are we too close? He focused the scope on the men chatting beside the hotel. They didn't notice the rumble.

The roar of incoming ordnance provided about a half second of warning. The men Robert watched in his scope took fewer than two steps before they were engulfed in the fireball of the explosion. He counted at least eight impacts of ordnance. Each one expanded the force of the previous blast. It was total devastation.

The job was done, and it was also time for them to leave. The four veterans quickly gathered their equipment and started the jog south to their Humvee. They would meet the advancing regular Army a few minutes to the south.

chapter 17

Los Angeles, CA – 10:05 AM PST

Lieutenant Mark Strattmann was still struggling with Colonel Zu's revelation of his faith. Although he had attended Sunday school as a child, little of his time or attention had been given to religion since. He went because his parents took him.

Colonel Zu calmly watched his troops move through their exercise to the constant commands of the officers guiding them. The sound of gunfire echoed between the buildings. Suddenly the radio burst with chatter in Mandarin. Zu sat up straight in his seat and looked down the street. He grabbed the microphone and rapidly shouted instructions.

Strattmann strained to look ahead to see what was drawing their attention. All he could see were the helmets of Chinese soldiers running in the street ahead of them. He grabbed his radio.

"Recon Five, this is Rover Six! Sit rep! Over!" he commanded.

"Rover Six, this is Recon Five! Sir, a group of what looks like forty insurgents has popped up between two Chinese light brigades. They came out of a building and fired on a group of Chinese north of us. Sir, the Chinese insisted we stay back. They're blocking us from engaging the enemy! Over!"

"Recon Five, this is Rover Six. What do you mean they're *blocking* you? Over." Strattmann asked.

"Rover Six, there are about fifty Chinese soldiers standing in front of us, in our way, just looking at us, smiling, and telling us to wait here. I don't get it, sir. Over."

Strattmann turned to Colonel Zu with a puzzled look.

"We are containing the insurgents for questioning," he responded.

Suddenly a loud buzzing noise followed by a bright red flash reflected off the buildings ahead. Strattmann stood and raised his radio.

"Recon Five, sit rep! Sit rep!" he shouted.

"Ho–ly crap! I mean, sir! Recon Five, sir! Lieutenant, they shot 'em with ray guns, sir! Just like *Star Wars*, sir! Over." Strattmann stood speechlessly staring ahead.

"What?" he finally spoke into the mike.

"Sir, the Chinese shot ray guns at the insurgents. That was the red flash. All EC's are on the ground. They're not moving, sir. Over."

Strattmann looked at Colonel Zu. "What the hell was that?"

"Plasma-pulse laser, lieutenant. Very effective little weapon," the colonel replied turning to Strattmann with a grin. "Maybe something else you guys can learn from China. Let's go take a look at the bad guys!" Then he shouted orders to his driver who immediately sped toward the scene ahead.

Oval Office, White House – 1:12 PM EST

The ride up from Pod One was slow. The elevator seemed to labor lifting the three of them. Mike convinced himself it was his imagination, even though the lift mechanism had seen more use in the last two hours than in the past twenty-five years.

The Oval Office was still empty except for the two bodies on the floor. The Chinese held the seat of American power by simply occupying the White House. The emptiness of the room was a silent and subtle insult to the Office. Even more insulting was treating it as a morgue.

Mike was puzzled why the occupying Chinese stopped trying to open the panel to the elevator. Perhaps they were working to find another point of entering the lower levels and capturing the president. Maybe they didn't care about apprehending him.

Their three ghostly forms made their way through the Roosevelt Room to the far side and the doorway leading to the Press Secretary's office. The two guards had returned to their position by the Cabinet Room door. *Glorified hall monitors*, Mike thought. The soldiers talked softly, keeping a wary eye for an approaching officer.

Mike reached behind him and gripped Steve's arm. He raised his face cover and mouthed to Steve and Sam. *"Guards!"* They moved toward the hall with extreme caution. Any noise would reveal their position.

Holding each others' hands and hugging the wall, they crept out the door of the Secretary's office. The three moved toward the West Colonnade where half a dozen guards stood.

To avoid the guards, Mike entered the Press Briefing Room. He guessed the press was being held in another part of the building, at least not in the briefing room. He was right. The room was empty.

The emptiness of the mansion was eerie. Hallways and offices normally bustling with activity stood empty and silent. Computer screens sat motionless, staring back at empty chairs. Phones waited in stillness, no lines blinking.

Their progress was slow but steady. The route they had planned to avoid the soldiers proved simple. Knowing where the enemy was located was helpful, but no guarantee of their success. Mike knew being invisible demanded his concentration. At the same time, it was very exciting.

Mike led his companions through the kitchen adjacent to the Center Hall. The whole time the radios in their ears were silent, indicating the way ahead was clear. The first objective was the stairway to the State Floor of the Residence, just outside the kitchen and across the hall.

They took the stairs slowly, watching above for anyone coming down. *If they come down the stairs like Elli, we're sunk*, Mike thought. Tension gripped him. The stairwell was wide open with nowhere to hide. At the top of the stairs Mike, Steve and Sam stopped. They listened. No guards were in the hallway by the Family Dining Room. Everything was quiet. They moved into the hall.

Suddenly, they heard voices. Loud voices speaking Mandarin were headed right at them. Quickly, the trio backed against the west wall of the hallway. They froze.

Mike's earpiece crackled to life. "Mike, someone's coming straight toward you!" warned Matt Kreiter in Pod One. All three were relieved the radios worked at that distance. "Oh, crap! Mike, he's wearing sunglasses!"

A chill hit Steve and Sam the same moment it hit Mike. They had seconds. They were backed to the wall and about to be discovered.

"Freeze! Don't even breathe!" Mike whispered just loud enough. He pressed himself as tight as he could against the wall. The officer and a small entourage turned the corner. He was talking loudly and sounded angry.

He stopped directly in front of Mike. The Chinese officer looked straight at him. He stared at Mike. Inside the cloak, perspiration sprang out on Mike's forehead. He held his breath.

"*Wèi shěn me fú zhuāng bì guà zhè lǐ?*" the officer asked moving his gaze to Steve.

"He wants to know why these garments are hanging in this hallway," Kreiter whispered through the headset.

"*Wǒ bù zhī dao,*" another answered.

"The other guy says he doesn't know." Mike was seconds from leaping out of the cloak and attacking the whole group.

"*Gān jìng! Sì hòu!*" the officer snapped. He spun and walked away, charging down the stairs the three shrouded Americans had climbed only moments earlier. Mike turned his head enough to see that they were backed into a coat rack. The officer assumed the cloaks were hung and carelessly abandoned by their wearers.

"They'll straighten this up later! Move!" Kreiter's insistence wasn't necessary. They were already headed into the Family Dining Room.

"Do you have a fix on the Secret Service agents?" Mike whispered as they moved through the Dining Room.

"They're in the Green Room. Employees are in the East Room."

Los Angeles CA – 10:17 AM PST

The scene was bizarre. Every enemy combatant was flat on the ground and unconscious. Not a muscle moved. Chinese soldiers and American Marines walked among the downed men checking for IDs. Few were found. They tagged and photographed each man. Once noted, the invaders were cuffed and carried to a waiting military transport.

"Fortunately," Colonel Zu began, "these men will remember everything very clearly. When they wake up in custody, they will be angry and ashamed. Exactly where we want them. Defeated." He was very proud they were able to conquer an army without bloodshed.

"So, you basically finished the technology that started here in the States?" Strattmann asked.

"Yes. Copied, then completed. I'm not saying it's the best way to conduct business, but in this case, it brought the best outcome, wouldn't you agree?"

"I cannot argue with the concept, sir." Lieutenant Strattmann's phone buzzed.

"Strattmann," he said briskly.

"Lieutenant, this is Brigadier General Westrup at Mainside."

"Yes sir!"

"I'm preparing to leave here to meet with you and the Chinese officer. Give me your exact grid location."

"Sir, our grid is 34°02'27.53"N, 118°15'51.11"W, sir!"

"Fine. Lieutenant, there is a parking lot at Pico and Hope about a block south. I want a full situation report. I'll meet you there at 1130 hours. Is that clear?" Westrup asked.

"Yes sir. Perfectly clear, sir," Strattmann replied. The call clicked off. With a slightly puzzled look on his face, Strattmann turned to Colonel Zu. "Looks like you're going to have the opportunity to meet our commanding officer," he said.

"Good!" Zu replied with a smile. "Let's get this mess cleaned up before he gets here."

North Lynn Ave., Oklahoma City, OK – 12:20 PM CST

Robert was eager to get to the Humvee in the next block and out of the neighborhood. As it was, they were sitting ducks.

Robert spotted their Humvee. His heart stopped. A crowd of armed men surrounded it and turned toward them. He called to his companions to halt, but they had already been seen. The men at the vehicle raised their weapons toward Robert and the SEALs.

"Cover!" he shouted as he dove to the ground. Robert whipped his M-16 from his shoulder and took aim. The other three men dumped the equipment and raised their weapons from prone positions.

The skills of the four SEALs far outweighed those of the men around the Humvee, but sheer numbers can offset skill. The distance between the two groups was static. The firefight erupted. They were pinned down.

The M-16s were more effective than the semi-automatic hunting rifles they had carried earlier. One by one the number of men at the Humvee dwindled as the body count increased.

More men began firing from between two houses to his left. One of the SEALs grunted and lurched when he was struck. They had to move.

"Quick! Back to the trees!" he yelled. With their M-16s on full automatic, Robert and the two other SEALs laid down massive fire as they pulled back to covered positions. Bullets zinged past him. Another SEAL dropped to the ground.

Robert and the final SEAL reached two large trees on the lawn of the corner house. "Cover to the right!" he yelled to the soldier.

Now men advanced from three sides. Robert fired on the men at the Humvee. Then at the three remaining to his left. Short of killing them all, he didn't see how he was going to get out of this one.

The soldier to his right grunted with the impact of a bullet. He fell limp.

"Can you hear me?" Robert yelled. There was no answer.

Suddenly, a hand grabbed his shoulder and spun him to his back. The stock of an AK-47 crashed into his face. Everything went black.

chapter 18

City Park, Lakeview, OR – 10:35 AM PST

Reggie Porter was a hero. He alone had braved the early morning walk through town. Never mind the fact that he was drunk. Never mind him passing out when he met the Chinese. Never mind the blinding hangover. He was a hero.

The full contingent of Chinese soldiers arrived in the park and began collecting the violent, evil men who had terrorized the town for days. As the terrorists awoke from the pulse laser blast, they were identified and taken away. Wherever *away* was, no one cared, especially Reggie.

"Reggie! Reggie!" an excited Corporal Woo yelled as he scampered across the park. Reggie figured it must be something important with all the yelling.

"Yes, Woo, what is it? Calm down!" Reggie said. He looked around hoping no one saw the young corporal's emotional display.

"General say you need help to run your town!" Corporal Woo was almost bouncing with excitement. Although Reggie never considered actually *running* the town, his newfound hero status opened new opportunities.

"Yes, the general is probably correct," he replied as he pondered the prospect.

"General say *I* be your helper!" Woo was out of breath with excitement.

Reggie opened his mouth to speak, but a series of significant questions flooded his mind, robbing him of words. *My town? Run my town? Hero? Helper?* It was all too much, so rather than ponder any longer, Reggie Porter accepted his role.

"You are very perceptive and perfect for the job, Corporal Woo," Reggie finally replied. He was delighted for Corporal Woo. A sense of pride swelled in Reggie's chest for his new friend.

"We have twelve soldiers stay here with us to help everyone be happy again!" Woo announced.

"Twelve," Reggie said in a considering tone, "do you think that will be enough?"

"Oh, yes! Soldiers very good. They work very hard to help people smile and be happy!"

Is anything not exciting to this guy? Reggie thought, but Woo's energy started to rub off on him. He could feel the excitement of the town coming to life again. It would be like Christmas and the Fourth of July rolled into one big day.

"Sounds like a great plan, Corporal Woo. What do you say we get started?" Reggie put his arm around the small Chinese soldier and strolled across the park to the general. *I guess I'll need to call a town meeting for all this*, Reggie thought. *Hope someone comes.*

State Floor, Red Room, White House – 1:40 PM EST

Mike, Steve, and Sam huddled in the Red Room by the window. Ten Chinese soldiers moved casually around the room admiring the furnishings and particularly interested in the small round table created by a French-born designer. The inlaid marble created a three-dimensional look with the shape and shade of the stone. The soldiers were fascinated.

Mike waited cautiously but was growing impatient. Standing absolutely still was nerve wracking. His right leg was asleep and tingled as if electricity was surging through it.

A loud voice in the Cross Hall drew the soldiers' attention. They exited the room briskly. The small, invisible team moved quickly across to the Blue Room. They skirted the edge of the room to the left, around to the small hall that led to the Green Room. Mike didn't want to stay in the hall any longer than necessary.

They swept into the Green Room and flattened themselves against the wall. Nearly sixty Secret Service agents and White House employees sat on the floor of the twenty-eight by twenty-two foot parlor. The furniture was pushed out of the way. Some of it was broken.

Six Chinese soldiers stood guard. Each man held a weapon Mike had never seen. They were large and bulky and maintained at a firing position.

Mike's earpiece crackled. "Raider One, this is Kreiter. Over."

"Send it," Mike whispered.

"You need to find Robert Nichols. The president told me he's the guy who questioned Ron Wallis. Can you see him in the room?"

Mike scanned the men and women sitting around the room. Some appeared groggy or drugged. A few seemed to have their hands bound behind their backs. He continued trying to see the downturned faces of the men. He felt Steve nudge his left arm.

"Over there," Steve said softly.

Over where? Mike thought. He couldn't see any gesture Steve made or where his eyes were focused. Then, a soldier moved, and he could see.

Robert Nichols was seated across the room, bleeding slightly from a wound in his scalp. He had obviously resisted and suffered because of it. The guard strolled toward the wall where Mike, Steve and Sam stood. He kept coming closer and closer. Mike feared the soldier would run into them. He almost did.

As the soldier leaned toward the wall between Steve and Mike, they separated. The armed guard was less than six inches from each of them—between them. He leaned against the wall, watching his charges. Mike breathed as lightly as he could. This was too close.

"You guys need to move!" Kreiter said in Mike's earpiece. It wasn't loud, but it was loud enough for the guard standing next to him to hear something. The soldier's head snapped to the right, looking directly at Mike. More like directly *through* Mike.

If he thinks the sound is from the next room, he's going to walk right into me to investigate, Mike thought. There was a sudden groan from the far side of the room. The guard left to investigate. Mike breathed again.

He moved to his left and reached for Steve. Steve wasn't there. Mike was alone, invisible in a room full of people.

Where did they go? He was unwilling to ask for help. It might betray his position this time.

Mike continued along the wall toward Robert Nichols. The room had been trashed. The Chinese showed little respect for paintings and furniture of profound historical value. It wasn't their history. They didn't care.

Robert Nichols sat against the wall a few feet away. Mike's earpiece crackled softly.

"Sorry about that last one, Mike," Kreiter said. The volume was lower. "I can see you on the monitor. From where you are there is a camera at eleven o'clock." Mike looked up and slightly to his left. The camera was nothing more than a dot in the felt border along the ceiling. He would have missed it had he not known what to look for.

"Mike, Steve is sitting beside Nichols," Kreiter continued. "Here's what we're going to do. When the guards are turned away, Steve, we want you to slip your cloak over Nichols. Loosen your tie and assume his position. Sit as he's sitting. Got it?"

"Right," Steve said into his comm. device. It must have been just a bit too loud because Nichols turned his head in his direction.

"We need a diversion," Kreiter said.

"Got it covered," it was Sam's voice. She had made the noise that distracted the guard standing by Mike. As he watched, the hands of the French Empire mantel clock made by Jean-Baptiste Dubuc began to move. It chimed at the top of the hour, more than fifteen minutes early.

Every guard in the room turned to the chiming clock, and then looked at their wristwatches. Several of the guards walked toward the mantel.

To Robert Nichols' immediate left, Steve Granger appeared, and Nichols vanished. Mike stepped toward Nichols and grabbed his forearm.

"It's Mike Trapper," he whispered. "We have to move!"

"Mike," Kreiter broke in, "Sam is beside the door you came through. Get there now!"

Quickly Mike and Robert Nichols moved toward the doorway. He bumped into Sam, nearly knocking her off her feet.

"Take it easy, Trapper!" she complained almost too loudly.

"Sorry!" was his only response. The threesome held hands and moved quickly into the Cross Hall. Cover was abundant in the long wide hall. The pillars and alcoves holding busts of past presidents kept them from the open areas. Once behind the pillars Mike pulled the three to a tight huddle so they could talk.

"Robert, we need to activate the VLF," Mike said. "You're supposed to be the one who knows how."

"Right," Nichols responded, "but we need to go back to the Oval Office or get to the president's private quarters."

"Go up another floor?" Sam asked.

"Yes," Nichols said. "We don't know who or what's there, but that's the closest point to activate the system."

"You lead," Mike said. The three cloaked Americans darted toward the Grand Stair.

Dallas/Fort Worth Airport, Grapevine, TX – 12:50 PM CST

The four giant planes filled the tarmac at the south end of both main runways. All four were surrounded by American soldiers. The large red star on the underside of each wing identified the owners of the craft. The Chinese.

General Herman Maris walked the length of the aircraft and peered into the cavernous interior through the tail. He was awestruck by the size of the thing.

"General! Sir, we have soldiers approaching!" one of his subordinates called out.

Maris turned to see an officer of the Chinese Army and about a dozen soldiers marching toward them from one of the service hangars at the edge of the tarmac. General Maris walked directly at them. Ten feet from him they stopped.

"General Maris?" the officer asked.

"Why, yes. How did you know?" Maris drew his head back and furrowed his brow.

"Please forgive us for monitoring your radio transmissions for the last several hours. We were expecting you. I am Major Han Chen of the Army of the People's Republic of China. I am honored to meet you." Major Han extended his hand and smiled at the American General.

"Pleased to meet you, major, but you have me at a disadvantage. Why are you here?"

Major Han's explanation for their presence was brief. General Maris's skepticism was not.

"Thank you for your introduction and offer, but I'm gonna ask you and your men to stand right where you are for a couple of minutes, if you don't mind." Maris turned and walked quickly toward his chopper.

Spend the entire morning chasing Mexicans and Arabs all over thunder, come to the airport and run into the Chinese Army! Damn! Somebody's gotta fill me in on what's goin' on!

"Command, this is Eagle Three! Over."

"This is Command, Eagle Three. Bring it. Over."

"Command, you need to patch me through to the Pentagon, right now! Over!"

I-44 & I-240, Oklahoma City, OK – 12:55 PM CST

All the teams responded in a timely manner and were returning to their base except one.

"SEALs Up One, this is Big Barker Six, come in." There was no response. They waited. "SEALs Up One, this is Big Barker Six, come in."

"Did you check other frequencies? Maybe the equipment is damaged?" Lieutenant Colonel Tom Crawford asked the sergeant at the radio.

"No, sir. The equipment shows that it's working fine. Nothing broken." The sergeant looked at the officer, "Sir, they're just not responding."

"Keep at it," Crawford said as he turned to leave. He entered the next room, and twelve Rangers snapped to attention. "As you were," he said, moving to the city map on the table.

"We have no response from SEALs Up One in the north central part of the city. I don't know if this is rescue or recovery, but you have to go in," the colonel said, "and go in hot."

They knew what he meant—fast and heavily armed. The team of Rangers hit the door at a run. The props on the chopper were beginning to swing overhead as they climbed in.

chapter 19

Second Floor, Treaty Room, White House – 1:59 PM EST

Getting to the Second Floor was simple. The ghostly trio ran up the steps of the Grand Staircase, but they came to an abrupt halt when they got to Presidential Personal Quarters. It was filled with curious Chinese soldiers and officers.

Mike, Sam, and Robert Nichols arrived on the landing only to discover the Center Hall nearly full of Chinese military. Nichols led them into the Treaty Room on the south side of the hall. The Treaty Room opened onto the Truman Balcony with its famous rounded view of the South Lawn.

Moving quickly past the windows of the Yellow Oval Room, they came to the entrance of the President's Private Sitting Room. Their goal was a small music box on the second shelf beside the fireplace. A twist of the ballerina inside the box would arm the VLF system and make contact with the lowest, most secret levels of the White House possible. Of course, raising the lid would set off the music box first.

Nichols spoke softly into his comm. device, "You wait here. I'll make my way over and arm the system." He didn't tell Mike and Sam that the music box would begin to play and possibly reveal his position. He felt if he were caught, they would have a chance to escape. Maybe.

The room wasn't packed with curious Chinese, but it was full. Nichols slipped along the east wall. He heeded Mike's advice to avoid the direct light of the windows. It still took nearly two minutes to move twenty-five feet to the adjacent corner. He stepped gingerly past the antique tables along the north wall, finally coming to the door leading to the Center Hall.

He waited. Soldiers sauntered in and out of the room. Their casual nature angered Nichols. They had illegally invaded his homeland, and their presence in the private quarters of the president of the United States enraged him. The soldiers stepped into the next room speaking softly to one another. That distraction was the break he had been waiting for.

Nichols dashed across the doorway and into the far corner. He scooted along the wall to the shelf beside the fireplace where the music box sat. It was his moment of truth. Would he sacrifice all for his country? This one act would probably be his end. He would be discovered and very likely shot. The time was now, not later. One final act of bravery and then pay the ultimate price.

He reached for the music box. Slowly his hand came close to the lid.

"*Chá kàn!*" a grinning soldier exclaimed as he walked toward the small box. The soldier lifted the lid and turned toward his comrades. The music began to play to the delight of several soldiers. Nichols quickly reached for the ballerina and gave her a slight twist.

Deep in the bowels of the White House the VLF system snapped to life. A simple flip of an automatic switch and new channels of communication opened to those in the lower sealed basements and in the Pods deep underground.

The music paused for only a moment. But when it played on, the soldiers smiled gleefully and talked loudly among themselves. Nichols quickly retraced his steps to the far corner of the room.

Mike and Sam remained rigid at the same place Nichols had left them.

"Come with me," he spoke softly and took Sam's hand. He hoped she had managed to grab Mike, and they took off. For the three of them to move out of the busy room was dangerous, but Nichols knew exactly where he was headed. He pulled Sam back into the Yellow Room and held fast against the northeast wall until he came to the bookcase.

He stood absolutely still. Nichols pulled Sam very close to his side. Sam did the same pulling Mike close to her. They waited. The soldiers milled about the room and wandered into the hall and adjoining rooms. Finally, three officers stood in front of the south windows where Ronald and Nancy Reagan had been photographed with Prince Charles and Princess Diana decades earlier. The officers looked out across the south lawn, talking softly.

Mike heard a barely audible *click*, and then felt the hard tug from Sam's hand pulling him forward into darkness.

Mainside Brig Observation Room, Camp Pendleton, CA
11:02 AM PST

Lieutenant Caleb Hamza sat quietly in the Observation Room, collecting his thoughts. He was still in mild shock over the morning's events. It was amazing to him that what he had encountered in Afghanistan was happening in the Camp Pendleton brig.

The door opened and Sergeant Major John Michaels walked into the room. Hamza began to stand.

"Sit, Lieutenant. Please sit down," he said pulling up a chair and leaning forward. "Tell me what you are discovering from the five men who claim to see this *Isa*."

"Oh, no, sergeant major, there aren't five. There are eleven men who have talked to Him." Hamza's words surprised the sergeant major. He sat bolt upright.

"Eleven?" he asked, "but we've only seen five."

"It seems Isa came to them while you were not looking," Hamza said calmly. "Every man tells the same story. They speak of how Isa knows their families, the names of their friends, and their hometowns. Each man has confirmed this to me."

"And there has been no contact between these prisoners?" Michaels asked. He knew contact was impossible.

"None, sergeant major," Hamza replied. "Please remember, I am on the same side as you."

"Of course, lieutenant. Of course, you are." Michaels was stumped. Protocol for such an event was unknown. The Field Manual provided no instruction on divine intervention or conversion of Muslim radicals to the Christian faith. "I just don't know what to say, lieutenant. A little flummoxed about it all. Know what I mean?"

"Yes. I have been, as you say, flummoxed over this for four years," Hamza said, "but sergeant major, it is becoming clearer to me. Perhaps we simply need more time to understand what is going on here."

Michaels was impressed with the young man's wisdom. He nodded in agreement. After a moment, he stood.

"Keep talking to the men, chaplain. Try to discover what they are thinking. And if you come up with any information on how they got here or who brought them, please let me know."

"I will," Hamza replied.

North Oklahoma City, OK – 1:08 PM CST

The mission to rescue SEAL Team One quickly turned into one of recovery. The bodies of three SEALs and more than a dozen terrorists were easily seen before the chopper landed.

The Rangers hopped to the ground and jogged to the fallen soldiers. They found the worst of outcomes. They were dead.

"Big Barker Six, this is Ranger One, come in."

"This is Big Barker Six. Gimme a sit rep. Over," Lieutenant Colonel Crawford said as he braced himself.

The Ranger's voice was somber. "Sir, we have three KIA. Sorry sir, we're too late. Over."

"There were four on the team. Who's missing? Over," the Colonel asked.

"Sir, the only man not accounted for is Robert Hitchens. He's a civilian, sir. Over."

"Affirmative, Ranger One. What else? Over."

"Sir, besides our men there are more than a dozen ECs on the ground. The Humvee is parked at the curb and has sustained minor damage. The only sign of Hitchens is a weapon that was left on the ground. It's probably his. Over." There was a pause.

"Soldier, I know Hitchens. I know his dad, too," the colonel said. "Wherever he is, the last thing Robert Hitchens truly needs is a rifle."

"Yes, sir. Over."

"Ranger One, pull the ECs out of the street so no one runs over them, then bring our boys home. Over."

"Yes, sir. Out."

Colonel Crawford had a phone call to make. One nobody ever wants to make. He had to call an old friend to let him know his son was missing in action. Slowly he picked up his phone.

East Los Angeles, CA - 11:15 AM PST

Reports of conflicts with the American military came to the headquarters of Colonel Alvaro Herrera with disturbing regularity. Frantic calls told of military units advancing on positions firmly held by his army of liberation. But none of the reports were clear on what was happening. They simply said the army was drawing near . . . then nothing.

Herrera looked out the window at the four trucks filled with the plunder of the Los Angeles neighborhoods surrounding him. He was surprised at how willingly the African American and Latino gangs gathered treasure for the new People's Republic of California. They were easy to manipulate and eager to serve his purpose. Sadly, they would not benefit from their efforts. He chuckled. The time to leave was drawing near.

"Estefan! Jahor! Come in here!" Herrera growled. Two of his closest confidants coolly strolled into the office. Both men were exactly like Herrera; their eyes were like ice; their hearts were stone. Killing was easy for them, a trait that increased their value to Herrera's purposes.

"Where is Cero?" he asked. "The reports of conflicts with the army are more frequent. We will need to leave soon. Where is *Cero*?"

"A young lady caught his eye, colonel," Estefan answered. "Do you want me to go get him and kill the girl, or kill them both?"

"Go get him, *now!*" Herrera snapped around the cigar in his mouth. "I don't care about the girl. Do what you like."

Estefan looked at Jahor as if he'd been given permission for some special pleasure. His face twisted into a sick grin as he wiped the blade of his knife across his tongue. Slowly he slid from the desk he was sitting on and ambled to the office door. It was clear he was preparing a special and particularly wicked end for the young woman.

"How long do we need to keep these monsters with us, colonel?" Jahor asked. "They make my skin crawl."

"My friend, we have four trucks. We need four drivers. Until we can procure two larger vehicles, we need them." Herrera's eyes were cold, his voice coarse and angry. In his opinion he only needed one truck. Everyone else was expendable.

"Jahor, go tell the men guarding the trucks we will be moving them soon. Tell them the Americans are getting too close to stay here. Then . . . send them toward the fighting," the colonel smiled.

The grin on Jahor's face made it clear to Herrera he understood. The vast wealth the people collected would soon be shared between two. Jahor was delighted to be so trusted. He sauntered from the room.

Herrera leaned back in his chair. His plan was working even though it wasn't what he was instructed to accomplish. He didn't care. They would all be dead soon enough. They would never bother him. His only regret was that he would not be doing the killing himself.

But for the treasure in four rental trucks just outside his window, he would forgo the pleasure. *Yes*, he thought, *it's just about time to leave.*

chapter 20

City Hall Parking Lot, Lakeside, OR – 11:20 AM PST

It had been years since anything like a town meeting was convened in Lakeside. Although City Hall seemed like the logical place for such an event, the twelve plastic chairs simply wouldn't hold the hundreds that showed up. Reggie was astounded.

He stood on the steps of City Hall with General Wang and Corporal Woo. The small contingent of diminutive soldiers flanked them at parade rest. The general was stately and proud of the liberation of the small town. The people seemed appreciative, yet skeptical. Woo smiled and bounced like a schoolboy.

"Ladies and gentlemen," Reggie began. He'd never led a meeting, but he'd heard someone start a meeting once by saying *ladies and gentlemen*. "Could I have your attention please?" The crowd slowly hushed and turned to him.

"Thank you. Thank you very much." Reggie cleared his throat and continued. "Today we have the honor of being liberated from the grasp of those stinking bastards that took our town from us." *Maybe that was a little strong*, he said to himself.

Two of Reggie's drinking buddies cheered feebly from one side.

"Thank you," he acknowledged. "This is General Wang, the officer in charge of taking out the bad guys. Let's give him a round of applause!" Reggie clapped along with perhaps a dozen others. Wang stepped forward.

"Ladies and gentlemen," he began, "my government, the People's Republic of China, sent us here to stop this terrible thing that has happened to America."

"What has happened? We haven't heard a thing in days. What's going on?" someone yelled from the crowd.

Reggie realized for the first time that the Chinese general was better informed than any of these poor people who had been treated so badly by the terrorists.

"General Wang, perhaps you could tell all of us what you know about the last couple of days."

The general bowed politely to Reggie and told the story of the invasion across the country's borders. Slowly the people began to piece events together. Many had been told to stay home while looking into the business end of an automatic rifle. That had been convincing enough, so no one knew the full expanse of the invasion.

The people were silent while the general spoke. Finally, it dawned on them the Chinese were there to help. As the explanation concluded, scattered applause came from about half of those gathered.

Reggie told of his first encounter with the soldiers early that morning. Corporal Woo demonstrated his cloak to the amazed cheers of the crowd. Three soldiers displayed the power of their pulse-plasma weapons by shooting a five-gallon drum, knocking it ten feet from its original position.

Reggie Porter won the day. Each of the soldiers who were staying behind to restore order to the town was introduced and ultimately welcomed. It was like the Fourth of July. It was a happy day again in Lakeside, Oregon.

Second Floor Safe Room, White House – 2:25 PM EST

The previous twenty minutes had been spent getting all the equipment up and running. Mike, Sam, and Nichols were in the President's Safe Room. It was small, cramped, packed with communication equipment, and once entered, sealed from the inside. Impenetrable.

Nichols knew all the systems. The VLF, Very Low Frequency system, allowed them to speak freely with the lower basements and the Pods beneath the White House. The Secret Service issued a full alert to all agents and reserves to assemble at locations surrounding the White House. In a relatively short time, defensive forces outside reached eighty percent, with more trained men and women arriving every minute.

The wound on Robert Nichols's scalp was the last item that demanded attention. Sam forced him to sit as she broke out the first aid kit. Between his complaining and her demanding, Mike had to laugh. *Do you two know you sound like an old married couple?* he thought and snickered.

"What are you laughing at?" Sam protested. She knew why he laughed.

"Not going there," Mike replied. "Are you doing all right?" He was serious, and Sam understood.

"You mean . . ." she said, imitating her emotional outbursts. "Comes and goes, Mike. Not sure what to make of it."

"Please don't take offense, but I've seen hardened combat veterans show the same emotions. Combat fatigue is nothing to take lightly."

"I'm thinking the same thing," she said softly. "Guess I'm not the emotional rock I thought I was."

"Nothing to be ashamed of," he said encouraging her. "This is more than I've ever dealt with. It's hard."

"Okay, I'll be good and hold it together until it's done." The fragility showed in her eyes, but along with it was chiseled strength.

"Good. I'm right there with you," Mike said. He looked at his cell phone. Elli had called four times. He listened to her last message.

"Doggone it, Mike! What are you doing? Why don't you call me back? Can't you tell I'm in trouble? Call me! Dang it!" Her message and the panic behind her voice alarmed him. He hit recall. Elli's phone rang once.

"What in the Sam Hill have you been up to? Why haven't you called me?" She finally stopped long enough for him to talk.

"Hey, we've had a major issue. Have you seen the news?"

"News? No!" she retorted. "I got bored, and we decided to go to the zoo this morning. Mike, I think I'm going crazy! Maybe it's the drugs, but I see ghosts everywhere! I mean, I don't know what to think. It's like no one sees them! I don't know what is going on!" Elli began to sob.

"No wait, Elli!" he began. "I can explain. They're not ghosts! They're Chinese soldiers!"

The sobbing stopped immediately on the other end. Mike told her the story. He gave her details about the parachutes opening along the north and south borders and the arrival of huge aircraft at airports all over the country. He also filled her in on some, but not all, of the happenings in the White House. He finished. Elli was silent.

"So," Elli replied slowly, "you've been pretty busy, huh?"

"That's an understatement, babe." Mike knew she understood.

"What should I do? It's kinda spooky with all these things around," Elli said.

"Tell me what you've seen. Honey, I need to know," he said.

"Well, Dad drove the SUV, so we didn't have to move the kids' seats. I rode in front. Mom was clear in the back. At first, it was just weird. About six blocks from the house I saw four yellow *ghosts* standing on the corner. Just standing there!"

"Did you have your sunglasses on?" Mike asked.

"Sure. Don't I always . . . oh," she drew her breath. "Do you think I wouldn't see them without my sunglasses?"

"That's what we discovered," Mike replied. "It has something to do with blocking certain bands of light. Were you wearing your prescription blue-blockers?"

"Yeah, the ones I bought just after Christmas because of the bright reflection from the snow." Elli's voice was filled with awe. "Then, as we went past the Children's Medical Center on Michigan Avenue, I couldn't believe it! Man, they were *all over* the soccer field! Hundreds of them! I didn't know what to say! No one else said anything. I thought I was crazy!"

"Okay, Elli, you're not nuts. Where are you right now?" Mike's question slowed the pace of the conversation dramatically.

"We're still at the zoo. I just thought I was seeing things, and as long as I didn't drive we'd be all right." Elli paused. "Mike, are we alright?"

He didn't want to spark fear into her already slightly drug-fuddled mind, but he had to be honest.

"I don't know for certain," he began slowly, "but I'd say it probably isn't the best day to visit the zoo."

"Oh, crap." Elli sniffed. He could tell her emotions were shot. "Here, Dad wants to talk to you." She handed her phone to her father.

"Hey Mike," he said, turning away from her. "I'm a little concerned about Elli. She's very easily upset, and I don't know, maybe you could come home in a while. It might calm her."

"That really isn't possible today, Dad. Things are pretty hectic right now," Mike knew his father-in-law understood, "but I was wondering if you would ask to borrow Elli's sunglasses for just a moment. Would you do that?"

"Sure. Hold on a minute." Mike could hear the soft voices on the other end and the ruffling of the phone in his father-in-law's hands. "Okay, what do you want me to—ho-ly cow!" He paused. "Mike, what are those things?"

"Dad, they're Chinese soldiers." Mike relayed the story, and what Elli was seeing all around her on their trip to the zoo. He encouraged them to quietly return to the house and stay there.

"Ho-ly cow!" Dad said for the fifth time as he looked around the zoo. "They're everywhere."

The apparitions stood well to the side, out of the way. For some reason, which Mike could not discern, they seemed to want it that way. Or was something else on the program?

"Dad!" Mike said trying to get his attention. "Dad, please listen to me. Do your best to quietly leave the zoo and head home. Please."

"Oh sure, Mike. Sure." The sense of wonder did not leave his voice. "Okay, kids let's head back to the car." Mike could hear the voices of his children complaining in the background. "No, come on. Grandma's gonna make homemade donuts when we get home. Let's go." He heard squeals of excitement from the children.

"All right, then," Granddad said. "Goodbye, Mike." The phone clicked off. Mike closed his phone.

"What was all that about?" Sam asked, firmly pressing the last piece of tape on Nichols's scalp.

"Elli and the kids are at the zoo," Mike said. "She saw Chinese soldiers everywhere. This could be bigger than we thought."

"Okay," Sam said. "What are we going to do about Steve?"

Los Angeles, CA – 11:28 PM PST

Lieutenant Mark Strattmann and Colonel Zu Cheng stood in the northeast corner of the parking lot at West Pico Boulevard and Hope Street. The immigration service across the street stood deserted and burned. The wave of rage that had swept through South Park was among the most violent.

Sweeping operations continued throughout the area, but this neighborhood was secure. Thousands of undocumented and foreign enemy combatants were in custody. And as they regained consciousness, new tales emerged, and with them a deeper understanding of previous days' events.

The Chinese soldiers displayed no brutality nor did kindness or gentleness explain the military maneuver. It was very matter-of-fact. Surrender into custody, or get zapped and taken into custody.

Strattmann watched the calculated moves of the soldiers and the US Marines keeping pace. *The ACLU would be having a cow about now*, he thought. Of course, that was part of the crippling effect on the American culture. It was politically incorrect to challenge anyone about anything. That didn't bother the Chinese. They performed their assigned duties flawlessly.

Four CH-53K helicopters thundered into frighteningly close positions overhead. Fifty-five Marines fast roped from each chopper to the asphalt parking lot with alarming speed. The soldiers took defensive positions around the perimeter. Four additional AH-1W Cobras hovered a few hundred feet up, one in each direction.

As swiftly as they appeared, the four CH-53Ks moved out of sight, and seemingly from nowhere a fifth AH-1W Cobra swooped to the center of the lot and landed. To Strattmann, the helicopter seemed to hop into the parking lot. The landing was fast, but the touchdown was feather-light.

As the blades spun to a stop, the back canopy opened, and very slowly Brigadier General Eugene Westrup climbed to the ground. His stride was firm as he walked toward Lieutenant Strattmann and Colonel Zu.

"Lieutenant! Good to see you again, son," the general said returning Strattmann's salute and extending his hand.

"And you, sir," Strattmann replied. "General, this is Colonel Zu Cheng of the Army of the People's Republic of China."

"Good to meet you, colonel. It is a privilege and an honor."

"As it is for me, General Westrup." Colonel Zu saluted, quickly bowed, and shook the general's hand.

"We've been monitoring your activity by satellite for the last couple of hours, colonel. Very impressive," Westrup said.

"Thank you, sir."

"What are your results so far?"

"In coordination with American forces, our soldiers have detained 11,316 men of undetermined national origin. It is safe to say they aren't American citizens, sir," Zu said crisply.

"And casualties?" Westrup asked, pulling his pipe from his pocket.

"None, sir."

The general stopped in the middle of lighting his pipe and looked blankly at his Chinese counterpart.

"You said none?"

"A few very minor injuries, twisted ankles or scraped knuckles, nothing serious. And certainly nothing from weapons fired." Colonel Zu maintained his charming expression and smile.

The discussion moved to the plasma-pulse weapon system and the effective use of the weapons en mass rather than in single firings. The science of it all was captivating for the older officer.

"But, please understand, General Westrup, we have five other battle groups operating in Los Angeles alone. I have not heard what their results might be. We have encountered significant resistance in this part of the city, but none that we haven't been able to master." Zu's confidence was evidenced in his broad smile and military posture. "The building-to-building, house-to-house sweep has been very successful."

"And what can we expect in the next ten to twelve hours?" Westrup asked.

"General, our sweeping maneuver will continue as we move southward. Are your forces engaging enemy resistance?"

"In the last sixty minutes, eight thousand Marines and an additional twelve hundred volunteer veterans have deployed in South LA. They are moving north at a rapid pace, meeting little resistance." The general's tone was tinged with both envy and admiration.

"Our base camp was located in Hollenbeck Park because of a large contingent of gang forces and insurgents at the LAPD at First and North St. Louis streets. Our reconnaissance teams identified it as one of the largest centers for the invaders. Our initial sweep will converge and conclude at that point."

"When will your sweeping maneuver be complete?" the general asked.

"In about eighteen hours, at the present rate," Zu answered without batting an eye, "but that is the entire operation. We expect to complete this course by mid-afternoon."

General Westrup couldn't find words to respond. Covering that much ground and searching that many buildings was unthinkable.

"And when you arrive at the police station up on First Street, what do you expect?" he finally asked.

"We expect they will either lay down their arms or be knocked to the ground by our weapons." Zu's voice was matter-of-fact and without a flinch.

"I would like to see that. May I join you?" he asked leaning toward the smaller man.

"General Westrup, I would be honored. As I am your guest, please also be mine," Colonel Zu said, and with a slight bow, he turned and led the American general to his waiting vehicle.

chapter 21

I-44 & I-240, Oklahoma City, OK – 1:34 PM CST

Sheriff Perry Hitchens pulled to a stop near the mobile command post for the 13th and 18th Field Artillery Regiments. Yolanda Vasquez exited the passenger side and ran to keep pace with the sheriff.

No one had stopped them or asked for identification. Everyone knew Robert Hitchens was missing. Sheriff Hitchens was well known by these men. Local elections tend to create a certain notoriety.

And not a single soldier dared challenge the beautiful woman with him. Her eyes were deeply shadowed by concern. She was with the sheriff and that gave her all the authority she would need.

"Anything new, Tom?" Sheriff Hitchens asked as he entered the trailer command post.

"Sorry, Perry. Everything's been either a cold trail or a dead end." Colonel Tom Crawford visibly flinched, realizing his poor choice of words, words that brought near collapse to the sheriff's lovely companion. "Excuse me, miss. That wasn't the best way to say that. We just haven't found him yet."

Perry Hitchens turned to Yolanda. He ached seeing the pain in her eyes silently yearning for hope. He could also see that not far behind that hope was a fear of the worst possible outcome.

"You know Robert can take care of himself, don't you?" he asked holding her gently by her shoulders.

"Yes," she replied. "I saw what he could do that night we drove down from Wichita. But then, I was there! I was there with a gun when he almost . . ."

She dissolved into tears and buried her face in her hands. Perry stepped forward and held her firmly. He knew she had faced danger with bravery. The soldiers working at their posts around them knew that even the strongest come to a breaking point. They didn't know her detailed story, and no one would stand in judgment of her.

"I'm sorry," she said gaining her composure. "I'm acting like a spoiled ten-year old."

"Honey, you're acting like an overly tired GI," Perry said correcting her. "There's not a man or woman in this room who's walked the path you have this week. Take a breath and give yourself a break. We *will* find Robert."

"Most likely, Ms. Vasquez, Robert will find us." Colonel Crawford was standing by Perry. "He's a very skilled soldier. *He* will probably find us first."

Yolanda nodded as she daubed her eyes. Her breath was ragged and her knees weak. "May I sit here for a while and wait?"

"Of course," the colonel replied as he motioned a sergeant to bring chairs for both of them. "There's a lot going on right now, but there is room for you here."

"Exactly what is going on, Tom?" the sheriff asked.

"About an hour ago we lost contact with Robert's recon team. That's when I called you. All the other teams completed their missions and returned to their bases. But all we got from up north was silence. We got a rescue team out to their last known location within thirty minutes. They must have been ambushed. The three other men on the team were KIA. Robert's gun was there. The radio was there and in working order, just no trace of Robert."

That was the first-time Sheriff Hitchens and Yolanda knew the other SEALs had perished. It was clear Robert was taken. *Why would anyone take him rather than kill him on the spot?*

"We aren't sure why he wasn't there, Ms. Vasquez. That's part of the mystery, but it's also what gives us hope. If Robert wasn't injured, and there is no indication he was, if he's able, he'll give them one hell of a fight."

It was little comfort, but it helped. All they could do was wait.

Trapper Home, Washington, DC – 2:38 PM EST

All the way home Elli saw the yellow ghostly forms standing in small groups at street corners, in the bushes at small parks, and spread along the parkways between the lanes of traffic. Even with the understanding that something huge was happening, and that the visions she saw were only people, it felt creepy.

The kids played loudly while strapped in their car seats. Grandma was the center of attention as they chattered excitedly about hot donuts. Elli and her dad were quite the contrast. They were quiet and sober. They heard the noise of the children without listening to them.

At the entrance to their street, the hair on the back of Elli's neck stood up. Two forms stood at the corner. Elli could swear they both looked directly at her and followed them as they made the turn.

"Dad!" she said softly, "there are two of them on the corner! They looked right at me!"

Her dad looked straight ahead down the street. "We'll get home and keep everybody busy. We need to think about this a little. Not lose our heads," he said. He drove to the driveway and pulled in.

The children freed themselves from their seats and leaped from the car. They bounced around grandma with excitement, talking loudly about the promised homemade donuts, the best snack ever!

Elli picked up Riley from his carrier and headed into the house. Her heart pounded in her chest. The wound in her shoulder throbbed, and she realized she shouldn't be carrying her baby.

"Dad, would you take Riley, please?"

"Oh, sure. Why did you pick him up? You know you aren't supposed to lift anything like that!" he scolded softly.

"I know, I know," she replied. "I just forgot." Elli felt wrecked inside. Her mind spun with wild imaginations. Her shoulder ached from the day's old knife wound, and the rest of her tingled with the stress of the day. The medications were something else, a different layer of odd sensation. She was glad to be home, and at the same time, she was terrified.

She entered the kitchen as Grandma began her magic. The children shuffled in their seats, then stood jumping with excitement, talking over each other constantly. Elli just wanted to lie down for a while. *Maybe a nap,* she thought. She walked into the living room and eased onto the couch.

"Wake me when this day is over," she proclaimed and pulled a blanket over her face. It was naptime.

North Oklahoma City, OK – 1:45 PM CST

Robert's forehead was split open, and blood pooled in the corner of his eye by his nose. The truck bounced hard along a rough, unknown road. It was dark inside. He figured he was in a van or an SUV with the windows darkened. Each bump slammed the floor against his forehead.

He lay still. The boots of three different men rested not far from his face. Surely they would relish stomping hard on him at the slightest provocation. His hands were tied behind his back. The plastic straps cut his wrists.

Robert remembered the men on his team were shot, then the hit to his face. He had no idea how long he had been unconscious or where they were taking him. Why did they keep him alive? What use did they think he would be to them?

Patience was his best weapon for now. The opportunity would present itself, and he knew exactly what to do. He just had to wait.

The vehicle careened to a stop. Leathered, brutish hands grabbed him and dragged him from the truck. He was thrown onto the dusty ground. The sunlight was bright. Through squinted eyes Robert discerned the shapes of six men. No one spoke. They stood around him waiting. *Waiting for what?*

Second Floor Safe Room, White House – 2:50 PM EST

Strategies were almost second nature to Mike Trapper. See the objective, then find the most effective method of reaching it. Mike, Sam, and Nichols ran the gamut of options. They had only one recourse. One of the captives in the Green Room would simply have to vanish.

Mike's greatest concern was for the remaining captives once Steve was rescued. They would need to work fast to execute the next step in the plan. The problem was none of the three of them could guess what that next step might be. They'd have to play it by ear.

Mike and Sam prepared to leave the safe room. Nichols was to stay behind and coordinate with those in the sealed lower levels of the White House basement, the president in the Pod, and the growing army of Secret Service agents at locations around the White House grounds.

Everyone had a plan. Unfortunately, none of the plans were coordinated. Until the VLF system was activated moments earlier, all the units of government and defense were operating on different channels of communication. As Mike and Sam made their final checks before leaving, the teams were beginning to talk. That made Mike a little uneasy. What kind of support could he expect? What would be the result if the plans changed and he and Sam were at the wrong place at the wrong time? He would have to depend on Nichols and the men and women in Pod One with the president.

"All systems check out, Mike," Sam said. Her determination bolstered Mike's confidence. She was like steel. She was determined to get to Steve and see him to safety.

"Great," he replied. "Is there anything we've overlooked?" he asked Nichols.

"Oh, gosh!" Nichols replied, "I almost forgot!" He reached into his shirt pocket and pulled out a small pair of glasses. "When I wrestled with one of the Chinese soldiers, he dropped these. I don't know what they're for, but after you mentioned the effect of the blue-blockers, I thought this might be something."

Mike took the lenses from him. They were red and had a small clip that held them on the bridge of the wearer's nose. He looked closely at the strange glasses.

"If blue-blockers can help us see the cloaks in regular light, could this be how they see each other while wearing the cloaks?" Mike pressed the red lenses over the bridge of his nose and pulled the cloak over his head. Sam pulled her cloak on as well.

"Holy Moses!" Mike exclaimed. "Sam, not only can I see your cloak, but I can see *you*! These things allow me to see through both our cloaks! That's how they can coordinate and maintain contact!" He knew there had to be some way the Chinese could see each other, remain in contact and operate as a single unit. The blue-blockers from the outside and the rose-colored lenses from inside the cloak!

"That also means they can see us, Mike," Sam said bringing a sudden bit of reality to their situation. Immediately, he knew she was right. Any foreign soldier wearing the rose-colored lenses would see them moving through the White House, but it was a risk they had to take.

"I guess we'll need to be careful about when and where we choose to be invisible." The fact simply added another unknown quality to their situation. "So far, they are confident they have secured the White House. I doubt there will be many, if any, lurking about in their cloaks. That gives us the advantage."

"Until we get Steve and the Chinese realize one of their prisoners is missing," Sam reminded him. "At that point, whenever it comes, our options will be limited."

Again, Mike knew she was right, and he knew there was no way those options could be assessed from inside the safe room. They would need to depend on those around them to watch and help them avoid capture. Mike secured the third cloak under his left arm and pulled down his face covering.

"Okay, we're outta here," he said.

"Be careful, Mike," Nichols replied. "The room is empty for now. Best you move quickly."

The china alcove in the Yellow Room inched forward a little more than a foot, and two ghostly forms swept into the room. The alcove panel silently closed and sealed.

chapter 22

North of Oklahoma City, OK – 1:53 PM CST

Two men grabbed Robert by his shirt and threw him against the rear wheel of the SUV. His hands were still strapped behind his back. His head ached.

"What is your name, gringo?" a swarthy man asked, squatting beside him.

Robert looked at him through a squinted eye partially blocked by dried blood. He huffed and smiled at the man. "What does that matter?"

"I want to know who I am saying good-bye to when I kill you," he said smiling. The other men laughed. They were looking forward to this.

"I'll let you know if you get the opportunity," Robert said, still smiling back at him. They had kept him alive to this point for a reason. He was curious what their reason was.

"Oh, a very smart gringo," the man mocked, kicking dirt at Robert with his boot. He leaned close to him. "Don't you know I can slit your throat right here and no one would care?"

"Sure. But you hauled me out here for a reason instead of killing me back in town." Robert was pleased to see confusion cross his opponent's face. It was now clear to him that this low-life thug was under orders to keep him alive. Slitting his throat was not within this man's authority, nor was it in the instructions he'd received.

"Maybe, maybe not," he snarled at Robert, as he dangled his knife near his throat. "But the time will come, and I will be happy to oblige."

The other men turned as a vehicle approached. Dust swirled through the air as the car slid to a stop. Two men exited the vehicle and sauntered toward Robert. They didn't look familiar, but they looked as threatening as the others.

"And who do we have here?" said the man who was clearly in charge. He walked toward Robert with a bit of a swagger.

The men who had brought Robert to this location stood more erect almost at attention in the man's presence. "He didn't tell us his name."

"That's because you are a stupid oaf who posses limited skills in gathering information." He swatted at the swarthy man to move him out of the way. He smiled at Robert.

"You are Robert Hitchens, son of Sheriff Perry Hitchens, are you not?" The man's smile faded slightly.

"Maybe, maybe not," Robert said mocking the swarthy man's earlier threat. "What does it matter to you?"

"Oh, it matters," he said drawing a huge knife from his belt and waving it threateningly. "It matters a great deal. And I think you *are* Robert Hitchens. You see, your father Sheriff Hitchens killed my father."

"If this sheriff you speak of is a murderer, he should be put in jail and tried for murder." Robert was testing the man.

"I am Mohamed Hussein, son of Colonel Baktir Hussein, leader of our forces in Dallas, Texas. He was traveling to meet us when your father ordered his minions to kill him in Norman. Your father killed my father. Now, my father's son will kill your father's son. Do you understand me?"

"It's not much of a riddle. You think since some sheriff supposedly killed your dad, you can kill me, right?" Robert smiled calmly. "Doesn't really make sense, but give it your best shot. We'll see."

"That I will. That is why I have men like this stupid oaf, this pig," Hussein replied. The swarthy man protested with a grunt. "But he is very good at killing. It will take a long time, I assure you."

Hussein motioned to the men who had come with him. He brought an old wooden chair from the back of the car. They lifted Robert from the ground and tied him to it.

"Mr. Robert Hitchens, we wouldn't want you to soil your pants in a pool of your own blood," Hussein sneered. "This way you can watch your blood soak into the dust. Unfortunately, I do not have time to waste watching you die. And you will die."

Robert shrugged his shoulders. "Others have tried and failed. Maybe this is your lucky day."

"You three, come with me," Hussein ordered, turning quickly toward his car. The three men followed him. Abruptly, he stopped and faced the swarthy executioner. "Oh, make it very painful. And make it last a long time." He smiled.

"Oh, si! Si, señor!" The eyes of the swarthy murderer sparkled gleefully. He faced Robert as Hussein and the three men climbed into the car and sped away. The dust from their departure lingered in the air.

DFW International, Dallas, TX – 1:55 PM CST

Sometimes even a general's *right now* takes time. General Herman Maris finally got through to the Pentagon. Although contact with the Chinese Embassy had been impossible all day long, it was determined the Chinese forces were not hostile, at least toward Americans.

It was mid-day in Dallas and the tarmac was hot. General Maris walked slower than usual to his meeting with the Chinese officer, Major Han. He surveyed the men before him. The major and his escort were standing in exactly the same spot he left them. The soldiers wore black, shiny helmets that shielded their eyes, and they carried bulky rifles unlike any rifle the general had ever seen.

"I'm sorry for the delay, Major Han. Things have been difficult this week. I'm sure you understand," Maris said in his best leader-like voice. He never spoke to his wife or his grandkids in that voice, but it was appropriate in this situation.

"Yes, we are well aware of the difficulties you face. We are here to be of assistance in whatever manner you deem helpful." Major Han smiled warmly. General Maris wasn't convinced.

"Let's get out of this sun while you fill me in on your capabilities. The US Marines are a crack unit and willing to face any challenge," the general said, intentionally dangling an implied warning. As they walked to the tail of the huge transport, Major Han told his story.

As a soldier, he was dispatched to an emergency in the United States. Their flight plan was pre-set. During the flight their orders were clarified and altered. They were not sent to occupy but rather to seal the borders against further assault and assist in re-establishing order.

The Chinese officer knew significant details regarding the murder of thousands of law enforcement officers. As they made their approach into DFW Major Han had wondered what role they might play in that arena. He knew the limits of their weapons. He also feared his men would be endangered by the high-powered rifles used by the terrorists. In view of that risk, Han outlined the procedures they were prepared to use in building-to-building or house-to-house searches.

"And that might be a contribution you can make," Maris replied. "But the first task at hand is determining the locations of the invaders. We have attacked several command centers, but we're not fully manned for house-to-house, building-to-building searches."

"General Maris, I am sure you know that Beijing is very good at keeping order. We have developed techniques over many years to root out dissidents in urban areas. I would be honored to demonstrate our abilities."

"And sir," Maris replied, "I am interested."

Thus, the unlikely alliance of long assumed enemies found a place of common need, ability, and trust, and the initiation of a huge task became possible.

North of Oklahoma City, OK – 1:58 PM CST

Three men stayed behind with orders to kill Robert in as painful a method as possible. They joked with each other in Spanish without realizing he understood every word. But these three were ready for a celebration.

The fat, swarthy man casually sharpened his knife on a stone. He stroked the ten-inch blade slowly and with precision, honing a razor's edge. The ivory handle extended behind the man's grip. The knife was designed for very serious cutting, and the man charged with the privilege of killing Robert knew just how to use it.

Another man, with a long, lanky stride retrieved a bottle of whiskey from the SUV to enhance the party atmosphere. They laughed and drank, fully enjoying their preparations for murder. Their coarse jesting allowed time for Robert to formulate a plan of his own.

The celebration ended when the executioner examined the blade in his hand, looked at Robert, and began to move toward him. His steps were more of a stumble than a swagger as the alcohol seeped into his brain.

Robert waited for the moment when the bumbling drunk was in range and kicked him in the groin with his right foot. The second kick was his left heel slamming into the man's face. Staggering backwards, blood gushing from his nose and mouth, the swarthy man fell flat on his back unconscious. Blood ran from his face into the dust on the ground around him and turned into thick, blood-soaked mud. The ivory handled knife rested in his limp, lifeless grip.

Robert leaped to his feet and faced the tall, gangly man to his left who made a stumbling charge raising his own knife. A third man grabbed him firmly around the shoulders from behind. With his hands still bound behind his back, Robert grasped the belt of this last attacker.

The years of elite training kicked in, and with perfect timing as though choreographed, he lifted the man behind him and spun to his left knee. The tall man slammed his knife into the back of his comrade with the full force of his weight. As the long blade penetrated his heart, the man threw his head back, screaming at his companion. Momentarily stunned, the tall man released the knife and staggered backward. That second gave Robert the advantage.

Robert's next kick was to the tall attacker's left leg. The bone snapped with a loud crack, and he fell to the ground in agony. Two more merciful kicks, and he was unconscious.

Using the full weight of his body, Robert dropped himself hard on the wooden chair to which he was bound. The chair shattered under him, and Robert's hands were free. He retrieved the keys to the SUV from the swarthy man's pocket. He leaped into the vehicle, hit the ignition, spun around in the dirt, and headed back toward town. He had another score to settle.

Lakeside, OR, – 12:05 PM PST

Reggie Porter and Corporal Woo entered Jenny's Diner as the regular lunch crowd assembled. A small cheer of appreciation rose from the group between bites of their first restaurant food in almost a week. It was feeble but appreciated.

In just over an hour the power was restored to most of the town. Electricity seemed to bring the little town back to life. The invading terrorists had forbidden this common convenience of daily life, and the residents had been miserable. However, once it was restored, it was readily taken for granted again.

Corporal Woo and Reggie sat in the last booth along the far wall of the diner. The young waitress scurried over and presented menus. Reggie scanned the choices before him and scratched his scraggly chin. Looking past the menu, he saw a puzzled and almost frantic look on Woo's face. Their eyes met.

"What this?" Woo asked indicating the menu. "Plate?"

"Plate? What do you mean by—" then it hit him. "No, that's not what we eat from. It tells us what we can buy for lunch."

"Oh, I no read English," Woo replied sheepishly.

"That's just fine, my friend," Reggie said comfortingly. "I'll order for you." Woo beamed at the prospect. "As a matter of fact, we need to get that recipe for Jenny. You know, the thing you gave me to eat this morning."

"*Ziao long bao?*" Woo offered smiling.

"Exactly!" Reggie replied. That particular delicacy was a wonder drug in his mind, and he was eager to share it with his late-night gang. The waitress returned with her pen and order pad.

"And what can I get for you two gentlemen, today?" she asked.

Reggie looked across the table to his bubbly young friend and made up his mind. "Why don't you bring us a couple of your quarter pound cheeseburgers with fries?"

"French fries?" Woo asked beaming. "Hamburger with fries?" Woo had only seen hamburgers on television commercials. He never dreamed he would some day actually eat one.

"That's the ticket, little buddy," Reggie replied. "That's the ticket." Reggie was pleased. This was turning out to be a good day after all.

chapter 23

State Floor, White House – 3:10 PM EST

Mike and Sam moved quickly across the hall and down two flights of stairs, headed directly to the Green Room. Time was in short supply. They could only guess what plans the Chinese might have for their American captives.

Fewer people were milling about than earlier, enabling Mike and Sam to move at a good pace and exercise minimal caution about making noise. The door to the Green Room was open. The two cloaked figures swept quickly into the room. Mike and Sam took positions on each side of Steve, preparing their move.

"Everybody stand up!"

Mike's heart stopped as he recognized the voice of the officer they had met earlier by the White House kitchen. Then the officer had been wearing dark sunglasses. Now, he wasn't.

At least he can't see us this time, Mike thought. Or so he hoped. The revelation of the rose-colored lenses left him uneasy. He was concerned about any other technologies he didn't know about. Mike felt more tension than before.

"Please, stand to your feet!" the officer commanded firmly.

People all around the room began to rise. Most had been sitting for the better part of three hours. Many were stiff, and their effort in getting up was significant. But Mike saw the moment and seized it.

As Steve began to stand, Mike and Sam stepped in front of him and held the third cloak open as he slid into it. The commotion in the room provided adequate distraction. They had arrived just in time.

"Please, follow me and come this way," the officer called to the White House staff members and Secret Service personnel in the room.

Mike noticed a handful of guards standing outside the room in the hall. They were counting the people as they exited the room. Time was crucial.

Quickly, Mike grabbed Sam and Steve by the hands and pulled them away toward the far side of the room. He drew them close.

"Steve, are you all right?" he asked, leaning toward him. Their heads were inches apart. Their voices hushed.

"I'm fine. We need to get out of here. They're counting as we leave and I'm going to be missed very soon."

"Right," Mike whispered. The noise of shuffling feet and people murmuring covered his voice. "We need to get to the elevator that goes to the lowest level of the basement."

"Won't it be locked down like the other emergency units?" Sam whispered back.

"No," he answered. "I watched Ray Jergins punch in a code the other day. It's not a number I'll forget. Let's go." Mike led them back down the stairs and toward the West Wing.

Their progress was erratic. Small groups of soldiers stood along the Colonnades outside the Press Briefing room. They were smoking and talking loudly, unaware of the small group sneaking past them in invisibility cloaks.

The threesome nearly jogged past the Cabinet Room and down the hall to the lobby. It was empty. Mike moved to the elevator, and after glancing over his shoulder, he pushed the button to open the door.

Once the doors closed, Mike lifted his face covering and opened the box in the elevator panel containing a phone. Without lifting the receiver, he entered four numbers on the key pad. The same numbers he watched Ray Jergins enter. 1 – 7 – 7 – 6.

Instantly the elevator dropped, leaving the occupants weightless for a moment. They were on their way.

LAPD Parking Lot, Los Angeles, CA – 12:12 PM PST

Colonel Herrera stood on the steps of the LAPD, watching three dozen men cheering each other on to what he knew was certain death. It amused him. His speech inspired them for the Republic, their foolish zeal was the only ingredient needed.

They had guarded the trucks with near religious devotion for two nights. Not a single question was asked about the new location of the treasure. Assurances were made they would receive their share. *After all, we are one people,* they were told.

Cero, Estefan, and Jahor stood behind him. The guards, encouraged by the three men, responded with cheers throughout the colonel's speech. The trio had played their roles well, and they were ready to claim their share of the gold.

As the last of the guards passed from sight, Herrera turned to the three with a smile. "Gentlemen, it is time for us to move."

The vehicles were fueled for the long trip. They would carry their own water and food to avoid unnecessary stops. After leaving Los Angeles, they would drive through the mountains east of the city and into the desert. From there it was a straight shot to their goal. Mexico.

ALI Map Room, White House Basement – 3:14 PM EST

Both Steve and Mike knew the likely reception when the elevator stopped. They quickly removed the cloaks and folded them inside-out, so they wouldn't be lost. Then, the three stood facing the doors with their hands in the air. A receiving committee would be waiting for them, and it would most likely be armed.

The carriage dragged itself to a weight-crunching stop. Mike took a deep breath and let it out slowly. Both Mike and Steve moved in front of Sam protectively.

The doors slid open quickly.

"Freeze!" No less than a dozen M-16s were aimed into the elevator. The Marines moved quickly, two of them grabbing Mike by his shoulders and pulling him from the carriage.

"Trapper?" Ray Jergins greeted them with wide-eyed surprise. "Hey guys, it's okay. Stand down!" Jergins pulled Mike away from the opening, allowing Steve and Sam to exit the elevator.

"How in the name of thunder did you get here?" Ray asked. He was a little nervous about someone *getting in* who wasn't really supposed to.

"Sorry, Ray," Mike replied. "I watched you enter the code and remembered it."

Ray was miffed. "I'll work on increasing my stealth capabilities." He grinned at Mike and greeted Steve and Sam. "Now what the hell is going on up there?"

"There are Chinese soldiers all over the White House," Mike began. "And from what I can gather, most of the city as well." He briefed the assembled group on what they encountered moving through the White House, as well as the events Elli had relayed to him from the zoo. "Has anyone made contact with the Chinese embassy yet?" he concluded.

"I understand they've made several attempts," Ray said, "but so far we've just got busy signals. What the heck are they doing to keep their lines full?"

"Maybe managing the overthrow of the American government," Angela Crain said, as she joined the group. Her voice was sarcastic. Mike decided that was just the way she was. He couldn't help but grin a little.

"Or maybe," Sam chimed in, "maybe they're trying to find out what's going on, like we are. Maybe this thing has taken an unexpected turn or is somehow out of hand."

"It could be just about anything at this point," Mike added. "For the life of me, I cannot figure out why China would want to take on the United States. They have troubles that make ours look like small potatoes. I can't see them doing this and presenting any advantage for themselves."

Mort the technician stood behind his keyboard. "Well, for the last two hours this massive observation hub has been trying to talk to someone who could help. We can watch a lot of stuff from down here, but actually talking to someone about it is more difficult."

"Any creative ideas?" Mike asked.

"We can talk to ourselves all over the place on the VLF, but the only location that actually has a phone line is over in Pod One with the president," Mort explained. "They've been calling constantly, but it's always busy."

"What contact have you made with the Secret Service units outside the White House grounds?" Steve asked.

"I'd say they should be at full deployment by now," Ray offered. "Once they can confirm where everyone is being held, they plan to storm the building."

"That explains why everyone was moved," Sam said. The fact the captives were moved was news to Ray Jergins.

"They're not in the Green Room anymore?" he asked.

"No," Mike answered. "We got to Steve as they were herding everyone out. We don't know where they went. Have you checked with the guys in Pod One?"

"Not yet," Ray said. "Mort, get on that, would you?" Mort descended behind his sea of monitors and keyboards.

"Who have you been talking to on the outside?" Mike asked. "Who's in charge of the maneuver?"

"Bill Ketcham. He's set up a command post on the top of the Chamber of Commerce Building across from Lafayette Square," Ray answered.

"I need to talk to him immediately," Mike said.

Ray Jergins turned to a desk, lifted a phone that was patched into the VLF, and handed it to Mike. He heard a couple of beeps then the familiar voice of Bill Ketcham, Director of Surveillance and Intelligence for the Secret Service.

"Ketcham." It was more a bark than a greeting.

"Bill, this is Mike Trapper."

"Mike! Where the hell are you?"

"White House basement with Ray Jergins. We just got here," Mike replied.

"We knew you left Pod One but had no idea where you went," Ketcham said.

"Listen, I need to bring you up to speed on a few things," Mike began. Quickly, he told Ketcham about the ghostly images the monitors revealed when the colors on the screen were properly adjusted. Mike also relayed the frightening trip Elli made to the zoo. Finally, he explained the rose-colored lenses that enabled cloaked soldiers to see each other.

"Bill, do you have a pair of blue blockers?" Mike asked. He could hear rustling and muted voices on the other end as Ketcham called out orders to those around him.

"Yeah. Right here," he answered.

"Do you have a clear view of the White House?"

"Sure. From where we are, I can see—ho–ly cow! They're all over Lafayette Square. Yellowish forms just standing in formation."

"That's what you're up against," Mike began, "but that's not all. They're all over the city, Bill."

The phone was silent. Bill had never encountered a foreign army standing in the nation's capital, surrounding the very seat of power of the United States. Bill Ketcham, never at a loss for words, was dumbfounded.

"Bill, are you there?" Mike asked.

"Yeah," he said slowly, "I'm here." The steam was out of his voice. Mike could tell he was still taking in the scene before him.

"Bill, I think an assault on the White House would be ill advised at this point," he said, surprised at the slow response.

"Uh, yeah, I think you're right, Mike. I think we're going to get some more sunglasses and do some counting." Bill Ketcham hung up without another word.

chapter 24

ALI Map Room, White House Basement – 3:25 PM EST

Steve Granger pulled a chair beside Sam who was working at a computer. She ignored him for a moment, and then stopped and looked at him.

"What?" Her face was deadpan. She showed no feeling, only minor irritation.

"Thought we could talk for a minute," Steve said.

"Your timing is rather uncanny," she snapped back. "Right here in the middle of a national emergency you want to *talk*. Kiss and make up?" Her stare was almost a glare.

"No, but since we are waiting for somebody else to do their job, so we can go do ours, I thought it might be a good time to see if we still liked each other." He could feel a familiar edge rising between them. One he didn't particularly like.

"Well, I like you most of the time," she said blandly. "It's just there is so much, I don't know, *tension* in the world right now. I think we're pretty miniscule by comparison."

"Perhaps we are," he answered. "But when all the crap clears, it's still going to be you and me trying to figure this out. I want you to remember that I love you. I want to be with you. I want to make this work."

"Yeah?" Sam snorted. She turned to him with eyes as cold as ice. "Got it. I love you, too, but right now, today, I don't know that I have room for that luxury. Maybe tomorrow things will be different. I don't know, maybe tomorrow you'll be dead, and I'm all by myself. Too many things I don't know right now."

The ice melted. Sam crumpled onto the desk. Serious overload. Steve scooped her into his arms and held her as she sobbed. Whatever happens next, the first thing this woman needed was someplace safe and quiet, and for a long time.

Steve caught Mike's gaze from across the room.

He knew Mike understood. *Its fine*, his look said, *just be cool*. The room buzzed with activity, but this particular corner was ignored. Everybody knew the story, but only Steve, Mike, and Sam had lived the story on the front line. Everyone knew battle fatigue was real.

I-44 & I-240, Oklahoma City, OK – 2:30 PM CST

Yolanda Vasquez sat quietly in the corner of the mobile command post communication room. The voices around her were hushed. The thoughts behind the voices held little hope of finding Robert alive, but to speak such a thing could bring it into being. At least that's what superstition feared.

Yolanda was in agony. She noticed how low and soft the voices were. She was convinced if she weren't there, everything would be much louder. But she wasn't going to leave. She wasn't going to move.

"Can I get you something to drink, Ms. Vasquez?" Colonel Tom Crawford asked.

"No," Yolanda said through a tight smile. "No thank you, colonel. You are very kind, but I am fine." Her eyes brimmed with tears that broke and ran down her cheek. She hastily wiped her face with the palm of her hand. "Not really fine," she said, "but not thirsty."

"I understand. If there is anything we can do, please let us know." The colonel fumbled his words.

"Just find Robert, please," Yolanda replied. "That's all I need."

"Yes, ma'am, we will do our best." He turned to his communication officer. "Have the boys run that northwest sector just one more time," he said. "Look for anything out of the ordinary. Anything."

ALI Map Room, White House Basement – 3:33 PM EST

The stunning effect Mike's revelation made on the Secret Service seemed to linger. Communication lines were very quiet, and it wasn't a peaceful quiet. Mike could feel the pressure inside to *do* something about it. The problem was, of course, what should be done and how it should be started? Those questions circled endlessly in Mike's mind.

Steve and Sam shared the weight of the situation. Steve sat at a computer screen making notes of the recently obtained video captures from rooms in the White House. The videos contained a time stamp that indicated they all were taken within the last twenty-five minutes.

Sam paced. Sitting around waiting for a solution to develop was not her method of doing business. Review, rehash, and reconstruct the events and conditions, looking for a workable angle. Then, do it again. Something would come to the surface. Something would fall into place, or so she kept telling herself.

"Hey! Come look at this!" Steve called. "Come here! You gotta see this!" He found the frames from the security camera in the Green

Room. "Look! I'm sitting right there." Sure enough, Steve Granger sat on the floor against the wall with his elbows on his knees.

The next frame showed the Chinese officer entering the doorway. Six frames later, when people began to stand, so did Steve Granger. The seventh frame revealed only the upper half of Steve's torso. In the next frame, he was gone.

"That is flat out cool," Steve said with a broad smile. "We need a couple hundred of those cloaks, and we could change the direction of this entire day."

"Easier said than done, unfortunately." Mike knew he had thrown cold water on Steve's idea. "I'm sorry, but I don't know how we could get a couple hundred without them noticing. I'm worried about these we have."

"Where do you think the cloaks used by the soldiers in the White House are now?" Sam asked. "They had to be wearing them when they came in. Where are they stored?"

Mike's eyes brightened at the prospect of finding a cache of cloaks. He turned to Ray Jergins. "Can we get the guys in Pod One on this line?" Mike asked leaning over Ray's workstation.

"Sure. Just a second." Ray picked up the phone, dialed in some numbers, and handed the receiver to Mike.

"Kreiter."

"Matt, this is Mike. We need you to begin scanning all the rooms in the White House with the altered resolution that revealed the invisibility cloaks. Can you do that?"

"Let me ask." The voices were muffled as Kreiter covered the mouthpiece with his hand and talked with Cliff, the technician. "He said that's no problem. What are you looking for?"

"We need to find where they are storing the unused cloaks," Mike answered pulling a chair next to Ray. "They should show up the same as the ones we saw earlier."

"We'll start looking," Kreiter replied.

"Any contact with the Chinese Embassy?"

"Still getting a busy signal. Not sure what to make of it," Kreiter said.

"All right, let me know as soon as you find something." Mike's mind was racing. *What if we can get a couple dozen cloaks? What if we can get more people into the White House? What if—*

"Mike." He looked at Sam only half aware of her speaking.

"I'm sorry, what?" he asked. Sam was smiling.

"I was going to say, we found where they moved everybody. We found the room." Sam looked at Mike questioningly. "You okay?"

"Sorry, I'm just distracted," he replied. "Where are they?"

"They're in the State Dining Room, just down the hall."

"That puts them near the West Wing. That's a good thing. It will be much easier to move them out quickly, once we figure out how." Mike knew his excitement was tempered by the challenge of actually pulling off such a move, but in his mind a plan was beginning to come together.

Frisco, TX – 2:36 PM CST

It took three days of persistent surveillance to find the American snipers. Insurgent forces had followed them from different locations to the National Guard Armory in Frisco. The arrival of the general's helicopter in late morning was the final clue in confirming the location. Now the invaders knew where the snipers were.

Through midday, more than three hundred angry men huddled under the trees along the meandering creek bed one hundred and fifty yards north of the Armory. As they surveyed the lay of the ground, they determined the trees to the north and east were good cover, and the higher ground to the west provided an advantage.

Slowly, one hundred men moved down the creek bed toward the bridge on Stonebrook Parkway. Another hundred crawled to the west behind the retirement home, making their way to the high ground on Parkwood Drive.

Revenge instills patience. No hurry to make their move. No need to rush. The odds were in the favor of the invading army. Surprise would give them victory. All they had to do was to wait.

chapter 25

Mainside Brig, Camp Pendleton, CA – 12:30 PM PST

Chaplain Hamza walked briskly down the hall toward the cell of Mustafa al Nubi. A new round of discussion with the prisoners had revealed important information. He wanted to see if Mustafa might confirm it.

The guard opened the cell door without knocking. Mustafa was surprised and turned to meet Caleb Hamza.

"I apologize for entering so abruptly. Please excuse my rudeness." Hamza was eager speak with the man. "I trust we may continue to speak openly as we have before."

"Of course, Caleb," Mustafa said with a wiry smile. "Are you going to interrogate me with a rubber hose or something?"

"Not at all. But I do need to ask you some questions, and I would greatly appreciate your honest answers." He glanced away.

"You do realize that I came here as your enemy," Mustafa said. "But it never occurred to me I would become your brother in faith."

"Yes, life is sometimes full of surprises. If I may, how you came here is the important question," Hamza sat beside him. "Where did you enter the United States, and what was the route that brought you to our borders?"

Mustafa's brow drew tight. His eye flashed at the cleric and just as quickly he sighed and relaxed.

"Forgive me. I suddenly felt I might betray my comrades. We are all your prisoners, are we not?"

"Yes. I have spoken with many of your men."

"About seven hundred of us crossed from Mexico at a small town called Jacumba. I thought it was a funny name. The Mexicans drove three large dump trucks through the border fence, making a hole about forty meters wide."

"And before that," Hamza asked, "how did you travel from your home?"

Mustafa's story was the same as the other ten men. They were all together, far from their homes, training in southern Afghanistan. The training was rigorous, even brutal. Food was scarce, and they lived in constant fear of American drones spying from above.

Shortly after the American presidential elections, they received word they would be leaving Afghanistan. In the middle of the night, they were rousted from their beds and loaded onto a truck. After a three-hour back-country trip down rough, dusty roads, they arrived at a base camp. They had no idea where they were.

"We stayed there for several weeks. Some left by fishing boat, others were loaded into cargo planes that flew to the eastern coast of Africa. We were allied with the Muslim Brotherhood who helped us there," he said.

Once across the African continent, hundreds of men were assembled at base camps in Nigeria. Then they were shuttled across the Atlantic on a private 747, owned by one of the Mexican drug cartels. After weeks of waiting and traveling, the full group was together again in the mountains of Nicaragua.

"We waited. Every few days we would move to a new location. We always traveled north. We knew we were coming to the United

States for a great battle." Mustafa stopped. He shrugged his shoulders. "Is that what you wanted to know?"

"Yes, it is. Did you ever know the names of the towns nearby or the people who were helping you?" Hamza asked.

"They were only known to us as Al Qaeda or the Muslim Brotherhood. They were our friends, or so it seemed."

"Why do you say that?"

"As I look back and reflect on the matter, it seems we were their pawns for a different game. We thought a great army was assembled against the weakened American forces. We never imagined we would be so easily defeated." Mustafa looked at the chaplain with clear, dark eyes. "They used us. We were their lambs sent to the slaughter."

ALI Map Room, White House Basement – 3:45 PM EST

The phone on the desk beeped. Mike grabbed it first. "Trapper."

"Mike, this is Kreiter," Matt said. His voice was light. He sounded like he was smiling. "You're not going to believe this."

"Believe what? What did you find out?" Mike asked.

"We found the cloaks. It's unbelievable. There are stacks of them right there in the open!" Kreiter was gleeful with the discovery.

"Where?" Mike pressed.

"We had to scan each room at lease twice and from different camera angles before we found them. I just couldn't believe it!"

"Where did you find them, Kreiter?"

"In the Yellow Room. Ha! Can you imagine that?" Kreiter thought it was hilarious. "They knew the cloaks would show up under the right conditions. They just stacked them where they would be least detected."

"What? We must have walked right past them when we left Nichols in the safe room," Mike said leaning back in his chair. He tossed his hands in the air, "and of course, we wouldn't see them. I had the rose-colored lenses, but I hadn't used them yet."

"Yeah, they're against the west wall to the left of the door going into the President's Sitting Room. That's incredible. We watched you guys go through there but never noticed the other cloaks."

"Okay, fine. We need to get up there and steal as many as we can." The wheels were turning in Mike's mind. The question remained, once they had the cloaks, how were they going to use them?

Frisco Armory, Frisco, TX – 2:50 PM CST

The armory was quiet. Siesta time. The men had been out most of the night, and the deployment to the Courtyard Hotel had added to the weariness. *And the fire ants!* Jim Parker shook his head in humiliation when he thought about it.

The breeze through the office window was soft. The weather wasn't hot yet. It would be a blast furnace soon enough. For now, they could catch their collective breath and see what the general might have in store for their evening.

Maybe grilled steaks and a movie, Parker thought, smiling. *Not likely.*

He knew they were in the middle, perhaps the beginning, of a real war. Lieutenant Parker and his band of Phantom Patriots had spent the last several days wounding and killing enemy combatants. He was aware of the risk they were running.

"You awake, sweetheart?" Sergeant Minks said peeking into the office.

"Oh, it's you," Parker groaned. Will Minks was always the troublemaker, but one of those guys who enjoyed it so much no one could fault him. Even when Parker found himself the target of one of his little jokes, he enjoyed it. When the deed turned back on Minks for whatever reason, everyone, including Minks, had a good laugh.

"Well, sir," Minks said strutting into the office, "I just wanted you to know *exactly* who the King of Canasta is in this outfit."

"As if I give a rip, Minks. Why aren't you resting?" Parker replied.

"Greatness never sleeps! Besides, you haven't had the chance to congratulate me or bow before my magnificence." Minks' royal pose was too much. Parker gave way and smiled.

"Congratulations, for, what was it? Canasta King?" Parker said tossing his hand in a single royal wave of approval. "The bowing thing simply ain't gonna happen, sergeant."

"I'll take whatever I can get. I am a humble man." Minks bowed deeply in appreciation.

"Okay, fine! You're it! Now get your hulkness out of here and rest. I don't want you falling asleep on a mission tonight." Parker's contrived anger had its effect, and Minks flitted out of the office.

Parker leaned back and propped his feet on the desk. He loved these men. The old *band of brothers* tag seemed a cliché, but it fit. They were more than a unit, more than the Phantom Patriots. They were brothers.

Trapper Home, Washington DC – 4:05 PM EST

Elli stretched her full length, still blanketed in drowsiness, unwilling to come fully awake. She could almost reach from one arm of the couch to the other. In the distance, no more than twelve feet, the kids were talking about Grandma's donuts. Their naps were over and behind them.

She felt better. Rested. The nausea was gone, as well as the achy feeling. *Maybe if I just stay here everything will be fine until Mike comes home*, she thought. That thought was immediately countered by a disagreement between Robbie and Sara. It was like every other day. Elli would get no real rest until all four kids were asleep in their own beds. Then, maybe.

Elli sat up and swung her feet to the floor. She caught her reflection in the hall closet mirror and quickly began pulling her hair into place. She was a fright. It never bothered Mike, but it did her.

"You still do it, you know," her mom said with a grin on her face.

"What, the snort?" Elli asked.

"Yup," she replied.

"What snort?" Robbie piped in. "Who snorts?" Suddenly the idea of someone snorting was the new antic. Robbie and Sara broke into laughter and snorts. Grandma smiled a broadly.

"Who snorts, Grandma?" Sara asked in a loudly.

"Ever since your mama was a little girl, she has almost always snorted just before she wakes up." The kids threw themselves on the couch flailing in laughter.

"All right, all right, cut it out!" Elli said with mocking seriousness. "Thanks, Mom."

Elli forced herself to her feet and went into the kitchen. Her shoulder felt stiff but the sharp pains were less frequent. She slid onto one of the stools at the center counter, and her mom gently shoved the last donut in front of her.

"Oh, thanks," she said. The donut was still warm. A glass of ice cold milk joined the donut on the countertop. Elli felt like she was seven years old again. She laughed.

A chorus of snorts erupted in the kitchen from two tiny tormenters with donut stuffed mouths and milk mustaches. Suddenly, she growled and lunged at the two little snorters.

"I'll get you two!" she said forming her hands to claws and baring her teeth. The snorting immediately changed to squeals as the badgering duo ran down the hall toward the stairs. Their shrieks of laughter and occasional snorts echoed behind them.

Elli sat on one of the tall kitchen stools, laughing. Grandma leaned against the kitchen counter, thoroughly enjoying the scene playing out before her, and because of her.

chapter 26

LAPD on First St., Los Angeles, CA – 1:08 PM PST

The neighborhood sweeps were bordered by I-5 on the west and south, I-710 to the east and I-10 to the north. The efficiency was nothing less than astonishing. Chinese troops continued to advance at a jogging pace, never breaking stride. The officers in charge moved as rapidly as their soldiers.

General Westrup and Colonel Zu sat in the back seat of the troop carrier that followed the search. Occasionally, a team of soldiers jogged to the tailgate and received water and a small bit to eat. Otherwise, they never stopped.

"How long can your men move at this rate?"

"Eighteen to twenty hours is as long as we plan for this kind of maneuver," Zu replied. "In China, it is a great honor to serve in the Army. Not everyone can make the cut. Those who do give one hundred percent and sometimes beyond. We train our soldiers to press to the end of the task. For that, they are well paid and greatly respected by our people."

"Any problem with insubordination?" Westrup asked.

"If a soldier is insubordinate, he will find himself working in a rice paddy somewhere. If he engages in insurrection, the punishment is swift and final. We see very little of that, but it happens from time to time." Colonel Zu recognized the lingering questions by the strained look on Westrup's face.

"General, please understand that most of our people are very poor. A very fortunate, hard working individual earns $20 a day. In our culture honor is more valuable than money. Pride runs very deep. That's a major reason the Chinese people have endured the Communist Party rule for so long."

"You're saying the people value honor over liberty or freedom?" Westrup asked leaning his elbows on his knees.

"The freedom and liberty you enjoy in America has never been experienced by the people of China," Zu explained. "For centuries our nation was many feudal dynasties, often ruled by evil men. During that time, honor, pride in one's family, was all the people of China could own. That's changing slowly and with resistance. But it is changing."

An officer ran to the side of the troop carrier and relayed information to Colonel Zu in Mandarin.

"They are ready to enter the Police Station. We'll move up." Zu turned and spoke to the driver. The troop carrier accelerated to the corner, turned to the right, drove over the curb, and parked on the walkway in Lani Vest Pocket Park facing the Station. The only sound was the breeze moving through the trees of the park.

Colonel Zu looked at his officer and nodded. The officer barked orders into his radio, and the sound of eight hundred soldiers coming to attention filled the air. Their boots pounded the asphalt as they marched toward the office building and maintenance garages of the Station.

General Westrup stood to watch. "Do you expect an explosion of gunfire at your troops?"

"We expect everything, and we are rarely surprised."

The main doors to the station were off their hinges from the original assault by the insurgents. The soldiers entered without resistance or response. It was disturbingly quiet. More soldiers streamed into the facility. More silence.

After several minutes, a single officer exited the building and jogged to the troop carrier. His expression was beyond sober. He marched directly to Colonel Zu and spoke softly into his ear. The colonel let out his breath and looked at the ground. He turned to General Westrup.

"General," he began, "the building is empty of the terrorists we expected. But my officer is very sad to report they found the bodies of more than one hundred police officers, men and women, stacked in a pile in the motor pool. My officer and his men extend their sympathies, as do I."

A detail of fifty soldiers was selected to identify and process each body. Westrup stood at the side watching. The soldiers respectfully inspected the bodies of those whose lives had been taken by brutal and inhumane slaughter. Desecration without honor.

Center Hall, Second Floor, White House – 4:15 PM EST

The hall was even less populated with Chinese soldiers on their return visit. Although the White House wasn't empty, it was as barren as Mike had ever seen it. Soldiers stood outside every door and window, but none faced in. Their backs were toward the inside of the building.

"Mike, where do you think everyone went?" Steve whispered into his VLF comm. device.

"Not sure," he replied. "Makes me a little nervous."

They moved across the broad hall, entering directly into the Yellow Room. The room was empty as well. Soldiers stood on the Truman Balcony, but again, they had their backs to the building.

"Welcome back!" Robert Nichols' voice boomed in their earpieces. "I was wondering when I would see you three again."

"Holy mackerel, Nichols, you nearly broke my eardrum!" Steve responded in a whisper.

"Sorry about that," Nichols said. "Listen, I'm almost finished in here. Could you guys use another hand?"

"That would be great!" Mike whispered back. "You just have to keep your voice down out here."

"Okay, okay, I got it." Nichols replied. "Get a cloak for me, and I'll release the door."

Mike, Steve, and Sam made their way across the room with outstretched arms feeling for the stack of cloaks. Mike reached into his shirt pocket for the rose-colored lenses and slipped them on the bridge of his nose. Although he couldn't see the cloaks themselves, he could make out a definite outline made by the fold in the fabric.

"Right here!" he whispered, pulling Sam and Steve toward the pile. Mike pulled one cloak from the pile and crossed to the opening for the safe room. "Nichols, I've got one for you!"

Mike heard a very soft noise he assumed to be the seal opening for the room. He quickly ducked inside, and the door closed. Mike whisked the cloak over his head and greeted Nichols.

"They're not too difficult to wear," he said. "You just have to walk as quietly as possible and remember to keep your voice down."

"I'll do better than that," Nichols replied, "I'll keep my big mouth shut!" Both men smiled. The day had been difficult, at the end of a terrible week, with much more still to be done.

"Let's do this." Mike pulled his cloak back over his head and vanished before Nichols' eyes.

"Wow! That is really something to see."

"Or not see," Mike answered.

The door of the safe room opened, and the two men stepped into the Yellow Room. They made their way toward the pile of cloaks. Sam and Steve were experimenting with how many cloaks one could carry and still remain covered by the cloak. The garments weren't bulky, but managing more than a few was a challenge.

A sufficient number was determined. Mike stood back, allowing the others a chance to gather a load under each arm. He watched the six guards standing just outside the room on the Truman

Balcony. He was puzzled. *Why are they looking away from the building?*

One guard turned slightly to speak to the man next to him. He was wearing rose-colored lenses. It hit Mike like a bowling ball. They were looking away from the building watching for someone escaping. They were looking for Nichols and his accomplices.

Mike tapped Steve's shoulder. He looked up and saw the guard. He understood their situation instantly. Quickly, they moved toward the hall carrying the cloaks. They were invisible to the naked eye, but at the moment, hundreds of Chinese soldiers were wearing rose-colored lenses and watching for them.

National Guard Armory, Frisco, TX – 3:20 PM CST

Lieutenant Jim Parker wasn't exactly in pain, but he hurt enough he couldn't rest. He was tired of hurting. The constant nagging ache in his buttocks was lessening, but the festering burn of the fire ant stings was constant. He was determined not to give in to the discomfort and turn nasty.

The first blast of gunfire ripped through the ground floor windows on the north and west sides of the building. Shards of glass flew at slower speeds than the slugs that shattered the window but with a similar threat.

Parker rolled from the table he had been resting on and scurried across the room to his rifle. He heard Minks run down the hall to his equipment and rifle. The other nine men grabbed their weapons and put on their MICH covers.

"Sit rep, guys," Parker yelled into his mike, "I need to know where you are. Now!" Suddenly, neither the shrapnel wounds nor the ant bites were an issue.

The nine men upstairs gave their positions as scattered throughout the second floor but unhurt. Minks was in the east end of the hall. Everybody was online.

"Can you see anything from upstairs?" Parker asked.

"Lieutenant, I can see muzzle bursts along the hill to the west," one reported.

"There are a bunch of them down along the creek," another said.

"Some over by the bridge on Stonebrook."

"Okay, bunch yourselves on the west end in one corner near Parkwood. You guys on the front side of the building move to the center, and those on the east end, meet in the major's office. When I give the signal, I want you to lay down a crap load of fire on those positions. Then move to a different position. We have to keep on the move, so they don't get us pinned down. Let me know when you're set. Minks and I will meet you upstairs."

The noise made by shuffling across the floor littered with metal and glass was covered by the zipping sounds of incoming ordnance. Plaster, glass and wood chips fogged the building under the barrage. Finally, everyone was in place.

"Fire!" Parker yelled into his mike. The return fire was deafening. Parker ran in a crouched position to the stairwell, and took the steps three at a time to the second floor.

"Now move! Move! Move!" he yelled as the men took new positions at the windows. Parker dropped to a corner in the hall and pulled out his cell phone. The number for Eagle Three, General Maris, was the last call he received. He hit Send.

The phone rang twice.

"This is Eagle Three."

"General Maris, this is Lieutenant Jim Parker at the Frisco Armory. Sir, we're under heavy attack! We need help!"

"You got it, son!"

Parker could hear the general yelling at the other end of the connection.

"Okay, I have three gunships coming your way. Where are the ECs from your position?"

"Sir, they're around us on the east, south, and west, and in pretty significant numbers."

"Parker, we're a little more than twenty miles from you, but we're coming! Put up a fight to keep them back but be careful!"

In the background Parker could hear the turbines of the Apache whining to life. The cavalry was on the way.

chapter 27

White House, Washington DC – 4:30 PM EST

Packing bundles of cloaks, attempting to stay covered by one, and making a quick passage through "enemy territory" proved to be difficult. The trek up to the Yellow Room was a breeze. The return trip was not. And knowing rose-colored lenses could see through the cloaks added to the stress.

Mike knew they must stay hidden at all times. The cloaks would help but were no guarantee of invisibility. He was certain the captive White House employees and Secret Service agents would be under heavy guard and those guards would probably be wearing rose-colored lenses.

The passage to the Ground Floor took several minutes even though no soldiers were stationed on the Second Floor of the building. The Ground Floor was a different matter. Soldiers peered out every window and doorway. The foursome moved as quietly as possible, carrying their burdens.

They had just reached the stairs by the Family Dining Room when Mike heard voices below. He grabbed Steve's arm and pulled him into the dining room. He only hoped Steve was in contact with Sam, and Sam with Nichols. He crept into the dining room and huddled behind the main table.

"Everybody here?" he whispered into his comm. device. The voices ascended the stairway and continued to the Second Floor. Mike was relieved it wasn't a search party working the inside of the building and that they hadn't met them on the stairs.

"Hey!" Sam whispered. "I found some of the rose lenses inside one of the cloaks!"

"Okay, check the cloaks you're carrying and see if you can find a pair," Mike responded. Steve and Nichols rummaged through the bundles they carried.

"Got one!" Nichols replied.

Mike slipped his pair over the bridge of his nose once again. The clarity was remarkable. His companions didn't appear in natural colors, but their features and shapes were distinct. He realized if they were spotted by any Chinese soldier, there would be no question they were Americans.

"Okay, I found a pair," Steve said. "Oh, my gosh! This is amazing!"

"Remember, any Chinese soldier wearing the lenses can see you with the same clarity." The thought was sobering. Sneaking through the White House suddenly became a more frightening matter.

Mike listened for voices in the stairway. It was quiet. All the captive employees and Secret Service agents were in the next room, the State Dining Room. The challenge was to get more than a hundred men and women safely out of the room, down the stairs to the Ground Floor, then to someplace safe.

Where the heck is it safe?

Jenny's Diner, Lakeside, OR – 1:35 PM PST

Lunch lasted forever. Curious townsfolk stopping at Reggie's table to extend congratulations interrupted practically every bite. Corporal Woo politely bobbed small bows in recognition of each person. He couldn't get out of the booth to greet each person because of the pressing crowd around them. Otherwise he would have bowed deeply to each person showing respect.

The mood in the town was steadily improving. More smiles appeared with every greeting. Some of the shops opened simply because they could. Others declared an early start for the weekend and began the celebration.

Corporal Woo finished his second quarter pounder. His face registered either culinary bliss or burgeoning gastric distress. Reggie wasn't sure. He decided to let come to pass what may. He would deal with it later.

"Mr. Reggie," Woo began with a new measure of respect, "I have never tasted food like this. Very, very delicious." Woo's eyes were glazed by a carbohydrate induced stupor.

"Yes, Jenny does have a reputation in these parts," he replied. "Glad you enjoyed it." He knew Woo would fall asleep at any moment.

"Reggie Porter! My goodness man, how have you been?" A large, meaty hand was extended in front of Reggie's face. He looked up to see his nemeses, Buster McGreer, the owner of the hardware store.

Reggie's sneer dissolved into a half smile. The full town council stood behind Buster, all wearing Cheshire grins that would make their mothers proud. It made Reggie suspicious.

"We have discussed the new lease on life our little town has been given," Buster began. Reggie squirmed not trusting a thing the man said. "We've decided you are the man in the know and with the right connections." Through his smile, Buster nodded at Corporal Woo.

Reggie looked at Woo. He was gone. Sound asleep. Reggie decided it was probably late at night or early in the morning where the small soldier was from. He let him rest.

"And well, we think you'd make a right fine leader for our town." Buster's smile was almost comical, but he held it firmly.

"Okay, I'm not sure what you mean by tha—" Before he could finish, Buster climbed onto a chair and turned to the full dinner.

"Citizens of Lakeside, Oregon, as acting head of the city council I hereby declare, for his heroism above and beyond the call of duty, Reggie Porter as mayor of our city!"

The cheer was deafening or at least loud enough to be bothersome. Woo stirred. Reggie was dumfounded. He looked at Buster in unflinching amazement.

What did he just say? he thought. *Mayor?*

And so it was, Lakeside was free, Corporal Woo had his first quarter pounder, and Reggie Porter was mayor.

White House, Washington DC – 4:40 PM EST

"Mike!" Sam whispered, "Why don't we just sneak people to the different escape elevators and get them down to the Pods?" Between the four of them they carried thirty-eight cloaks. Just over a third of the captives could "vanish" at one time. It would be a slow process.

The idea was clumsy at best, catastrophic at worst, but it presented an option that could work. The first objective was to determine the number of guards watching the captive agents and employees.

"Steve, go see how many guards you can count through the serving area, and I'll check the hall," Mike whispered to Steve. He moved to the doorway leading directly into the State Dining Room. What he saw didn't surprise him, but it still made him sick.

The stately room was transformed into a holding cell for a hundred prisoners. Tables and chairs were shoved to the walls, stacked, some broken, in a massive heap. Men and women were huddled together sitting with their hands secured behind their backs.

Ten soldiers stood at the massive windows looking across the White House grounds. Mike and his team knew they were most likely looking for them fleeing across the compound wearing invisibility cloaks.

"Ten to four odds," Steve said through his comm. device. "Just about even." He was a little concerned about Sam taking on two soldiers, even with the element of surprise. Then again, the guards expected someone running away, not an attack from behind.

"Right," Mike replied. "Steve, you and Sam go through the serving area doors and deal with the two men by the fireplace. Nichols, come with me."

"Got it!" Sam answered as she moved toward Steve in the serving area.

Mike beckoned Nichols to follow him. They moved quietly back through the landing and into the Cross Hall. The door to the Red Room was standing open, and they entered. Another door stood closed at the far end of the room, past the fireplace.

Mike and Nichols moved toward the closed door. Opening the door might alert any soldiers on the other side, but it was a chance they had to take. Most of the furniture was stacked against the east wall of the Dining Room, and the captured employees were crammed together against the pile. Going through the far door was the only option.

Slowly, he pressed against the tall wooden door. It moved slightly and smoothly into the Dining Room. No response. He pressed further into the room. The guards stood, casually chatting as they looked out the tall windows. Mike entered the room, followed by Nichols.

Mike motioned Nichols to move behind the first two guards. He moved himself forward to the next pair. The men stood with the sheer curtains pulled behind their shoulders for a better view to the outside. Glancing to his right, he could clearly see Steve and Sam already in position. Only two guards remained uncovered. He would need to move fast.

"Now!" Mike yelled out loud. At the same moment, he delivered a crushing blow to one guard with his right fist. In a recoil action, he threw his elbow into the surprised face of the second soldier. Both men dropped to the floor.

He turned quickly toward the two remaining guards. Both were surprised but had time to react. Wearing their rose-colored lenses, the soldiers turned into the room. They instantly knew where the missing invisibility cloaks were, and at this moment, they were coming directly at them on two Americans.

The two guards raised the bulky, odd-looking rifles, one toward Steve, the other toward Mike. Mike knew he was facing his end and charged anyway.

"She ji!" one soldier cried.

No bullets came from the weapons, only a soft hum and a bright, red flash. Mike and Steve were hit. They were stunned, felt dizzy, as if their bodies instantly fell asleep. Mike staggered, then he pulled strength from deep within himself and surged ahead.

The bulky rifle held by the guard whined to a higher and higher pitch as it recharged, but Mike's charge arrived first. He plowed into the soldier, slamming him against the wall by the window. Steve crashed into the second soldier. The fistfight was brief. Two Chinese soldiers crumpled to the floor.

Steve spun toward Sam. She was in trouble. One guard was down and beginning to recover from her initial attack. Sam was fully engaged in hand-to-hand combat with the second guard. Steve sprinted across the room, spun the guard around, and smashed him with a right hook. A similar jab rendered the recovering soldier unconscious.

"Hey! I had it under control!" Sam protested whipping off her cloak. A gasp rose from the hundred or so American captives seated on the floor of the large room. It had not occurred to Steve, Sam, Mike, or Agent Nichols what the scene looked like to those held in the room. A shout, then guards slammed around the room by an invisible force. It must have been terrifying.

Quickly, Mike removed his cloak, followed by Steve and Nichols. A second and third round of amazed gasps and shocked expressions filled the room.

"Okay, you need to please keep quiet!" Mike said to the group as he walked toward the center of the room. "We're here to get you out as quickly as we can. We don't have much time. First, I need ten of you to take these soldiers' jackets and hats and stand near the windows. We want those outside to believe you are still being guarded in here."

Immediately, twenty-five volunteers sprang from the floor. Mike selected the ten smallest of the volunteers and quickly removed the restraints from their hands. Steve, Sam, and Nichols were busy removing the jackets from the unconscious Chinese soldiers. The freed Americans donned them and took positions next to the windows.

The maneuver took nearly a full minute. The final touch was the rose-colored lenses for each of the imposter guards at their stations. Mike hoped no one had glanced up during the fight or in the minute no guards were visible from the ground below. Hope was all he could afford. An officer or another group of soldiers could pass at any moment, and they would be discovered.

Nichols and Mike hurried to undo the plastic restraints on the captives. When properly released, the restraints fell off easily. The reusable ones were placed around the wrists and ankles of the unconscious Chinese soldiers. All of them. Each soldier was bound by ten to twelve restraints. Once gagged, they were placed in the center of the room and tied together with an extension cord.

"What *is* that?" Steve asked walking toward the rifle next to the downed soldier. He'd never seen anything like it. Sam was already examining the weapon.

"I'm not totally sure," she began, "but I think it's some kind of plasma-pulse technology we abandoned a few years back. The effect of the discharge was too weak."

"That's evident by the fact that Mike and I are still here," he replied with a cocky smile.

"Don't remind me," Sam said, wrestling with the memory from the Oak Mountain Power Plant. "I know you had to rush him, I'm just glad I didn't have to watch it again."

"What do you think about these things?" Mike asked as he approached.

"Not sure," Sam said looking up at him. "But I think we need to take them with us."

"Good enough. Get everybody ready."

Only a third of the people in the room would be able to leave at one time. They would all wear cloaks and make their way to the elevator locations that would take them to the Pods below. Time was short, and Mike knew it could be over in an instant. They had to get moving.

chapter 28

I-44 & I-240, Oklahoma City, OK – 2:30 PM CST

The speaker in the mobile command center finally crackled to life.

"Big Barker Comm., this is Hawkeye Six. Do you copy? Over."
Behind the broken communication, one could hear the pounding thumps of the chopper's blades overhead.

"Hawkeye Six, this is Big Barker Comm. Bring it."

"Big Barker Comm., we have a situation a couple miles north of the Sundance Airpark. Three men are on the ground and seem to be badly hurt, possibly KIA. Over."

"Hawkeye Six, this is Big Barker Comm. Is that it? Only three men? Over."

"Sir, one man is on the ground with his leg bent at a very unnatural angle, another looks like he has a knife in his back, and the third is flat on his back, spread-eagle, out cold it seems. Please advise. Over."

"Hawkeye Six, go ahead and approach. Give them some help if you can. I'll send a detail to bring them in. Over."

"Roger that, Big Barker Comm. Hawkeye Six out."

The radio operator signed off as Colonel Tom Crawford turned to Sheriff Hitchens and Yolanda.

"I think we found our boy," he said with a slight grin. "At least where he's been. We'll know more after we talk to the men he crumpled into broken bones and meat."

"If they *can* talk," Perry replied.

At the very least, it was a sign of hope. The sheriff looked at Yolanda and smiled. Hope burned in her eyes, restrained by the fear to say too much, to hope too much. It was something to cling to. That was enough.

I-10, West of Palm Springs, CA – 1:45 PM PST

Alvaro Herrera hated driving. He always demanded a driver, so he could spend his time constructively. That might mean interrogating a captive during the drive or, on rare occasions, entertaining a young lady. Driving was tedious.

For a Friday afternoon in Southern California, there was little traffic. The interstates normally packed with commuters and tourists were bare of travelers. Every few miles a truck heading into the city might pass, but other than that, it was quiet.

Suddenly, one of the rental trucks swerved to the shoulder and came to a stop. Herrera cursed and slammed on his brakes. He leaped from the cab and stomped angrily toward the parked truck.

Cero was standing on the far side of the vehicle, relieving himself.

"What are you doing, you fool!" Herrera shouted. "I said no stopping!"

"I am sorry, sir," Cero answered zipping his trousers. "I was ready to explode, and I couldn't take it any longer."

"You waste *my* time!" Herrera growled. However, the change of position climbing down from the truck made it clear he bore the same affliction. "All right! Everybody take care of this. Then, *no more stopping*!"

Four angry, dangerous men stood at the side of the road and left their mark on the desert.

"Now, *no more stopping!*" Herrera snarled as he stomped back to his truck. The desert ahead would help. They would sweat it out.

National Guard Armory, Frisco, TX – 3:48 PM CST

More than thirty minutes passed since Jim Parker had spoken with General Maris. Help was long overdue. They kept a constant, varied rotation of their locations for returning fire. Sometimes they all fired from the same window then split to two sides of the same room.

As far as they could tell, none of the enemy combatants attempted to cross the open ground between the armory and the safety of their positions. If they charged the armory, he knew they wouldn't stand a chance.

Then it dawned on him.

They're gonna stay put and shoot at us until we run out of ammo! The truth of the matter was that they were already running low.

"All right, listen up!" Parker called out to his men. "No more heavy fire. Lay down short bursts. I think they're waiting us out before they attack. When they think we're out of ammo, they'll charge. That's when we unleash on them."

The incoming was steady. It was clear the ECs weren't worried about running out of bullets. But the return fire was reduced to a smattering response. Then, the guns of the Phantom Patriots fell silent. The waiting game began.

Slowly, the incoming fire dwindled and stopped. The silence was overpowering. Waiting fostered unbearable tension.

Suddenly, the war cry of three hundred men broke the silence. As they emerged from hiding and charged the armory, the men inside braced themselves. Parker paused just a second or two, hoping more of the enemy would be in the open and easier targets.

He was forming words in his mouth when the thunder of three Apache AH-64s roared over the building. Almost simultaneously, strafing fire of twin .50 caliber machine guns tore into the attacking insurgents. Overhead gunships from III ACR took on the enemy. The cavalry had arrived.

"Open fire!" Parker shouted, and the Phantom Patriots joined the counterattack. It was a killing field, and no mercy was shown. Every man that raised a weapon against the U.S. and the strength of the 3rd Armored Cavalry Regiment paid with his life.

As the gunfire ceased, a cheer arose from the armory. The odds had been against them but had quickly changed to their favor. It was a victory.

Parker walked down the center stairway, crunching glass every step. He looked toward the east end of the building. His heart stopped when he saw the legs and boots of a man at the base of the east steps.

"Minks!" he shouted and ran down the hall. Sergeant Will Minks lay on his side, a large pool of blood surrounding him.

"Minks! Can you hear me? Medic! Medic!" he yelled.

Slowly, Will Minks opened his eyes just enough that Parker knew he was alive.

"Minks! Stay with me! Don't let go! Stay here!" he shouted as members of the Phantom Patriots ran to his aid.

"Did we get 'em boss?" Minks whispered with half opened eyes and a sly grin.

"Yeah, buddy. We got all of them . . . every single one."

"Good," he replied, and he fell limp in Parker's arms.

"No! Minks! Don't—" Parker cried, but it was too late. Sergeant Will Minks' eyes glazed, and the breath left his body. He was still smiling.

White House, Washington DC – 5:05 PM EST

Moving through a virtually empty White House was beyond strange. Doing so silently with more than forty people was unnerving. Mike had given specific instructions about the need for silence and how to walk quietly. He had also reminded them that although they were invisible to each other, the Chinese could see them if they were wearing the rose-colored glasses.

Still, keeping forty pairs of feet quiet was nearly impossible. Mike knew the risk was great, but they had to try. If they could move to their destinations quietly and not arouse suspicion, they just might make it to safety.

The group moved in pairs, holding hands between them and grasping the cloak of the person ahead. Some found rose-colored lenses inside the cloak they were given, but most of them didn't. They were required to hang on, be quiet, and trust those ahead and behind them. It was awkward.

Mike led them down the stairs by the Dining Room and to the Kitchen on the Ground Floor. They slipped between the tables and food preparation stations, making a ghostly snake through the room.

He came to the door leading into the Center Hall and stopped. It was only a few feet to the first escape elevator located in the corner of the Press Corps Offices. The location was selected to provide escape for Secret Service agents to Pod Five.

That elevator had not been used earlier when the escape was made from the Oval Office, so it would not need to be retrieved. One of the Secret Service agents who knew the access code led the first group of ten. Nichols collected the cloaks from each person entering the safety of the small elevator.

The door quietly closed on ten thankful, smiling faces. Mike moved on with the remaining twenty-six agents and civilians. The next escape elevator was in the Cabinet Room. They carefully navigated their way through the press offices and the Press Briefing Room. Chinese soldiers maintained their posts, watching the outside grounds around the White House.

The last section for the large group to move through was the hallway leading from the West Colonnade into the presidential offices. Mike turned to the group huddled against the wall behind him. He opened his face cover to speak.

"When we make it through the hall, the first eight will turn into the Cabinet Room and use the escape elevator there. Nichols, you go with them and collect their cloaks. Do any of you know the access code?" he asked quietly. One agent toward the back raised his hand.

"Good. Sam, you'll take eight with you to the vice president's office where you went earlier. Steve, you take eight to the Oval Office and use that lift. The rest of you will come with me to the President's Dining Room by his study. Got it?"

Heads nodded confirming the plan. Mike leaned against the door, peering toward the Colonnade. It was clear. He moved out.

chapter 29

Mainside Brig, Camp Pendleton, CA – 2:15 PM PST

Lieutenant Caleb Hamza was euphoric. He was waiting for Sergeant Major Michaels and Captain Bob Prescott. The information he had gathered from the detained invaders was remarkable. Initially, every man told a different story. Nothing provided linkage of any kind between them.

Hamza understood why. Each man was trained to deflect and deceive any captor. They were prepared to concoct wild tales hide the truth. Their stories were fiction. He soon learned to play their game and could catch them off guard by slipping a real event he had learned from another prisoner into their tale.

The door to the Observation Room swung open, and Michaels and Prescott walked in briskly.

"Gentlemen, this has been a very interesting day for me," Hamza began. "I don't remember a time in my life where I have been so encouraged."

"Please, go ahead and enlighten us, lieutenant," the sergeant major said.

"This morning, as you know, I began meeting with several of the men. I was particularly interested in those who experienced the vision of the man in white."

"You mean this *Isa* character?" Captain Prescott asked. Michaels and Hamza both looked at him with surprise. For a man of great learning and skill, Prescott had a bad habit for poorly selecting his words.

"Well, yes, the men who met Isa," Hamza replied, then he continued. "Most of the detainees shared fanciful tales of magic and preposterous feats of superhuman strength and ability. Each story was as if they were reciting from a comic book.

"But as I focused on the men who shared the common vision of the man in white, the truth began to emerge. Those eleven men told exactly the same story. Even minute details confirmed simple observations of a base camp or modes of transport.

"Many of the others spoke of feasts and celebrations that any good Muslim would shun simply because of the audacious display of carnality. Nothing they said matched what others said, but those eleven men shared one and the same tale." Hamza paused.

"Do you believe the visions of the man in white have affected them in some way?" Michaels asked.

"I do," Hamza replied. "I believe them. I believe they are speaking honestly."

"Gentlemen, science has shown us that some people react to extreme confinement with varying degrees of hysteria and often hallucinations. Wouldn't that provide a better explanation for these visions?" Prescott asked.

"I might agree with you, sir, if these men were held under harsh conditions," Hamza replied. "You fail to understand that this experience is possibly one of the best in their lifetimes. Here they have a clean cell, clean clothes, and three excellent meals a day. They are neither freezing nor suffering heat stroke, as they might in the extreme weather conditions of the Middle East. The mountains or the desert provide very harsh environments. To them, this is heaven on earth. They've never had it this good."

"So, from their point of view, all they need to do is string us along with a bunch of fables and lies, believing we'll learn nothing from them," Michaels said.

"Yes, sergeant major. That is exactly what they believe." Hamza paused and smiled as he looked at the two men. "These eleven men have experienced a life changing encounter with the man in white."

"Jesus," Prescott said with an edge of mockery.

"Careful, Bob," Michaels cautioned. "If Jesus is talking to these men and you discredit it, you might be next on His list." Prescott chuckled, but stopped abruptly when he realized the sergeant major wasn't joking.

"You're not serious, are you, John?" Prescott asked.

"I am," Michaels said as he leaned forward. "Bob, we're dealing with one-hundred-sixteen radical Islamists. These people have been trained their entire lives to a specific code, a hard and demanding lifestyle. And in a matter of hours, eleven men, not one or two, but eleven men have undergone a transformation of their nature. *One* might crack and do something really strange. Here we have *eleven* who, in a remarkable way, have come to their senses."

"Actually, twelve," Hamza said with a gentle smile. "You have forgotten me. I know what these men experienced. I know how dramatic that change is, and I'm telling you, what has happened to them in this place is real. Very, very real."

Captain Prescott was silent. He looked at Lieutenant Hamza. "You think this is real," he said.

"No, sir. I know it is real." Caleb Hamza spoke with inarguable certainty. Truth, when seen as truth, removes all doubt or question.

"Hmm." Prescott let out a breath. His eyes did not leave the lieutenant. He shrugged. "I don't know what to say."

"Sergeant major," Hamza asked, "have any plans been established for these men?"

"None that I'm aware of," Michaels replied. "What's on your mind?"

"I would like to meet with these eleven men all together. I think it would be of great benefit to them and to us as well."

John Michaels gazed steadily at the lieutenant. "I need to run all this by the CO, Brigadier General Westrup. I'll get back to you, son."

The meeting was adjourned.

White House, Washington DC – 5:40 PM EST

Mike ran through the Press Room and offices with Sam, Steve, and Nichols, headed back to the remaining captives. Twenty-six waited patiently in the State Dining Room with ten Chinese soldiers bound and gagged in the center of the room. An additional ten Secret Service agents posing as "guards" stood at the windows.

One more trip, he thought. The fact that the number to take to safety this time was larger than the other two groups bothered him but not enough to stop. The biggest concern was the timing in removing the "guards." If they left too soon, the Chinese might enter the building and catch the last group in their escape. If they stayed too long, they themselves would be caught.

The foursome swept through the kitchen and headed up the stairs. Halfway up Mike heard voices. He stopped, blocking the rest of his team. The voices indicated men were coming down from the Second Floor. Mike surmised they had spent the last several minutes on the roof, scanning the grounds for escaping Americans.

Quickly, Mike and the rest retreated into the kitchen. He knew they would be visible to the Chinese officers if they were wearing either the dark glasses or the rose-colored lenses. He was also aware that a visit to the State Dining Room would reveal that an escape was underway.

The sound of the conversation continued to the State Floor. At that point, they began to fade. Mike's throat closed. *They're visiting the captives!* Mike signaled, and all four hit the stairs at a dead run.

"Freeze!" the Chinese officer shouted into the State Dining Room. His eyes were angry. Most of his captives were gone. All five Chinese soldiers drew their weapons, real ones with real bullets.

The imposter guards standing at the windows turned toward the main door where the armed Chinese officers stood. They laid their weapons aside and raised their hands. The remaining American captives were still seated on the floor. Their disappointment was visible.

The highest-ranking officer strode into the room with just a little too much swagger. He removed his sunglasses and leered at his captives. The four other officers moved to either side of their commander. Even though they were outnumbered thirty-six to five, the Chinese held the guns. They had the advantage.

"So," the officer began, "you are in the process of leaving us?"

He turned to the two officers on his left and spoke in Chinese. They quickly holstered their weapons and moved to the Chinese guards who were tied and gagged right in the middle of the Americans.

"Now!" Mike shouted as the four phantoms threw off their cloaks and dove on the officers from behind. On cue, the Americans leaped on the two officers attempting to free the guards. The scuffle was brief. The officers were swiftly overcome and forced to the hardwood floor of the Dining Room. Their handguns spun as they slid across the wood surface.

"No disrespect intended, sir," Steve said to the senior officer. "We simply needed to increase our bargaining position." He smiled at the man who sneered at him through the duct tape covering his mouth.

Mike grabbed the sunglasses the officer was wearing and took them to the Secret Service agent posing as a guard on the west side.

"Put these on and watch the hallway by the Colonnade," he said. "When you see us go past the windows, get to the president's bedroom and take the emergency elevator there."

"Do any of you know the access code?" Sam asked. No one responded. She looked at Mike. Of course, he knew the code. He was assigned to the president.

"Right. Okay, I'll stay here with the guards, the rest of you get going now!" Mike also knew the president's escape elevator was smaller than all the others. Since less space was available on the Second Floor, fewer people were expected to use it. Ten small people might fit. Eleven was impossible.

Quickly, the cloaks were distributed to the remaining captives, and twenty-six of them scurried from the Dining Room, led by Steve, Sam, and Robert Nichols. Mike took a position beside the guard at the west window to watch them pass. Everything had just changed. It was time to improvise.

Northwest Oklahoma City, OK – 4:45 PM CST

It didn't take long for Robert to figure out where he had been taken. He could see the city to the south as he turned the SUV from the dirt farm access road onto Sara Road. He was less than two miles north of the Sundance Airpark.

He knew teams like his were sent to four locations across the city. He was certain the bad guys received similar barrages from the big guns on the south side of town. The American command had suspected one location as the headquarters, the La Quinta Inn at South Yukon Parkway and I-40.

That had to be the place he'd find Mohamed Hussein along with the rest of his team of killers. It was probably the next target for ground forces from Fort Sill. Regardless, that's where Robert was headed.

He exited the interstate and turned onto Mustang Road. He was pretty sure he would be expected. At least the SUV was expected. Hussein had instructed the men to give Robert a long, drawn-out, painful death, and the timing was about right.

But Robert was driving the vehicle, not the fat, swarthy man left with orders to kill him. He could probably drive right up to the hotel without raising suspicion. He entertained the thought but dropped it. If the Army was on its way any time soon, there would be scouts on site. He just had to find them.

He drove past the entrance to the hotel and turned right onto West Reno Avenue. On his left was an apartment complex. It was likely abandoned by its residents, and "home" to a couple hundred invaders. He passed the apartments.

Robert turned the SUV onto Willowood Drive. Only a few days ago, these had been nice homes. That was before they were plundered and torched by looters. He drove to the last house in the row and turned into the driveway.

Quickly, he emerged and opened the back doors of the SUV. He was pleased and not altogether surprised to find a number of weapons in the back of the SUV. He took four items with him; a pair of binoculars, a .40 P229 DAK model with a Nitron finish, complete with silencer, a knife with a ten-inch blade, and a roll of duct tape. It was just enough to do some damage without slowing him down.

The next objective was to find the advance team for the Army. Certain they would not have driven anywhere near the hotel, Robert determined they probably parachuted early in the morning several miles to the west and jogged to their position. The most likely surveillance location was the tree line and brush at the north end of the vacant lot adjacent to the hotel.

The open field gave clear sight to the entrance and the parking lot on three sides of the building. The ten-foot privacy fencing to the south and west of the hotel eliminated any distracting activity in the background. That was the spot.

The soldiers would be armed, and caution was a must in any approach. He decided to cut a wide path around them before making his presence known. Robert jogged northwest along Willowood Drive, past the playground and park.

The trees at the back of the residential lots provided excellent cover. Robert made his way through the brush, veering to the northeast. He passed through another neighborhood before he reached the field.

No one was in the tree line. That was his first choice to survey the hotel activity. He took his position, retrieved his binoculars, and began searching for the recon team. The flat, open terrain limited the selection.

He saw them. Not really *them*, but a group of branches that shouldn't move together as they did. He guessed one man on the team checked his watch. It was just a flash. Not much to go on, but he was certain. A camouflaged team of spotters was less than one hundred yards from the hotel.

chapter 30

White House, Washington DC – 5:50 PM EST

Mike stood against the brick wall next to the window. He wore a pair of rose-colored lenses and looked over the shoulder of the agent wearing dark sunglasses. The minutes stretched out of time. Waiting was agony. Did they escape? Did they make it to the lifts?

Mike's comm. device was silent. Not a word had been spoken since the large group left the Dining Room. *They should be there by now*. He had to take the risk and use the comm. device.

"Raider Two, this is Raider One, do you copy?" Mike said. His voice was crisp and clipped, and just above a whisper.

"Raider One, this is Raider Two. Copy." The sound of Steve's voice brought a surge of relief to Mike. "First group away. Ready to proceed."

"What's your twenty?" Their time in the Dining Room was running short, and he still had ten people to get to safety.

"Moving through the Press Briefing Room. Almost there. Over."

"Roger, Raider One," Mike answered. "Move it!" As he finished, he could see the crouched forms of cloaked Americans scurry from the Press Briefing Room into the hallway leading to the West Wing.

Mike counted as he watched. He recognized Sam, then Steve, and finally Robert Nichols at the very last of the line. They made it.

"All right, everyone follow me!"

Holding his cloak under his arm, Mike ran for the stairway leading to the top floor. The American agents shed the Chinese jackets and hats and carried the weapons with them. He hoped they would all fit into the elevator. Carrying the weapons would be a problem.

They ran as fast as they could up the stairs and down the hall toward the president's bedroom. The doors to the Sitting Room were open. Mike charged through the Sitting Room and into the bedroom. He led the agents into the president's dressing room and to a shelf in the far corner. He lifted a small sculpture on the bookcase below the window, revealing a keypad. He entered the code, and a panel immediately to the right slid open. It was as he remembered. It was small.

"Everybody in!" he commanded. The agents filed into the small chamber, each one raising their arms and holding the weapons over their heads. "Hurry, hurry!" They squeezed tightly together. The last one barely squeezed in, but they fit.

"See you soon," Mike said and tapped the close button. He smiled as the panel slid closed, then he slipped the cloak over his head and left the dressing room.

Trapper Home, Washington DC – 5:58 PM EST

Elli watched her mom skillfully move through her kitchen, whipping together another evening feast. She was glad to sit. Her shoulder ached, and she didn't feel like doing much of anything. Sitting was fine.

Her mom was quite the talker. News from home, things the kids said and did rolled from her, story after story, often comparing their hi-jinks to those of Elli and her sister. And as always, the apple didn't fall too far from the tree.

Elli toyed with the items scattered across the kitchen island, one of Jackson's toy trucks, her sunglasses, one of Robbie's socks.

"Mom, why is it always one sock?" she asked laughing to herself.

"One of those real mysteries," Grandma answered. "I always thought it better one sock than a pair of underpants!" They both laughed, knowing the possibility of finding either was very real.

The glare from the afternoon sun reflected harshly off the cooktop, and Elli playfully slid on her sunglasses. She made a face at her mom, reflecting the attitude of a starlet. She turned on the stool and stretched. Suddenly, she froze.

A tall, yellowish, ghostly form stood in the far corner of the living room.

Highway 86, Salton Sea, CA – 3:05 PM PST

The desert was Alvaro Herrera's home not because he enjoyed heat or liked a barren landscape, but he preferred the desert because very few people would bother him there. He only needed a few to help with his needs and desires. Other than that, people were an annoyance.

The long, flat stretch of highway both bored and mesmerized Herrera. His mind wandered from the exciting times he had planned for spending his wealth to schemes of using the money to get more. The world was waiting for him to harvest its treasures for his personal use and consumption.

Still, he faced the problem of disposing Cero and Estefan. They simply didn't fit into his plan. And there the matter of downsizing from four vehicles to two. Moving his plunder from its present location into separate trucks would require a great deal of work.

Then it dawned on him. The crossing point. Three large dump trucks had been employed to level the fence at the border. Certainly the trucks were left after the army crossed the border and moved north as they were much too cumbersome to drive to Los Angeles. He only needed two but would have his choice of which two would carry his wealth back into the Mexican desert.

The idea pleased him. They would transfer the valuables, leave the rental trucks and then dump the bodies of his unnecessary companions a few miles into the desert. A perfect plan. In Jacumba, California, he would finish his quest.

A smile crossed his face. *Perhaps I will find more occasion to smile in the future*, he thought.

National Guard Armory, Frisco, TX – 5:10 PM CST

Lieutenant Jim Parker had witnessed the ritual in Iraq. Back then, he had been too busy, or the threat of attack too imminent to really watch. But for his friend he stood with the Phantom Patriots and did just that.

The four medics moved Will Mink's limp body with the tenderness and care one might show a child. Every move was discussed softly and applied in reverence. With a quiet command, the four soldiers lifted him and placed him in a body bag. Even zipping the bag closed was done with care.

It is a Marine custom for an officer from the fallen soldier's unit to accompany the Marine to his or her final resting place. Jim Parker had already volunteered in his own heart and mind to be that officer.

Will's body was placed on a gurney and slowly moved through the demolished building. As it passed, every soldier stood in respect. Conversations stopped mid-sentence. Every man removed his cover. A fallen hero was passing by. Jim Parker and the Phantom Patriots walked in a solemn line behind him.

Outside, General Maris removed his cover and stood beside Jim Parker as Minks was loaded into a UH-60 Blackhawk for transport.

"Sorry we were too late, lieutenant," the general said. "If we had moved sooner, well, we wouldn't be doin' this."

"Sir, I think he was hit early on," Jim said. "He had lost a lot of blood. He was probably hit before I called you. We were just so busy I didn't think about him not getting upstairs."

"You ridin' with him?" the general asked.

"Absolutely, sir," Parker replied.

The general nodded and bit his lip. Every loss was personal to him. The general knew it, and he couldn't change it.

The two men shook hands. Parker snapped to attention and saluted the older officer. Maris's old frame stiffened and returned a perfect salute in expression of a warrior's gratitude.

Parker hopped into the Blackhawk, and the crew chief pulled the large sliding hatch closed. As he looked out the side glass, the remaining members of the Phantom Patriots fell into formation. The props spun over the heads of nine soldiers—two mechanics, an insurance agent, a guy who drove a bread truck, a machinist, two construction workers, a dentist, and a kid starting law school. They stood at attention and saluted.

Jim watched his men as the chopper lifted off. The dust from the wash of the giant props stung their faces. These were ordinary men, yet men of extraordinary courage and valor. For that, Lieutenant James Parker was thankful.

City Hall, Lakeside, OR – 3:15 PM PST

Reggie Porter stood on the very spot he first saw the invisible Chinese soldier's face. The gravel was still scuffed where he passed out. *So long ago. So much has happened.* He heard a small voice behind him.

"Reggie?" she said softly.

He turned. It was Arla Dell, his wife. He hadn't seen her for a week. They had fought over his drinking, and the day came when she'd had enough. Arla Dell had moved to her sister's house two blocks away.

"Arla Dell!" Reggie's face brightened with a warm glow. She was smiling. "I'm so happy you're, and—"

"I'm very proud of you Reggie," she said with a blush. "Everyone has told me about how you led the Chinese Army to fight against those terrible men!"

"Well," he kicked his toe in the dirt, "to be perfectly honest abo—"

"I think that is one of the bravest things I have ever heard. Oh, Reggie, I wish I could have been there," she said sidling closer to him.

"Oh," Reggie shook his head and held a grave scowl on his face. "That would be much too dange—"

"Well, I guess it would be dangerous! Oh, my! But you were right there out front, like you weren't afraid of anything. My goodness, Reggie, who would have ever thought you were so brave?"

As he opened his mouth to answer a valiant attempt at the truth, he saw the waitress from Jenny's coming toward him. Corporal Woo was almost comatose, leaning heavily on the young waitress, only half awake. Then Arla Dell turned and saw the dismal scene.

Her smile vanished instantly, returning to her look of intense disapproval he'd seen too many times. "Why, Reggie Porter!" Arla Dell shouted. "You got that poor Chinese boy drunk! Just when I think you're a changed man, you turn your worst—"

"No, Arla Dell," the waitress yelled back. "He's not drunk. He just ate too much."

Arla Dell sighed with compassion. "Well, the poor boy, and so far from home . . . and his mother." She smiled at Reggie and slid her arm around the sleeping Woo. Reggie could never explain or understand her. Instantly, she was as sweet as she could be.

"Reggie, dear, why don't you help me get this poor boy to the house and put him to bed. He needs rest," she said smiling. "Then, I'll take good care of you, Mr. Mayor." Her smile would have sweetened a bucket of sauerkraut. He was mayor and a very lucky man, who was about to get luckier.

chapter 31

White House, Washington DC – 6:18 PM EST

The trip down the stairs from the Second Floor to the State Floor was nerve wracking. If the soldiers had managed to free themselves in the State Dining Room, Mike would be facing more than a dozen fighters he had disgraced. He moved slowly and deliberately from the stairwell.

He darted into the Dining Room used by the presidential family and peered around the corner into the State Dining Room where the hostages had been. It was empty. In the few minutes it had taken him to run up the stairs and send the agents to safety far below ground, the Chinese had freed themselves.

Why didn't they follow us upstairs? Maybe they couldn't tell if we went up or down? None of the Chinese soldiers had been in positions to watch the Americans escape.

He eased back into the Family Dining Room and reviewed his options. He could simply hide and wait for the inevitable assault to reclaim the White House, he could make a run for it, or he could make his way up to the safe room behind the bookcase in the Yellow Room.

"Mike, this is Steve. Do you copy? Over."

"Hey, Steve," Mike whispered, "do you have a twenty on the Chinese?"

"Yeah, we just found out they got loose," Steve said. Mike noticed Steve's voice had lost its optimistic bounce. "They've fanned out all over the Ground Floor. I mean, they are covering every inch. The officer went outside for reinforcements. Mike, they're looking for you. Over."

"Do I have a clear path to the safe room? Over." Mike asked.

"Maybe. Still a half dozen soldiers on the Second Floor doing the room-to-room," Steve replied. "And, Mike, they're all wearing dark glasses. They can see you. Over."

He had figured as much. At this point, the only people using the invisibility cloaks were escaping Americans, and the total number seeking escape was down to one.

"Right. Listen, I'm going back up. Check it out and tell me what to expect. Over."

"Checking now. Over." The pause of a few seconds seemed like minutes to Mike. He peeked again into the State Dining Room. Still empty. He turned to his right and looked into the Cross Hall. He could see the doorway to the Red and Blue Rooms but no farther down the hall. To lean farther out for a better view could expose him.

Mike listened carefully. The voices he heard were distant. Were they upstairs? Were they down the hall? Steve's voice boomed into his ear.

"Mike, do you copy?"

"Copy, bring it," Mike whispered.

"They're at the east end of the floor. Queen's Sitting Room and Lincoln Bedroom, but they'll be coming your way fast. If you're going to move, now is the time to do it. Over."

"On my way. Out."

Mike edged toward the stairs and listened for distant voices. The only sound he could discern was the ticking of a clock. He sprinted down the stairs two at a time to the Second Floor. At the top of the stairs, he turned to his immediate right, went through the Cosmetology Room and into the President's Dining Room.

The path with the least chance of being seen was through the West Sitting Hall. Mike hoped the doors would be open, and as long as the soldiers were looking in other rooms, he might have a chance to get by unseen.

He stopped next to the door casing in the West Hall. He leaned forward to get a clear view of the Center Hall. It was empty. Mike's cell phone vibrated in his pocket. He looked at the screen.

"Elli?" he said softly.

"Mike!" Instantly, he heard the panic in Elli's voice.

"Hey, what is it?"

"Mike, I woke up from a nap, and one of those things was *standing in our living room!*" Elli began to sob uncontrollably. Mike nearly stumbled at the news. *In their home!* His head spun.

"Okay, wait, say that again?" Mike asked, moving to lean against the wall.

"When we turned on our street, there were two of them at the corner that *looked at me!* And when I woke up, there was one *standing* in the corner of the living room!"

"All right, you're sure you saw one in the liv—"

"Mike Trapper," Elli growled, "I love you, but right now I would strangle you if I could get my hands—"

"Okay, I'm sorry! I know you're terrified, I'm sorry!"

"I need a gun!" she demanded. "You've got a gun around here, right? For the last ten minutes I've torn our room apart looking for it. I have to have it, right now!" Mike feared that was the last thing she needed at the moment. She was at the brink, and he knew it.

"Is your dad there?" he asked.

"Yes, but where is *your gun?*"

"All right, my old handgun is on the top shelf on your side of the closet. The shells are right next to it. Do you remember how to load it?"

"You showed me, and I have not forgotten," Elli replied angrily.

"Okay, honey. Listen, there's that old double-barrel shotgun in the hall closet. Have Dad get that. The shells are with it."

"We're going to fix this *right now!*" Elli said firmly.

Mike heard her sniff. She was crying, facing a terrifying unknown, and he was helpless.

"I'm sorry! Sweetheart, please be careful." Mike felt awful. He thought he heard something like a growl as she hung up.

He shoved his phone deep into his pocket. Elli needed him, and he was powerless. He didn't even have time to call for help. Even if help was sent, could he trust them? *Too much!* he decided.

Mike ducked across the hall and into the president's bedroom. Moving at a fast walk, he crossed the sitting room to the doorway.

"Steve, do you copy?" Mike whispered into his comm. device.

"Copy, bring it."

"What does the Yellow Room look like? Over." He wasn't winded, but his breath was short. He wrote it off to tension.

"It's clear," Steve replied. "Do you have the safe room code? Over."

"Affirmative. Back to you shortly. Out." Mike glanced into the room. It was quiet and empty. The stack of cloaks was to his immediate right. The bookcase opening to the safe room was to the left of the doorway. *Only eight feet to go!*

He entered the Yellow Room and moved to the bookcase. He heard the now-familiar rustle of a cloak and the cocking of a handgun, then a voice.

"Good evening, Agent Trapper. I've been looking forward to meeting you." The Chinese officer sat beside of the stack of cloaks. His pistol was pointed directly at Mike.

He let out his breath, leaned against the bookcase, and removed his cloak. Mike was caught.

Avenida Cesar Chavez, East Los Angeles, CA – 3:22 PM PST

The campus and buildings of the East Los Angeles Community College became the central location for members of the invasion, partly due to it's being named Cesar Chavez Avenue. Students and faculty had fled, abandoning everything, on the first day of the invasion. The advance of the Chinese and American forces was unstoppable. Those who had witnessed the capture of their fellow invaders congregated on the campus. The old baseball diamond and the solar-panel covered parking lot rapidly filled with men telling stories of the blinding red flashes from rifles carried by armies dressed in black. Some told stories of their survival of the assaults at Camp Pendleton a few days earlier.

"Have any of you seen Colonel Herrera?" one invader asked.

"We saw him at the LAPD on First Street a few hours ago. Why do you ask?"

"He had the gold and the plans for our resistance against the American Marines. Did he tell you what we should do?" the first man asked.

"No, they were taking the gold to a safe location to the north, but he said nothing of the battle."

"To the north, you say?" another man shouted from a few feet away. "Did you say to the *north*?"

"Yes, he showed us on the map." A handful of men who helped guard the bounty harvested from Los Angeles homes, confirmed the location.

"I came *from the north*, you fools!" he shouted angrily. "No Colonel Herrera came to the encampment in the north! He has stolen the treasure for himself!"

A roar of disapproval swelled from the crowd of several hundred armed men. They raised their rifles and shouted words of disbelief mixed with the guilt and the shame of being duped by a thief, bit instead of focusing their anger on the man who had stolen the treasure, they directed their fury at the American Marines who had dared to move against them.

The crowd was quickly whipped into a frenzied rage. Hundreds more joined the men on the field. The ranks swelled from hundreds to thousands in mere minutes. The shouting increased, and hoarse voices screamed for revenge and victory.

One man was lifted to the shoulders of two others. "Follow me! Follow me! We will face the Americans and win victory!" The cheers rose even louder as their new leader waved his rifle over his head.

The crowd surged toward the gate in a furious rant. As they turned to exit the old ballpark, they fell silent instantly.

Facing them along Bleakwood Avenue stood an army of small, ninja-like soldiers, hundreds of them. Shiny black helmets with facemasks covered their eyes. Body armor covered their arms, chests, and legs. Their large, black weapons were pointed to the sky. They stood in perfect symmetry and silence.

"Where did they come from?" one man asked.

No one offered an answer.

Stillness hung in the air over the standoff. Unseen by the terrorist horde, hundreds more soldiers dressed in black moved toward them from the north. An additional brigade deployed along the Avenida Cesar Chavez to the south.

The new leader, still seated on the shoulders of two men, looked perplexed, but his brutish confusion quickly found its way to a new rage. He raised his rifle over his head and shouted, "*Revolution!*"

The crowd instantly sprang to life and surged toward the army in black.

Sharp commands echoed through the ranks of the Chinese soldiers. The front row dropped to one knee, the second row leaned forward in a semi-crouch, and the third row stood tall. Another command and the bulky weapons snapped into firing position.

"*She ji!*" The flash bathed the advancing mob in bright red. Hundreds dropped to the ground. The throng paused but only for a moment. Their rage rekindled almost immediately, and they ran forward.

"*She ji!*" The flash from the second row of soldiers slammed into the raging mass. Hundreds more fell into the dust.

Without a pause the third command came. "*She ji!*" Again, hundreds of men crumbled to the ground.

From the north and south, more of the soldiers dressed in black swarmed into the area around the old ball diamond. Confusion overtook the army of miscreants spread across the field.

The same commands were heard to the north and south that brought the initial brigade of Chinese soldiers to fighting position. The armies moved with robotic precision and raised their weapons.

The men in the field froze. Slowly, they dropped their weapons to the ground and clasped their hands over their heads. They were defeated. Their cause was lost.

chapter 32

Northwest Oklahoma City, OK – 5:25 PM CST

Robert Hitchens didn't care much for military procedure. He respected the discipline, but keeping the rules and staying between the lines was more for the report after the fact than action in the field. He didn't have a radio to contact the advanced team of soldiers. He decided to just show up.

As he slid into the tall grass beside a heavily camouflaged Army sergeant, he simply said, "Hi."

All three men nearly jumped out of their skin. He wasn't camouflaged, he hadn't spent three hours crawling one hundred and fifty yards on his belly as they had, and he hadn't told them he was coming.

"Who the hell are *you*? What are you doing here?" The sergeant jerked to his side as a furious flush cross his face.

"I know, guys. I'm sorry." Robert introduced himself, and the tension dropped a notch.

"Were you with the three guys who bought it up north?" a specialist beside the sergeant asked.

"Yeah," Robert answered. "None of them made it?"

"Nope. They were KIA at the scene. How'd you get out?" the sergeant asked.

He told his story, or all that he could remember. He also told them he had a personal score to settle with one man in particular. The team filled him in on all the activity they had seen in the previous hour. It wasn't much.

"We figure there are only a couple dozen men in the entire hotel. HQ is hesitant to drop three-quarters of a million in munitions on a nice building so close to private homes," the sergeant said.

"Are there troops en route?" Robert asked.

"They're ready to deploy, but everyone has been looking for you. They're concerned you might be in the hotel getting interrogated."

"You have a radio. Call them and tell them that's exactly where I'm headed." He wished them well and quickly moved out as twilight settled in. Darkness was his blanket of safety and would give him the cover he needed.

White House, Washington DC – 6:31 PM EST

The irony was too much. Agent Mike Trapper was seated on a chair in the middle of the room, his hands bound behind him. He was a captive in his own country, held by a foreign army, in the personal residence of the president, and he was being detained in the Treaty Room on the Second Floor of the White House. The Treaty Room was the room in which major conflicts in the history of the United States had been initiated and resolved.

Presidents Andrew Johnson and Ulysses S. Grant had used the room for Cabinet meetings during their administrations. William McKinley oversaw the signing of the peace treaty for the Spanish-American War on August 12, 1898. John F. Kennedy sat in this very room and signed the Nuclear Test Ban Treaty in 1963. And, it was from the Treaty Room that George W. Bush addressed the nation announcing the beginning of the War in Afghanistan on October 7, 2001.

The depth of history surrounding Mike Trapper was profound. Literally millions of lives were challenged, altered, and many ended by decisions made in this room. The table Grant used for Cabinet meetings, and on which the Spanish-American War Treaty was signed lay on its side, pushed against the wall. *A desecration.*

Mike was humbled, no, humiliated. Bound like a criminal in the People's House. He was held by a foreign army in the residence of the nation's head of state, useless to his president, his country, and his family.

The restraints around his wrists were tight and cut into his skin. In his mind, Mike exercised every possible option that might present his escape. The more he thought about getting loose, the more his options diminished in number and availability.

The ten guards he fought earlier with Steve, Sam, and Robert Nichols stood around the room. This time they were not facing outside watching for escapees. Their eyes were locked on Mike Trapper. Each man had a score to settle with him, and each man firmly gripped a Chinese made QBZ95-G rifle. The weapon was capable of firing eight hundred and fifty rounds per minute. A thirty-round magazine on fully-automatic fire would empty in just over two seconds. Those were odds Mike knew he could not outmaneuver, and the odds against him were multiplied times ten.

The officer who had captured him strode through the open doorway into the room. He glared at Mike. His swagger spoke loudly of his self-proclaimed superiority. This man had commanded the seizure of the White House, and by the anger in his eyes, Mike could see that he was angry that the captives, his bargaining chips, were now gone. And that the Chinese office probably held him responsible for their escape.

However, he still had one chip, Mike. And now the officer would try to get the information he wanted. Mike braced himself. He knew the Geneva Convention meant nothing to the officer.

"Agent Trapper, we have many things to discuss, but first I want to bring a number of items to your attention." The officer sneered as he spoke. "We have searched the entire White House complex and found none of your comrades. You will be happy to know they seem to have escaped. We do not yet know how this happened, but I am confident you will tell us soon.

"You may not be aware that we not only control your government, but this entire city, as well as every foot of your nation's borders." His sneer spread into a smile, but not one of friendship. "You Americans are lazy and arrogant. You believe your technology is your salvation. Well, Mr. Trapper, our technology has overcome yours. You have no help from your allied nations. You have no one to call on. We have beaten you."

Mike shifted in his seat. He longed for an opportunity to stand toe to toe with this runt-captor and settle the issue.

"And, as a simple reminder," the officer said walking toward Mike with a very cocky air, "we have soldiers around and *in* your home at this very moment."

Mike felt his cheeks flush. It was not news to him, but it made him angry. *Just one free hand,* he thought, *just one!*

"For now, they are safe." The officer paused at Mike's left shoulder. He leaned toward Mike's ear with a twisted smile on his face. "How long their safety continues depends a great deal on you. I am more than certain you will be very willing to help us, don't you think?" Very slowly the officer drew a blade from a casing on his belt. It looked sharp even from several feet away.

"You see, I can be very persuasive when I need to be. So, let's begin with you," he said stepping toward Mike. "Why don't you tell me where all those people went?" He leaned forward and placed the blade against the lobe of Mike's left ear.

Mike gritted his teeth and glared back at the officer. He said nothing. The tip of the blade pressed firmly against his neck. Suddenly, the officer flicked the blade, cutting across Mike's cheek. He felt the sting of the cut and the warmth of his own blood trickling down his cheek.

"On the other hand, perhaps there is a better way to do this."
The officer shouted a command in Mandarin, and two soldiers
scampered to Mike's side. Each man gripped a shirtsleeve and
ripped them downward, baring Mike's arms.

"I'll just keep track of how many times I need to ask you the
same question before you break," the officer sneered. "Where did all
those people go, Agent Trapper?"

The point of the blade pressed against Mike's arm. Then, it cut.

I-44 & I-240, Oklahoma City, OK – 5:33 PM CST

Sheriff Perry Hitchens and Yolanda Vasquez stood outside the
mobile command center in the interstate median. Both were tired
and stiff from doing nothing. Waiting for anything was difficult for
both of them.

But the fresh air was nice. A gentle breeze blew through the
grass and carried whiffs of dust off the ground. The setting sun felt
warm on Yolanda's bare arms. The command center air conditioning
had chilled her a bit.

The door on the trailer squeaked open. Yolanda looked up to
see Colonel Crawford beaming. "We found him!" he shouted as he
stepped to the ground.

"Where?" She started quickly toward him. "Can we go there? Is
he all right?" Yolanda moved to the edge of her seat, full of
questions.

"Well, we don't really *have* him, I should say," the colonel
responded. "The little smartass plopped himself down in our
spotters' nest without any warning. Scared those boys to death.
Then, he up and headed right into the middle of the bad guys'
hideout all by himself. Never seen the like."

"He went in alone?" Yolanda slunk back into her chair. The
color washed from her face.

Sheriff Hitchens smiled at her and put his arm around her
shoulders. "Sweetheart, you're gonna learn some things about that
man today. He is the nicest person anyone might want to know, but

if someone crosses him far enough, he's one tough mother-f—," he coughed sheepishly. "What I mean to say is, that man has a particular set of skills that few possess. He's not one to be trifled with."

"Ms. Vasquez," the colonel broke in, "there are few men like Robert, and those men are an army all by themselves. Besides, I just sent plenty of help his way to pick up the pieces when he's done."

She knew both meant their comments to comfort her, but the thought of her Robert taking on six, ten, or a dozen men all by himself frightened her. She smiled, yet the fear lingered. Her eyes glanced quickly away from the older men, and then she turned to face them.

"Can't you do something to get them there faster?" she asked.

"Miss, our guys are underway as fast as the Army can move them. We just have to understand that Robert is already there and will most likely have the situation under control before we arrive." The colonel shrugged. "It's what he's been trained to do, ma'am."

Yolanda feigned approval. It still didn't feel right.

Avenida Cesar Chavez, East Los Angeles, CA – 3:36 PM PST

Brigadier General Gene Westrup watched the entire display of force from less than seventy-five yards away. He was both impressed and disturbed. Impressed by the precision and effectiveness of the maneuver; disturbed about the possibly of facing their advanced technology in combat.

"Very impressive, colonel. Very impressive," he said to his Chinese counterpart. "Total control of the situation without as much as a paper cut."

"Thank you, general," Colonel Zu responded. "But you must understand this technology is effective in very limited ranges and under specific situations." The two men turned and walked toward Zu's command vehicle.

"What do you mean?" Westrup walked with his hands clasped behind his back

"The weapon has an effective range of less than two-hundred yards," Zu said. "Beyond that, dissipation reduces the impact. So we need to be in close proximity. That creates a higher risk. We cannot wait. We must deploy and act within seconds.

"Secondly, getting this close is often impossible," he continued. "If we are dealing with a band of brigands such as these, it is not a problem. A more sophisticated force, such as your Army and Marines, would probably see us coming from miles away. These undisciplined rebels didn't know we were on the next block."

"This morning we didn't see you coming from the other side of the planet!" Westrup admitted with a blush.

"That is a different matter entirely, general," Zu responded, beaming with pride. "Your scientific efforts have been of great help in what we have achieved. Don't think for a moment we are unaware of your technologies."

General Westrup nodded with a tinge of pride. At the same time, he wondered how much high-tech American hardware the Chinese might already have.

"What's next on your agenda, colonel?" Westrup stopped and turned toward the colonel.

"Of course, these will be processed and turned over to your military police," Zu said. "Most of our forces will move to another sector. You see, our plan is to move, you might say *herd,* as many as possible to a location like this and deal with them en mass. It is much quicker and simpler."

"I get it. They run like rats into your net, right?"

"Yes, general, very much like that," Zu motioned with his hand and they continued walking.

"This has been most informative, General Zu. Now, if you'll excuse me, I'm going to head back to Pendleton. Our joint chiefs are to meet in a couple of hours, and I want to have a full report ready for them. Lieutenant Strattmann will continue to coordinate our forces if that is fine with you."

"Excellent, General Westrup," Zu replied smiling broadly.

As the general stopped to take one last look across the old baseball diamond, he noticed several groups of soldiers standing together with their heads bowed.

"Colonel Zu, what are those men doing?" he asked.

"General, they're praying. Probably giving thanks that any injuries are slight, and no one had to die today," the colonel replied. "I've seen it quite often."

"You mean the Communists allow such a thing in your country?"

"Officially, no," Zu said. "Our country may be restrictive in many areas, but we are not stupid. Many of our citizens are Christian—hundreds of millions of them. Unofficially, our leaders have discovered they are also some of our most productive workers and excellent soldiers. Productivity and loyalty are rapidly becoming very important in China."

"I'll remember that, Colonel Zu," Westrup nodded thoughtfully. "I'll remember."

Mainside Brig, Camp Pendleton, CA – 3:40 PM PST

The door to the Observation Room opened halfway. Sergeant Major John Michaels stuck his head into the room.

"Lieutenant Hamza," he said, "I spoke with General Westrup moments ago. He's returning from Los Angeles and would like to hear from you. He should be back in thirty or forty minutes. Just wanted you to know."

"Thank you, sergeant major," Hamza replied. "I'll be ready."

Michaels closed the door as he left. Caleb Hamza was excited. He was eager to provide the details to his commanding officer. But the real excitement was what was going to happen as the eleven men met each other for the first time. Especially for the first time since meeting the man in white.

chapter 33

La Quinta Inn, Oklahoma City, OK – 5:42 PM CST

Robert Hitchens entered the backside of the hotel unobserved waited by an ice machine to allow his eyes adjust to the brightly lit hallway. He was in no hurry. He would do this his way and in his time.

He listened. Music drifted down the hall from the lobby but no voices. Slowly, Robert moved to the hall. Peering around the corner, he saw it was empty. Surely someone was in the lobby "guarding" the entrance. He went the other way.

He stopped at every door to listen. The rooms were quiet. Every room was quiet.

He arrived at the back stairs and eased into the stairwell. Silently, he ascended the steps, taking two at a time. At the top he cautiously rounded into the hall. Again, he checked each door, listening for any sound inside.

At the sixth door, he heard music. It was soft, romantic music, not the loud Mariachi he expected. He listened very carefully.

Two voices, a man and a woman. They spoke and laughed softly. Their words were indiscernible, but it was clear they were having a good time. *He'll be busy for awhile*, Robert thought. He moved on down the hallway.

At the far end of the building, Robert came to the Jacuzzi Suite. He leaned against the door, listening to more than one voice engaged in a heated discussion. He listened to the different voices and counted four.

Carefully, he knelt and placed his head on the carpet. Beneath the double door, he was able to distinguish four distinct pairs of shoes; two to the left, one dead ahead, and one a few feet to the right. *The man on the right must have his legs crossed*, he thought. Only one foot was visible. That meant a slower response time.

Robert assumed the man he wanted was the one in the middle conducting the meeting. The others would not be a problem. He slowly rose from the floor. He had one chance. If he failed, he died.

He summoned all his strength and smashed the double doors from their hinges with his right foot. Robert was in the room before the splintered wood hit the floor.

Tuft! Tuft! To the left. *Tuft!* One shot to the right. Left standing was Mohamed Hussein, commander of the invasion forces in Oklahoma City. His face blanched white in disbelief. He glanced at his officers on the left and right. None of them moved or gave any indication they would ever again.

"So, you have beaten my pigs and cowards," he said with a sneer. "You fool! You have landed yourself in the belly of the beast! My soldiers are all around us! All I need to do is raise the alarm and they will come!"

"Then, perhaps we should remove that option." Robert stepped forward and smashed his fist into the face of the commander. Mohamed Hussein crumpled to the floor. The man was not a fighter, just a terrorist. Now, that career was finished.

White House, Washington DC – 6:45 PM EST

Death by a thousand cuts is no one's choice method to leave this world. Mike was beginning to think it might be his. The nasty little officer attempting to interrogate him seemed to be enjoying inflicting fine cuts to Mike's arms, each several inches long.

His left cheek burned from a three-inch razor slash that began at his ear lobe. The sleeves of his shirt hung at his elbows, torn from the yoke at the shoulder. Both of his biceps trickled angry streams from fine cuts that burned from his shoulder socket downward. The cuts weren't deep, but they were deep enough.

The officer stepped directly in front of Mike and smiled as he pressed the blade firmly against the thigh muscle in his left leg. The point pierced the fabric of his slacks and then sliced its way into the skin. Mike flinched against the pain and stared into the eyes of his tormentor.

Suddenly, the door from the Center Hall burst open. Voices shouted in Mandarin, and the soldiers around the room snapped to attention. The officer wielding the sharp knife stood at attention and hid the blade between his arm and side. The commands were loud and gruff. Whoever this new man was, he was not pleased with what he saw.

The new officer walked briskly to the center of the room and to the officer. Mike noticed the insignias on his shoulder. Two stars on a field of blue. He was a lieutenant general, the second highest rank possible in the Chinese Army. *Why in the world are you here?* Mike wondered.

The general looked at Mike. His eyes filled with tears of rage. He shook with anger. The general turned his gaze to the officer who had been torturing Mike and exploded. The words needed no translation for Mike to understand the general was violently angry with the younger officer. He spat on the man as he screamed his displeasure.

The room filled with dozens of soldiers carrying carbines like the guards standing around the room. Behind the last soldier walked a man who looked very tired. It was Wang Zhu, the Chinese Ambassador to the United States of America.

The general issued a command, and the young officer revealed the razor-sharp blade he'd hidden behind his arm. The general snatched it from his hand. Pointing it at the officer, he growled his words of scorn and judgment. Then quickly, he thrust the blade into the chest of the officer, piercing his heart. The young officer crumpled to the floor. Mike's mouth dropped open.

Both the general and the ambassador came to Mike. Their faces were flushed with anger and embarrassment. They ordered soldiers to loosen his restraints and called for medics to tend to his wounds. The ambassador was first to speak in English.

"Agent Trapper, I apologize for the injury inflicted on you by this man. He was part of a rebellious faction that had no authorization for seizing the White House. Please understand, much of what has happened in your country today was a plan arranged by *some* in our military when your president was assassinated, but not this. Please accept my nation's apology and hear our explanation of what we attempted to do."

"So, you're not here to kill us all and take over?" Mike asked with a measure of well-earned skepticism. He winced at the sting the antiseptic as the medic treated him. Mike watched the medic closely.

"No," Ambassador Wang replied. "It is important that I speak with President Makin. The general and I want very much to confer with him as soon as possible. It is vitally important."

"Would you have someone bring me that little head-set over there?" Mike indicated the small comm. device with the VLF setting. The general barked a command, and a soldier scurried in response. He brought the radio to Mike.

"Did you guys catch all that?" he asked slipping the earpiece in his right ear.

"Every word, Mike." Steve Granger's voice carried frustration and anger, but it filled Mike with relief. "Sorry we couldn't get there."

"Not a problem, Steve," Mike replied. He sighed deeply and looked into the eyes of the ambassador.

"Okay, here's the deal," he said to the ambassador. "Before we do anything more, I want every Chinese soldier out of the White House and off the grounds immediately."

"Yes, of course. That is already underway." The ambassador looked at the general who nodded in agreement.

"Fine," Mike replied. "Then it's going to be you, Mr. Ambassador, and the general meeting the president in the Oval Office. When your soldiers are clear of the premises, I'll ask President Makin to meet with you. We can wait for him there."

Trapper Home – Washington, DC – 6:50 PM EST

Elli slammed the magazine into Mike's .40 Smith & Wesson and chambered a round. Her father stood behind her, holding an old 12-gauge, double-barrel shotgun. He had seldom seen Elli in such a mood. She was enraged and reacting furiously to another threat to her family.

She turned to face her dad as she checked that the safety was on. Not a glimmer of patience or mercy showed in her eyes. He was looking upon the face of a stone-cold killer. His stomach dropped a little. He couldn't blame her for what she was feeling, but he hoped he could guide her and avoid a tragedy. He leaned the shotgun against the wall.

"Elli, please listen to me," he said gently taking her by the shoulders. "I want you to think about something. Are you hearing me?"

She looked at him and focused as her eyes cleared. She was surprisingly calm.

"Sure, what is it?" she said.

"We're going to go downstairs and confront whoever or whatever is down there. That's going to happen very soon," he said softly. "Then, one of two things is going to happen next. That person down there is going to surrender and reveal himself, or you're going to kill him right in front of your kids."

Elli opened her mouth as if to speak. She stopped. Her face contorted through expressions of denial, confusion, fear, and anger. She shook her head. "No, I'm not going to kill anyone, am I?"

"That gun means only one thing. And if the person you're pointing it at chooses the wrong thing, you only have one choice and a split second to decide if you'll pull the trigger." He held her gaze. Her eyes went suddenly soft and moist.

"Dad, what am I doing?" she said burying her face in his chest. He wrapped her in his arms and held her. Fathers never expect to see their daughters forced to be brave. Other things, fine. But gunfights and real bullets are nothing anyone ever expects.

"You're protecting the most important things in your life–your children and your home. We just need to be very clear with what we do. Does that make sense to you?"

"Yeah, I just didn't think about what was really happening," Elli's voice was hushed. "Hold me one second, please?"

Elli's father shifted his embrace and felt the soft hair of his child under his chin. Elli breathed deeply and exhaled two, long breaths before briefly holding the third. After the third, long exhale, Elli inhaled as she raised her head and looked at her father.

"I think we need a plan."

chapter 34

La Quinta Inn, Oklahoma City, OK – 5:53 PM CST

Rapid deployment requires special training and is not usually requested from artillery brigades. But the Army is the Army. All that is asked is that a soldier pays attention and gives his best when called upon. The call came.

In a matter of seconds, six Apache AH-1W Cobras dropped from the sky and surrounded the hotel. Troop carriers careened into the parking lot, and soldiers in full field dress poured from the back.

The "army" of Mohamed Hussein was taken by surprise while waiting for a second round of pancakes at the Bob Evan's next door. Nearly sixty men surrendered without ceremony, gently placing the few handguns they held on the floor in front of them. Not a hero among them.

Half of the troops stormed the hotel. In the lobby, they found Captain Robert Hitchens sitting in a chair with Mohamed Hussein bound, and on the floor at his feet. At the same time, three camouflaged spotters ran down the hall from the west to greet the reinforcements.

"Good to see you, Captain Hitchens," the sergeant spotter said, removing his leaf-covered helmet. "Impressive show. We filled HQ in as you did your work. Very impressive."

Moments later a handful of GIs escorted a man wearing only a pair of boxers down the stairs from the second floor. His lady of the evening was sent packing, unpaid. The captured man was beet red from embarrassment, and his eyes glared angrily at Robert.

Following them were soldiers carrying three body bags from the Jacuzzi Suite. The response to the terrorists' invasion had come with stunning finality. Quick and decisive action had been the rule of the day.

Robert rested his elbows on his knees and stared at the carpeting under his feet. The skills he had learned came back to him too easily. He didn't want a life that depended on brutality and the quick kill. That was why he left the military. The time had come to once again begin the search for a normal, quieter lifestyle.

Trapper Home, Washington DC – 6:55 PM EST

Granddad walked casually into the kitchen. Grandma's eyes widened when she saw he was carrying the shotgun beside his right leg. He put his index finger to his lips to quiet her next and obvious question.

"How's the donut business, Granny?" he said as he motioned her to move behind him. "Come over here kids. Look what I found." The children scurried off the kitchen stools and scampered toward their grandparents. Grandma pulled them close to her in the corner of the kitchen and hushed them.

Suddenly, they heard Elli's voice from the living room. "All right, whoever you are, I can see you, and if you don't tell me what's going on right now, I am going to shoot you!" Enough panic remained in her to make a slight tremor in her voice.

As she spoke, Granddad stepped around the corner of the living room and raised the shotgun.

"Grandma, why is Mommy going to shoot the china hutch?" Robbie asked in a heavy whisper, confused by the scene.

"And if you're thinking about making a run for it," Granddad said, leveling the shotgun, "you can forget it." Whoever it was in the corner knew he was trapped.

Silence reigned in the room. Seconds stretched.

"Please. Please don't shoot," a strange voice spoke from the corner of the living room.

"That's not very convincing," Elli growled at the apparition. The gun in her hand clicked loudly as she cocked the hammer. "Who are you?"

"Okay, I'm going to open the face cover. I have no weapons. I'm not here to hurt you, please believe me." The voice was as genuine as the caution behind it.

"You move slowly, mister," Elli demanded. "I can see you, and if you move one inch, I will shoot."

Slowly and astonishingly, a human face appeared in front of the china hutch. "Please," the man said, "let me take off the cloak, and I'll explain."

Reluctantly, Elli nodded and motioned with the pistol for him to remove the cloak. In a flash the man appeared.

"Cool!" Robbie exclaimed, peering around the corner of the room.

"Robbie, you stay back!" Elli yelled as she removed her sunglasses. The boy ducked back toward his grandmother. "Now, who the hell are you? You've got about ten seconds." Elli held her pose, and granddad slowly crept forward into the room.

"Please, Mrs. Trapper," the man said. He was dressed in black and carried no weapon. "Please forgive my intrusion into your home. I am not here to hurt any of you. I have been assigned to protect you."

Oval Office, White House – 7:05 PM EST

The Chinese ambassador and lieutenant general stood in the center of the room. Mike was by the window to the right of the Resolute Desk, looking across the White House lawn. Feelings of anger, failure, and injustice swirled through his thoughts. As a boy, he would have run into his backyard and struck the oak tree with a baseball bat as hard as he could to relieve the stress. That wouldn't work today. He didn't have a bat.

The room was silent with the exception of Mike's broken conversations with the Secret Service agents and Steve Granger in Pod One below. The words were clipped, angry. No one was the least bit pleased with this day. A great deal of explaining would be required.

Mike struggled inwardly with the presence of the Chinese in the Oval Office. Although the bodies of the two men who died there earlier were gone, their blood stained the carpet, an ominous reminder of unwanted events between two adversarial nations. He kept his back to the Chinese. He wasn't sure if it was anger or a show of disrespect. He really didn't care.

"Trapper," Bill Ketcham's voice crackled in his earpiece.

"Go, Bill," Mike replied.

"The last of the Chinese soldiers have left the White House lawn," Ketcham said.

"I want the entire area cordoned off. I want police, SWAT teams, Federal marshals, Secret Service, and the United States Marines on the ground, armed to the teeth, and about four feet deep on every square foot surrounding this place. Now!"

"Two steps ahead of you, Trap. Police and SWAT teams are being deploying as we speak, and the Marines are only seconds out. We're locking it down."

"Fine," Mike replied. As soon as he had spoken that one word, the building was swept by the thunder of AH-64 Apache attack helicopters fanning out over the grounds. Chinook CH-47Gs deployed troops to the lawn below.

The display of strength wasn't made against the Chinese army, but rather as a formal declaration that enough was enough. From this point forward, the message would be clear. Americans were ready to protect and regain control of what had become a cultural, political, and military mess in a matter of hours. While a nation dozed in luxury and self-acclaim, its sovereignty had been taken. That outcome was not acceptable, at least for many Americans.

With a scowl on his face, Mike turned to the Chinese ambassador and lieutenant general. He walked to the side of the president's desk.

"If you gentlemen will please be seated, I'll summon the president." Mike heard commotion in the hallway. Three Secret Service officers stepped into the outer office and let Mike know the building was being secured from within.

"Raider Two, do you copy?"

"Affirmative, Raider One."

"Bring him up."

Trapper Home, Washington DC – 7:15 PM EST

Tensions had eased dramatically. Granddad and Elli stood in the living room with their weapons at their sides. The young man sat on a straight-backed chair with his hands in his lap. Grandma and the kids were again in the kitchen, paying equal attention to the inquisition in the living room and Grandma's dinner preparations.

"Now, you need to tell me everything," Elli began. "You're here in my home *watching* me and my family in secret. That's just a little too weird. And who are you?"

"Yes, we were assigned to protect you," he replied. "I am Nathan Hoste. I was born in Wisconsin, a child of the Chinese Agricultural Diplomatic Corps. I attended American schools until I was twelve when my parents returned to China."

"Okay, but Hoste doesn't sound very Asian, if you don't mind my saying." Elli added.

"While in American schools, my parents felt it best to fit in as much as possible. We adopted the name from Dixon Edward Hoste, an English missionary to China who introduced my great-grandfather to Christianity. It sorta stuck." Nathan's eyes met Elli's. She could see by his look he was searching for her trust.

"You said you were assigned to us. Assigned by whom?" Elli demanded.

"By my government," he answered, "but please, there is much to tell."

"You bet there is," Elli said, her brow furrowing deeply. "Get on with it."

"I am an agent of the People's Republic of China assigned to protect you from any foreign agent or threat of danger." His gaze was steady.

"What?" Elli asked. She shook her head in shock and unbelief. "You're here to protect me and my kids from what?"

"Mrs. Trapper, there are three of us. We have been here for several days in preparation for the events happening today in Washington."

"*We! Three of you?*" Elli yelled, rage resurfacing, and quickly becoming explosive. "You've been here for *how many days?*"

"Elli," Granddad said stepping toward her, "take a breath. Let him speak."

She looked at her father and calmed herself. She looked back at the man.

"How many days?" she said in a flat tone.

"Eight. We arrived here eight days ago," the man said softly. "For several months, an investigation has been underway in my country. Evidence was uncovered of a threat to the president of the United States. We were unaware how far it had developed until the assassination last Sunday in St. Louis."

"But why are you *here?*" Elli asked. "Why in the world are you watching us?"

"Your husband, Mr. Trapper, was very close to President Marshall and her family. We were sent here to defend you in the event access to the president was attempted through your husband.

We feared they might use you, his family, to get close to President Marshall."

"You knew the president was going to be assassinated?" Elli asked in amazement.

"No. We knew of a possible plot to kill the American president," Nathan replied.

"You've been here eight days," Elli said flatly. "You were here late Sunday night when my husband came home."

"Yes."

"You knew about the people who were watching from across the street."

"Yes."

"Why didn't you stop them?" Elli asked.

"They were fools, buffoons. We stood near them every day. If any attempt had been made to enter your home, we would have stopped them."

"And when I left to go to my parents . . ."

"You nearly knocked me over in the garage." A grin passed over Nathan's face, and Elli remembered when she barged into the garage it felt as if she *had* run into something. She had.

"What about at my parents' home? Were you there?" Elli pressed.

"No, that was an error on our part," Nathan said with embarrassment. "When you left, we determined you were away from danger. We didn't realize they might follow you. We didn't know about the traitor still in the White House."

"And what about our privacy upstairs?" Elli flushed at the idea of someone watching her and Mike.

"We have never been upstairs. We know nothing of your private matters," Nathan assured her. "We are to be invisible eyes to defeat an unwanted threat, nothing more."

"So, do you have weapons? Are you armed now?" Elli pressed.

"Only these," Nathan said holding up his hands. "But we are very good."

"You probably weren't afraid of my gun, were you?" Elli said as a smile crossed her face. Her cheeks flushed.

"Concerned, but not afraid." Nathan smiled at Elli and her father. "Now, it would be best for me to join my fellows outside and tell them of our conversation. We will maintain our vigil from outside your home. I will also inform my superiors. You have nothing to fear from us."

Elli looked at her father. Granddad shrugged his shoulders.

"Okay. I don't want you in here anymore, is that clear?" Elli asked. "And you need to remember that I can see you."

"Very well, Mrs. Trapper. You may rest assured we will be here, but not *in* here." Nathan stood and pulled his cloak over his head. He vanished.

"Cool!" Robbie said from the kitchen.

"Hush, Robbie!" Elli snapped harshly at her son. She immediately put on her blue blockers and watched the yellowish form walk out the front door, closing it behind him. Elli sighed deeply. She needed to apologize to a little boy.

chapter 35

Oval Office, White House – 7:20 PM EST

The Chinese ambassador and lieutenant general stood from their seats as the panel slid back and the president entered the Oval Office. Behind him were Steve Granger, Samantha Long, Robert Nichols, Ray Jergins, and half a dozen Secret Service agents. The room filled quickly.

"Mr. President, I am pleased to introduce you to Ambassador Wang Zhu, of the People's Republic of China," Mike said, leading the president to the ambassador, "and Lieutenant General Deng Hê, Commander of the Army of the People's Republic of China. Gentlemen, President Al Makin."

The greetings were curt and not without an undertone of suspicion, especially on the American side. President Makin was clearly and rightfully uncomfortable with the events of the day and appeared doubtful of any explanation.

The president requested those who accompanied him to the Oval Office to excuse themselves. He wanted to speak privately with the Chinese representatives. Mike alone was asked to remain in the room.

"Please, sit down," President Makin said as he pulled a chair forward to face the couch. The president did not sit behind his desk. He wanted to face these men straight on and hear their assessment and reasoning behind the outrage. "I expect," he continued, "you have something to say that will help us understand the actions your country has taken today."

"Yes, Mr. President," Ambassador Wang said taking his seat. "I am greatly relieved for the opportunity to speak with you. Please understand that today's events, specifically here in the White House, were not at the direction of the Central Government of the People's Republic of China."

"That's a little difficult for me to follow since hours ago we were overrun by thousands, if not tens of thousands of your countrymen, Mr. Ambassador," the president said.

"Yes, your nation's borders were sealed by one hundred and thirty-six thousand soldiers of our National Army. That is true, and I will explain," the ambassador replied. "But what happened here in your office and the brutal treatment of your people in the White House was not part of our plan."

"Very well," the president replied folding his arms across his chest. "But that gives me little comfort."

"President Makin, we are very conscious of the competitive nature of our two great nations, both politically and economically," Ambassador Wang began. "We are also aware our nations have become more intertwined in each other's affairs since the mid-1990s. That relationship has strengthened our economy tremendously. It has also stressed our politics to a dangerous level."

"We know you carry a significant portion of our national debt," the president interrupted. "We are grateful for your investment in America. We are also grateful for your patience in the difficult times we face. But," he shook his head, "what's your point?"

"Yes, Mr. President," Wang pressed his hand together and leaned forward. "For many years, we have purchased American dollars to add strength to our national currency. More recently we have purchased vast sums of gold to add validity to our economy. There is still much to be done, and as you may know, change is difficult to accomplish much less master."

"I am eager to hear your explanation, Ambassador Wang," the president said. "Please continue."

"Mr. President, the assassination of President Marshall on Sunday afternoon sent a shock wave through our Central Government. We held high expectations for President Marshall and our relationship with the United States. Every member of the Politburo and the State Council was alarmed. Lieutenant General Deng was sent to our embassy in Washington that very evening. What had not come to light on that horrible day was activity inside the National People's Congress that amounted to acts of treason within our government."

"How does treason in your government relate to the assassination of an American president, Mr. Ambassador?" President Makin asked.

"Yes, I'm coming to that," the ambassador stood, took a step to the side, then he faced the president. "For years, decades, actually, discussions with our leaders have posed the question, 'What is the most effective manner of competing and ultimately defeating American global influence?' In the early years of the Republic, the military option was the most obvious since we had been at war with either the Russians or the Japanese for decades. We were a warring nation, many times to our shame, against our own people. But as American military might advanced, and with an ocean between us, the strategic maneuvering and supplying an army in a land war in America was beyond our reach."

"That strategic capability of yours has obviously changed recently," the president said dryly.

"Well, yes," the ambassador shrugged, "but please allow me to continue. Our next method of engagement was economic. We were able to attract many new business contracts using our cheap labor force. Our trade increased, but we lacked the industry, and frankly, the capital to compete with your industry. So, we sent our best and brightest students to America to be trained and educated, hoping they would return and help our nation to develop. Some did return home, but many—far too many—did not. Our economy and industry continued to struggle for years."

"Ambassador Wang, prior to my entering politics I served in the diplomatic corps. I lived through many of the events you describe." The president leaned forward with his elbows on his knees, spread his hands, and nodded. "I'm very interested in your perspective."

"Yes, Mr. President. When we realized our best option was to copy, and yes, steal your patents and designs, we found an avenue of success. Our students returned home filled with ideas and projects they studied in the States. We began comparing notes. Students worked on a project at one American university, while at a separate university aspects of the same study were approached in a different manner. We began to see the projects were related.

"Then, we sent students with specific instructions to target and enroll in your universities working on government projects. Military equipment, avionics, weapons systems, technical development of any kind became our primary interest.

"We were amazed at the resources available to us. We compiled information from students at many different universities. We learned to copy computer programs, automobiles, even space vehicles with remarkable precision. Our advances in science and engineering were unprecedented. That was where the division in our government began."

"You turned your exchange students into spies. Yes, we know that, but how did that create a division in your government?" President Makin asked.

"The younger members of the Politburo and our Army began to see the power of free enterprise, particularly in development and engineering. They pressed hard for reforms, allowing citizens to own businesses, own homes and property, also to have the freedom from the Central Committee to decide *how* to run their businesses.

Those reforms have come and gone and come again in different sectors of our economy over the past twenty years. The success of those ventures was undeniable, yet the older members of our government resisted change."

"And you believe this *division* gave rise to the assassination of President Marshall and the invasion of the United States?" the president asked.

"We suspected a conspiracy several months ago, but we had no proof. Suspicion can bring fierce judgment on a citizen of my country, but proof is difficult to discover when the suspect is a high-ranking officer in the Army." Ambassador Wang turned his gaze to General Deng.

"Mr. President, it was one of my immediate subordinate officers who acted on his own. He betrayed us," the general said.

President Makin could see both shame and indignation in the eyes of the Chinese military leader. A betrayal of the highest order had insulted his professional integrity.

"May I ask the extent of this betrayal? Do you know where it has spread, when it began, who was involved? Have the details been discovered?" President Makin asked leaning back in his chair.

"We believe most of the details have been discovered," Ambassador Wang sighed before finishing his response. "When President Marshall was assassinated in St. Louis, Major General Ma Chen spoke boldly in a joint meeting of the National People's Congress and the State Council, saying now was the time for the invasion. Weakened and in turmoil, he postulated the United States would fall in a matter of hours—"

"Actually," General Deng interrupted, "it was only a small percentage of the NPC that voiced support. The rest were shocked. The State Council was enraged that such a plan had been set in motion without their approval and oversight."

"And when did all this planning begin, if I may ask?" The president looked directly into the eyes of the ambassador, who visibly flinched with discomfort at the directness of the question.

"It was set in motion in the early 1970s, Mr. President." He was clearly embarrassed.

"The Kahmir Arrangement?" Mike added to the surprise of the Chinese.

"Yes. You knew of my country's role in this?" the ambassador asked.

"No, but we discovered several links to China through weapons caches found in Iraq and an arms dealer being held in Singapore," Mike replied.

"Renee Broussard, no doubt," the ambassador said. "That criminal was expelled from our country three weeks ago for illegal arms trading. It seems we acted too late."

"We believe the weapon that killed President Marshall was a Chinese-made imitation of a Barrett M-107," Mike said.

"Our attempt to copy that weapon failed." General Deng inserted abruptly. "The material used to make the rifle lighter proved too soft for extended use. The project was abandoned nearly a year ago. The prototypes we manufactured were to be destroyed, but they were illegally sold on the black market. Was that the weapon used in the assassination?"

"I'm afraid so, general. The Secret Service has the weapon we found in St. Louis here at the White House," Mike replied. The silence in the room was palpable. The commander of a traitorous Chinese general sat within inches of the man who had attained the presidency of the United States through assassination by a Chinese-made weapon.

"So, more than forty years ago, this General Ma Chen conspired with agents of other nations to assassinate our president," President Makin began. Both the ambassador and General Wang silently nodded. "Then, working with agents in Iran and the United States, arranged for us to bring students into our country under the guise of an educational exchange program."

"Yes, but the Shah of Iran resisted and would not endorse espionage against the United States. Our leaders at that time desired a more radical regime for their purposes," the ambassador said. He paused. Glancing at the president, then at Mike, he said, "The shah was, well, removed."

"His cancer was *induced*," Mike said, resurrecting on old conspiracy theory.

"Yes, it appears so." The ambassador spoke haltingly, unaware of how much the president and Agent Trapper might know. "General Ma Chen was not the only Chinese military officer initially involved. He was the youngest when it began and was the only surviving original member of the conspiracy."

"And his present condition?" The president asked.

The general stiffened and sat upright on the couch across from the president. His face flushed in humiliation. "He was executed Wednesday afternoon when his disgrace was fully revealed."

"And this long-range plan was left to the imagination of unknown persons in the Middle East to complete. Is that correct?" Mike asked.

"Yes, as far as we know," the ambassador answered.

"And Jalal Uddin?" Mike turned his gaze from the ambassador to the general. "Uddin is the Egyptian ambassador we took into custody for threats against the president a few days ago."

"Not an agent of ours but one of the early planners and the only surviving member of the original Middle East group," Ambassador Wang offered. "We know they used your southern border with Mexico to bring men and arms into your country."

"Several thousand it seems," the president said.

"Six-hundred and twelve thousand to be precise, Mr. President," General Deng said. A quick look from the ambassador signaled his disapproval of that revelation. "I am sorry. We only discovered those numbers recently in examining General Ma Chen's records. Your president's assassination was the call-to-arms."

The four men sat in silence. After a full minute the president spoke.

"Then, why are your soldiers occupying our borders?" he asked.

"Our economy is struggling to develop. A failure of the American financial system would be a disaster for China," the ambassador answered.

"Your currency has been artificially supported by money that doesn't exist, correct?" Mike asked. "Isn't the system almost like a ponzie scheme, with values shifting from one place to another, bolstered by double counting and false numbers?"

"Perhaps not quite that simple," the ambassador replied, "but not unlike the real estate disaster you experienced a few years ago. If the American dollar collapses, the Chinese Yuan is affected. For years, we hoped to replace the dollar as the world currency. We now know that effort would fail. Our economies, as with much of the world, are more inter-dependent than we realized."

"When we discovered you were under attack early Wednesday morning," General Deng began, "we used a system our students learned about at Louisiana State University to track the position of cell phones. I think you call it ALI mapping. Am I correct?"

Mike turned quickly toward the general, his eyes widening. "Yes," he said, glancing at the president. "Do you have a similar system?"

"Yes, but only of the United States. Our satellites do not possess the capability as yet. We simply tap into your system from China. Perhaps, I speak too openly." He looked at the ambassador who simply shrugged his shoulders.

"General, I don't know if that matters at this point. We employed your system to watch the events of that day. Even though we suspected an invasion was happening, we couldn't act fast enough to stop it. General Ma Chen knew the significance of the assassination. He also was aware that the funeral was the signal for the invasion. It was then he ordered a call-up of our troops and their deployment to the United States. All this was done before he addressed the joint session of the State Council and the NPC. His plan to seal your borders and seize control of your country was already underway. The troops were airborne.

"When we learned of General Ma's deceptions, our planes were more than halfway to their destinations, beyond the point of return. We decided to allow the deployment of troops to continue. We simply changed their orders.

"We knew your communications were interrupted, and activating your Reserve and National Guard troops would be delayed. There was no reason for us to wait. Since they arrived early this morning, our soldiers have been working with your Marines and Army units along the West Coast and throughout the Southwest," the general said, smiling.

"And your troops in Washington DC?" President Makin asked.

"They were under the command of a rogue officer closely aligned with General Ma Chen and some older members of the NPC. He executed the orders given to him by General Ma. Once we discovered what was happening, I took command," General Deng explained.

"Was that the guy you stabbed upstairs?" Mike asked.

"Yes," he replied. "Our troops have been instructed to set their arms aside, remove all invisibility cloaks, and establish billets in several of your parks until we arrange their departure."

"Mr. Ambassador, General Deng, I want to thank you for speaking openly with me," President Makin said, his voice quavered under the stress. "I'll assemble the joint chiefs and my key advisors to discuss this situation. We will begin working toward the earliest possible date that you and your forces can return to your homeland."

"Thank you, Mr. President," Ambassador Wang said. They stood, shook hands, and the Chinese left the Oval Office.

The president leaned back in his chair, sighed, and buried his face in his hands.

chapter 36

Trapper Home, Washington DC – 7:35 PM EST

Dinner came to the table slowly that evening. Elli sat at the head of the table with Robbie still on her lap. The confusion surrounding the man in the living room and Elli's firm rebuffing had left her son with hurt feelings. Little boys don't often understand big events, and adults frequently overreact to them.

The smaller children, Sara, Jackson, and Riley clung to their grandma in the kitchen. They had never seen their mother as angry or as violent as that day. Uncertainty or fear, or both, gave them caution. Granddad was busy putting the guns away.

Elli cuddled Robbie on her lap with her arms wrapped around him and talked softly to him. The words were private, prayer-like. Robbie wiped his eyes confident that no one was looking. It really didn't matter if someone did look. Elli turned her face to him and spoke in a whisper. Robbie nodded he understood.

Robbie had seen a lot that week. The president had been shot and he knew his dad had been right there with her. Grandma and granddad's house had been blown up for no reason he could understand. The bad man attacked and stabbed his mommy when she had always been nice to everyone. And his mom yelled and aimed a gun at the china hutch for no reason until the invisible man appeared. It was a tough week.

"Mommy, is all the bad stuff over now?" he asked softly.

"I think so, Robbie. All kinds of things happen around us every day, and most of it is good. Some will be bad, but I think we've had our share for a while, don't you?"

Robbie nodded his head in fervent agreement. "It's gonna be good now, right, Mommy? I know I'll be good." Robbie smiled and hugged his mom as hard as he could. Elli winced with pain and smiled with glee. The hope for good behavior can be fleeting, but forgiveness is priceless.

Granddad came slowly down the stairs to a rising cacophony in the kitchen. Grandma carried the hot dishes to the large table in the dining room as children climbed into their seats.

"Mommy, is Daddy coming home soon? I haven't seen him all day!" Sara whined and stuck her lower lip out in a pout.

"He will probably be late, honey. It's been a very busy day." The answer satisfied the puzzled looks around the table. Daddy often worked late. After all, he worked for the president of the United States. That was important.

Elli and her folks took their seats. The family joined hands around the table, bowed their heads, and gave thanks to God for their many blessings. After Granddad said "amen," Robbie spouted off, "And thank you, Lord, that Mommy didn't shoot the china hutch!"

Roosevelt Room, White House – 7:45 PM EST

The Chinese Ambassador Wang Zhu and Mike Trapper sat in the large, plush chairs at the far end of the conference table. The two men shared a great deal in common. They were fiercely devoted to their respective nations but neither to the point of willful blindness. Both shared concerns for justice, the pursuit of liberty, and individual freedom. And both men were fathers.

Ambassador Wang was a radical to some of his countrymen. To others, he was the future. China was changing, but change would not come quickly, and those who cared understood that. The old China, the China of the Southern Song Dynasty and warriors like the legendary Yue Fei, was long past. The new China lay decades into the future.

General Deng was overseeing the reorganization of his troops and discussing terms of departure. The huge stealth transports were called *Tí hú*, Mandarin for *pelican*, the original name for the cancelled American project. The massive planes were being fueled in preparation for their return flight.

"What time did the president tell you the joint chiefs would arrive?" the ambassador asked.

"Shortly after eight this evening," Mike said as he checked his watch. "Fifteen minutes, maybe a little more." Mike was drained. The cuts in his arms and thigh burned in spite of the excellent medical attention.

"Good," Wang replied, "it's about time to get this day behind us." Although the Chinese Embassy in Washington had been the focus of rival groups in China for two days, full knowledge by Chinese intelligence of what was actually underway was only minutes ahead of the real events. American intelligence was hours behind everything.

"I know there were hundreds of soldiers in the parking garage of the Old Executive Building across the street," Mike said, watching Wang closely. "Whose side are they on?"

"Those soldiers are General Deng's personal brigade," Wang said. "They were preparing an assault on the soldiers holding the White House when you returned to the Oval Office. It would have been very quick, but your presence stopped that offensive."

Mike swiveled his chair away from the ambassador feeling a twinge of foolishness. Perhaps a pause of only a few minutes would have changed the day. *And I wouldn't be sitting here all sliced and diced*, he thought groaning inwardly.

"We all considered your actions very brave, and each of us watching would have acted in the same manner." Wang looked at Mike, showing earnest respect. Mike nodded.

"Wait. You said *each of us watching . . .*" Mike slowly turned toward him. "What were you watching?"

"We watch your security cameras in our embassy all the time," the ambassador replied softly. "I apologize for the intrusion, but we are very good spies."

Mike looked at Wang. The ambassador was smiling. Mike smiled in return.

"Maybe this time it wasn't a bad thing," he said grinning.

"Our countries are so different, yet our struggles are so very similar," Wang said.

"What do you mean by that?"

"We both struggle under the weight of tremendous change and treat it with very different efforts and attitudes," the ambassador added. He stretched his shoulders and let out a breath. "Our culture reaches back nearly four thousand years, and those old ways are deeply engrained in our thinking and behavior. We cling to them, perhaps more than we should."

"And our nation, just a couple hundred years old, seems to want a complete overhaul every election cycle, right?" Mike replied. He understood him perfectly.

"Yes. Exactly. Why is that?" Wang asked.

"I think as Americans, we feel we can fix just about anything," Mike said. "Give us a little time and room to work it out, and we'll set it right. Every politician seems to have a new answer. It's the same as in business. Last year's model is, well, so last year. Now, it's time for a *new* one."

"Would you call that American ingenuity, perhaps?" Wang ventured.

"Ingenuity, arrogance, bull-headedness, I'm not sure."

"Creativity, I believe," Wang said. "It is our considered opinion there is a creative notion that belongs uniquely to the American people, your melting pot. Our culture has remained pure, inbred, in a sense. You have benefited with the best minds from every culture on the planet. It is a gift that perhaps your Christian God has given you."

"Could be, Mr. Ambassador. Could be." Mike's thoughts drifted to the historical accomplishments of the American people in little more than two hundred years. It was unique, imperfect, and unparalleled by any other nation. "You've thought about this a great deal, haven't you?"

"Since I arrived here I have been puzzled, challenged, and amazed by it," the ambassador confessed. "Even in school I was intrigued by what made America work. The idea of individual achievement was strange to me then."

"And now?" Mike asked.

"Not so strange," the ambassador smiled. "I am both amused and delighted to talk about large concepts in such a simple way. We should discuss this more."

"How about in my backyard with our families, over some barbeque?"

"Sounds distinctively American, Mr. Trapper," Wang said smiling. Behind him the door to the Roosevelt Room swung open. The joint chiefs were arriving.

Mainside Brig, Camp Pendleton, CA – 4:50 PM PST

Brigadier General Eugene Westrup and Sergeant Major John Michaels stood together in the Observation Room. It was late in the day for coffee, but it just seemed the right thing to do.

The two old friends watched the group of twelve men talking quietly in the dining hall.

These men were different. They looked different. It was in their eyes. The glare of hatred common in the others was replaced with eyes of clear and serene understanding. Their voices were pleasant to each other. They laughed.

With them was Chaplain Caleb Hamza, dressed in beige cotton pants, a matching kurta and an embroidered kufi, not as a US Marine, nor Muslim cleric. He was one of them.

Each man had had a life-changing encounter with the man in white, Isa. They shared their stories quietly with each other. Every one acknowledging the teaching they had received from the man in white dramatically transformed them from the inside. They called it the "inside birth."

The part of them that was dead, filled only with anger and hate, had been changed. It wasn't a matter of their changing their minds, nor were they trained in a new way of life. Their entire meaning for life and its value was remade.

As their time together drew to a close, the first to arrive was the first to be taken back to his cell, escorted by two Marines. Before each man left, the men remaining in the room embraced him warmly.

The last man to leave Caleb Hamza was Mustafa al Nubi. The two men spoke for several minutes before Hamza called the soldiers to return Mustafa to his cell.

Seconds later Hamza entered the observation room where Westrup and Michaels watched sharing reasonably tasty coffee. The two men stood as Hamza entered.

"Share with us your evaluation of meeting with these men, Chaplain," the general directed, pulling out a chair for the younger man.

"Sir, I have to admit I have never in my life had a more fulfilling experience. As far as Middle Eastern men go, they are a new breed. They have been changed," Hamza replied. His face glowed as he spoke.

"They do understand they will be detained here for some time, don't they?" Michaels asked.

"Yes, they do," Hamza said. "They know what they were a part of was wrong. They realize laws were violated, and they have a debt to pay to our country. Not one of them complained about that."

"What about the future?" Westrup asked. "Do they want to file for political asylum? They don't want to go home do they?"

"Yes! Yes, they do!" Hamza pounded his index finger into the table.

"But their lives will be endangered when people discover they've converted from Islam to following Isa, or Jesus, won't they?" Michaels asked. "I mean, didn't they want to execute that pastor in Iran?"

"They understand that very well. It is also something Isa spoke to each of them about. He said they should not worry but to trust Him. The Bible teaches we should not love our lives more than God, right?" Hamza said.

"Yes, it does," Westrup confirmed, "but they will be facing certain death. They know that, don't they?"

"Gentlemen, they came here to a land they hated, willing to die for a cause that taught them to hate. These men are ready to return to the land and people they love, eager to share a faith that teaches love." Caleb Hamza looked into the eyes of his superior officers. "Sirs, at the appointed time they will be ready to go home."

Porter Home, Lakeside, OR – 4:55 PM PST

Reggie Porter sat in his favorite chair. It was command central. He had a great reading lamp, the central position in the room, and the remote. That chair held an important part in many of Reggie's best memories of being home. Those memories, however, were few. Too many of them were lost in a drunken haze.

When those thoughts passed through his mind, he was flooded with regret. Too many foolish, selfish choices he longed to correct, but that was impossible. The past was gone, whether broken or grand. He could only hope for a better future.

Then, there was Arla Dell. She was a dear lady to him. True, she was quick-tempered and tougher than nails. Maybe that wasn't her fault. She was a great cook. And she could be funny. But, there was that temper.

The aroma from the kitchen was vaguely familiar. He was glad to have her back home, especially since his last real home-cooked meal was the one she threw at him the day she left. Since that ill-fated day, he'd survived on a mostly liquid diet. Whatever was cooking smelled good and familiar.

Reggie scrambled from his chair to investigate. The chair, a recliner, didn't return to the upright position with the same ease as when it was new. He wrestled the footrest down and made it to his feet.

When he poked his head around the corner, he was surprised by what he saw. Arla Dell and Corporal Woo stood side-by-side, rolling piles of meat, vegetables and spices into fist-sized rolls. It was the wonder meal Woo had given him that morning! And Arla Dell was learning to make them.

"Sweetheart! You're making those . . ." he paused, unable to remember the name of Woo's wonderful dish. ". . . things!"

"*Ziao long bao!*" Woo interjected with what seemed a broader than normal smile.

"That's the ticket!" Reggie replied excitedly.

"And iced tea." Arla Dell's smile was gone; so was Woo's. Reggie hoped that was temporary. He also hoped the pause in the preparation of the meal was temporary. But she was staring him down, insisting on his agreement. Poor Woo was silent, looking first to one, then the other.

It was Reggie's call. Iced tea or the fury of Arla Dell. He nodded and acquiesced.

"I'm for tea and that *zippy-long*-whatever," he said pointing at the food being prepared. His mouth watered at the thought.

Both Woo and Arla Dell smiled and returned to their preparations.

Reggie leaned against the door. He thought about the day's beginning with Woo helping him from his drunken stupor, then watching the Chinese dispatch the hooligans in the park, becoming mayor, and Arla Dell. A strange feeling began to rise in his chest. One he had missed feeling for a very long time. It was hope.

US Border, Jacumba, CA – 5:00 PM PST

The town was deserted. Law enforcement officers as well as all border guards and employees had been killed in the initial assault sixty hours earlier. Anyone opposing the invading army of terrorists had been eliminated. If one had survived that day, it was certain they were still hiding, too terrified to venture out.

The site had been chosen months earlier because of the long, straight road leading to the fence from the Mexican side. The three huge trucks had smashed into the fence at forty-five miles an hour, blasting a hole more than thirty feet across.

Much to Herrera's delight, the massive vehicles were parked less than fifty feet inside the border. It could not have been a better arrangement. The four rental trucks lumbered over the rough terrain between the highway and the border strip. The lift gates on the rental vans would be almost level to the bed of the trucks. The transfer would be simple.

Herrera pulled his truck to the back of one of the dump trucks. He climbed from the cab and signaled the others to park nearby. The heavily laden rental trucks lurched to a halt, and Cero, Estefan, and Jahor climbed out.

"First, we will unload my truck, and then transfer the valuables from your vehicles into two of these monsters. Let us move quickly. We don't have a great deal of daylight left." He pulled on the handle and lifted the back door of the rental. He raised the movable lift to its highest level. All four men jumped on the lift and began transferring their plunder.

"Freeze! Stop what you are doing!"

The voice brought a puzzled look to Colonel Herrera's face. *Who the hell could that be?* he wondered. He peered around the back of the truck.

Forty small men wearing the funniest get-up Herrera had ever seen stood in a line facing them. They were dressed entirely in black. They wore helmets that covered their eyes and revealed only their lower faces. Each man held a huge black weapon Herrera had never seen.

"Look at this," he mused to his companions. "This has got to be a joke!"

"Everyone, out of the truck! Immediately! Stop what you are doing and get out!" The command came from one of the small men in the black ninja-like uniform. He was the only one not carrying a weapon.

The four men slowly moved from the truck beds with amused expressions on their faces. They looked closely at the small army confronting them. They were Chinese.

"These little toy soldiers are going to try to stop us?" Esteban remarked with a laugh.

"You are Colonel Herrera!" the commander said pointing directly at him.

"Yes. How do you know my name, little soldier?" Herrera smirked. *How could he possibly know who I am?*

"The *soldiers*, as you may call them, the ones you abandoned in Los Angeles, were captured several hours ago. They were not happy you stole their treasure. We were told everything. And since you were driving rental trucks, each equipped with GPS tracking equipment, it was a simple matter to find you. We have been waiting here for over two hours."

Herrera's jaw dropped. *How stupid to forget the GPS.* His face glowed with a crimson rage. He cursed the three men with him. "How could you be so stupid you, cowardly dogs?" he said in Spanish. "Do you not think? Do you not have a brain? Do you suppose these little men can understand Spanish? I don't think so! You cowards! When I count three, we kill them all! Ready? One, two—"

Several of the 'toy soldiers' spoke Spanish fluently and understood every word. A sudden buzzing sound and a bright red flash froze time and space for the four rebels.

Weeks later, as Alvaro Herrera recounted the episode, it seemed to him that after the red flash encompassed him, he floated very slowly to the ground. Every muscle in his body had become rigid. His eyes were fixed on the small soldiers. He remembered every detail, yet he could not remember hitting the ground.

The four thieves, sprawled in the desert dust, were quickly collected by the soldiers, restrained, and taken into custody. The commander of the group pulled his phone from his pocket and dialed. After two rings, someone answered.

"Sir, we got them. All four are in custody, and the treasure is intact."

"Very good work, nephew. The Marines know your location and have two helicopters en route. Well done!"

In Los Angeles, Colonel Zu Cheng turned off his phone. He looked at the Marine officer beside him and smiled.

"Lieutenant Strattmann, we have the scoundrels in custody!"

chapter 37

Roosevelt Room, White House – 8:15 PM EST

The Joint Chiefs of Staff entered the conference room. For most of the day, they had been sealed in the lowest bowels of the White House complex working desperately to catch up with the events of the last several days. After much work and deeply appreciated help from a new and surprising ally, a foothold had been established.

Joining the president and the chiefs was the ambassador from the People's Republic of China, Wang Zhu. By video conference they were joined by Brigadier General Eugene Westrup, Camp Pendleton, CA; Lieutenant General Martin Crawford, Fort Sill, OK; Colonel Herman Maris, 3 ARC Commander, Fort Hood, TX; and Colonel Aaron Stevens, Mid-west Office of Counter Terrorism, Little Rock, AR.

Mike Trapper stood behind and to the right of President Al Makin. To the left was Special Agent Matt Kreiter. The others around the room included Major Steven Granger, of the president's Secret Service; Samantha Long, U.S. State Department; Alex Hodson, Federal Bureau of Investigation; Angela Crain, Department of Homeland Security; Ray Jergins, Department of Justice; and Donald Stewart, Director of Secret Service, retired.

"Gentlemen, and ladies," President Makin began, "we've clearly encountered one of the most defining weeks in our nation's history. Thousands of our countrymen and women have lost their lives in this outrage, but basically, we ourselves hold the blame. Our weaknesses in immigration, border security, international diplomacy, and in some cases, loss of common sense, have cost us dearly.

"High-tech weapons and extensive intelligence measures have failed to serve us in the manner we expected. It is time we review our positions and take steps to effectively re-establish ourselves as the strong and compassionate nation we are. It is my personal hope that as we review these events we will learn how, where, and what we missed that permitted this catastrophe."

The discussion of the timeline of events began with Donald Stewart, who highlighted details of the Kahmir Arrangement. Allowing foreign students access to American colleges and universities had sounded like a good idea in the beginning, however the flood of applicants seeking the opportunity to live in the United States was overwhelming. Eventually, many were allowed into the country, some without the required screening and background checks.

"From our perspective," Stewart concluded, "it was considered a gesture of friendship, but there was another side of which we were unaware. I'll let Ambassador Wang tell what he has learned. Ambassador?"

"Thank you, Mr. Stewart," Ambassador Wang began. "Many years ago, the leaders of the Communist Party in my country convinced Chairman Mao there was an opportunity for a long-range plan to work inside the U.S. When the Russian Army moved into Afghanistan, our leaders doubled their efforts to ally with Iran and Iraq, the principle benefactors of the Kahmir Arrangement. It was then the contacts were secured, money paid, and the plan initiated. The code word for the initiative was *Dragon*.

"Of course, infiltrating the United States government was not a stand-alone program. Spying, bribes to obtain military secrets, and flat-out theft of American technology were rampant. Eventually, Chinese students joined exchange programs and made the process more fluid and precise."

"So, even as far back as the '80s and '90s your students on exchange programs in the States were stealing our technology? Is that when this whole plan was hatched?" Colonel Maris asked by the video link from Fort Hood.

"No, sir. Long before that," Wang replied. "Chinese leaders were aware of efforts by the Japanese to encourage Mexico to invade the southwest United States as far back as World War I. At the time, Mexico was embroiled in its own civil war and had no interest in opening another front, especially against Americans.

"But times change, as do the actors in a drama. Rather than joining with the Mexican government, Chinese agents found better access with drug cartels throughout Central America. The profits of the drug trade removed the threat that China might be seen as the one bankrolling the program. It was self-sustaining espionage."

"You're saying the increase in illegal drug consumption in the U.S. was part of a plan to weaken the nation?" Angela Crain asked.

"Yes, the mystic draw of Chinatown's opium dens was a tremendous fascination for the youth in the 1950s. Little was known of the long-term effects of drugs at that time," Wang said.

"Creating an atmosphere of addiction in our nation was a plot of subversion?" Crain pressed.

"Yes, addiction was the weapon of distraction," Wang continued. "Our intelligence agencies were able to deepen their penetration into the affairs of the United States, and through drug use, weaken your culture. Insiders knew this as the *Dragon's Claw*, the hook. While agents in your Department of Alcohol, Tobacco and Firearms worked to eradicate the drug trade, agents of the cartels slipped into the States and vanished into the undocumented population.

"After more than a generation of planning and training, the stage was set. The borders of the United States were open and provided easy access. Agents working for China within the US Government acted as aides to men and women in Congress. They encouraged them to introduce programs that would create stress in the nation's economy during a time of financial difficulty."

"The dot-com bubble and the crash of the housing market," Mike interjected. "Both were brought on by federal intervention in the markets."

"Yes, both encouraged by our agents, but their effect was too small to bring collapse. Two earlier attempts to initiate the plan involved the World Trade Center in New York City," the ambassador explained. "As the figurative and financial capital of the free world, it was a natural target for those who hate capitalism. The first attempt in 1993 was a dismal failure. A resurgence of their efforts began with a new plan offered by the terrorist leader, Osama bin Laden.

"The use of hijacked airliners full of fuel was intriguing. Would massive destruction of the financial center in New York bring the free markets crashing down? As horrific as the attacks on September 11, 2001 were, they were unsatisfactory. Several of the hijack teams never made it onto their planes. In St. Louis, Dallas, Atlanta, Los Angeles, and Seattle, the alarm was raised too quickly, and the planes never became airborne. In the final analysis, not enough buildings were destroyed. Not enough cities were affected. Not enough people died for those men to call their plan a success."

"All this time it was Chinese agents working to destroy the United States?" President Makin asked.

"In a way, one might come to that conclusion. There was a small group of leaders in the Communist Party in China that wanted to destroy America," Wang replied. "But through much of that time period they simply gave their approval for others to make an attempt. It wasn't until the strain of two wars in Iraq and Afghanistan, combined with the collapse of the housing market, that the plan was propelled into action. Markets tumbled, the dollar weakened, and the opportunity long hoped for was in hand."

By now, everyone understood the assassination of President Harriet Marshall had been the signal to prepare for the invasion.

Both Mike Trapper and Special Agent Matt Kreiter presented summaries of the investigations, events, and actions taken over the previous five days. Samantha Long introduced details of the weapons smuggled into the country to arm a silent army of 612,000 common laborers hidden among millions of undocumented immigrants. Men and women who worked by day in restaurants, fields, and factories across the United States answered the call. Thousands banded together at assigned locations for the Day of Conquest.

The effort to explode the Oak Mountain nuclear reactor near Washington DC on the morning of the presidential funeral, and scatter radioactive material over tens of thousands of mourners was foiled by a small team of American agents. Mike Trapper and Steve Granger provided eyewitness testimony of those events.

But the explosion of the nuclear reactor was only a distraction for the larger event, the invasion.

"In the years prior to the assassination," Wang continued, "several scenarios were considered to find the most effective method for the invasion. They learned in Mumbai, India the most efficient plan required the removal of law enforcement. The ruthless slaughter of police officers and patrolmen and women was the first assault. The invasion was launched in coordination with the president's funeral.

"Our leaders knew that having a plan and making it work are two separate matters," Wang continued. "Factions inside our government caught wind of the possible assassination of the American president months ago. They confronted those suspected of leading the effort in secret meetings. And though they opposed them, it came to nothing. It wasn't until the discovery of an illegal gun-running operation by a high ranking military officer in the Chinese Army that we found the first loose thread in their tapestry of deceit."

"Renee Broussard was the gunrunner, and Major General Ma headed up the scheme. Is that correct, Mr. Ambassador?" Sam asked.

"Quite true. As we discovered the details of the plan, in a matter of minutes, or sometimes a few hours, we watched them become reality in a crippled and terrified America. Everything was already in process. General Ma dispatched an army of nearly two hundred thousand soldiers in our stealth transports to seal the borders of the United States.

"It was in those hours that the tables turned, both in China and the United States," Wang said. "When the treachery of Major General Ma Chen was revealed, immediate steps were taken to issue new orders to the massive army. The planes were already too close to their destinations to safely return. This invasion by stealth was the final step in the plan to conquer the United States of America. It was called *Dragon's Breath*."

Quick glances were exchanged between Mike, the president and Matt Kreiter. Kreiter had called it. *Dragon's Breath* was the code name he identified a few hours earlier.

"The orders were sent by the Chinese High Command, and the Chinese Army was reassigned to a new role?" President Makin asked.

"Yes. Those orders were received only minutes before the troops deployed," Wang answered. "They were not to occupy but to assist the American recovery."

"Were you aware of the fact that within the United States, tens of thousands of veterans of the Iraqi and Afghan conflicts rallied to resist the invasion?" General Westrup asked from Camp Pendleton.

"We had no actionable intelligence to prove it, but we expected vigilante groups to rise and join with regular military forces," Wang said. "We have studied Americans for many decades. We have learned there is an inner strength that makes Americans unique. We were not surprised when ordinary citizens took up weapons against the invasion. We have long suspected any effort to conquer the United States would be met by more than a standing army. That attempt would also face an armed citizenry, a most unpredictable factor.

"It was that unpredictable factor, combined with the logistics of bringing an army to America that precluded a land invasion. Our military could not have accomplished that during the Cold War. More recently, our financial arrangements in owning American debt to support our frail economy, proved to many in China that our fates as nations were intimately entwined. In the last several months, we have come to realize the collapse of the United States would bring disaster to China."

The ambassador paused briefly. The Americans listening were numb with disbelief. The evidence provided by the ambassador touched details known by the Americans, but the details were never linked or proven, until now.

"If I may continue, please," Wang leaned forward in a pleading gesture. "Regardless of the new orders sent to our soldiers, treason and treachery lingered in the minds of a few. Some Chinese Army officers remained true to their original instructions, particularly those assigned to Washington DC. Disregarding the new orders, an army of several hundred commandeered the White House to affect the overthrow of the nation.

"That rebellion resulted in the destruction and terror in the White House today. Those responsible are either in our custody or have been executed." Ambassador Wang paused and hung his head before continuing. He faced the president. "For these actions and events, we offer our sincere apologies and, as a nation, ask your forgiveness."

The men and women in the room sat in overwhelming silence. Those who had lived the story, walked, fought, and bled because of it, were exhausted. Individuals looked at the floor, the wall, anywhere but at someone else. Each man and woman knew they shared a role in letting down the nation's security. At one point or another, each found blame in their arena of responsibility.

President Makin stood at the head of the conference table. His words were halting, his face pale and drawn. Nothing would be as it was a week earlier. Moving forward was a difficult and uncertain path.

"I have decided to call the Congressional leaders together tomorrow morning for a hard look at where we are," he began. "It is my opinion that a Constitutional Convention may be needed. We have lived as a free people to the extent that liberty itself was taken from us. We must renew a conversation about how we think of ourselves, how we teach our children and train our workers. We must reconsider how we assist business and industry development, as well as how we relate to faith, both nationally and personally.

"There is no question in my mind that each of us must face the challenge of what we can do to help right this terrible wrong. I cannot tell you what to believe, but I can urge you to begin that inward search for an answer. If you pray, do so earnestly. If you once prayed and no longer feel it is needed, I urge you to look again. Humble yourself and begin anew. If your trust rests in the imagination and strength of human ability, we have seen that fail us miserably. I leave that challenge before each of you. The days ahead are of tremendous importance. Let's not allow this event to pass without serious reflection and forward-moving action."

The arrogant bluster of American strength sat in silence. Eyes bored holes in the desktop.

"This meeting is adjourned." The president turned and left the room.

I-44 & I-240, Oklahoma City, OK – 7:45 PM CST

Robert Hitchens hopped from the Apache the instant it touched down. He was tired but satisfied that his work had been effective, and that it was over. He walked toward the communications trailer to file his report, turn in his equipment, and head home, or at least someplace quiet.

"Robert!" He spun around She was running as hard as she could and leaped into his arms as he opened them.

"What are you doing here? I mean, why did you come?" His questions were muffled in her embrace and kisses. Tears ran down her cheeks. She spoke in Spanish too quickly for him to understand her, other than she thanking God for his safe return. Then, she held him tightly.

"Babe, why are you here? Why didn't you stay in Norman where it's safe?"

"We came because you were missing. No one knew where you were. Robert, I was terrified!"

"We?" he asked.

"Yeah, her and me." Robert turned to see his dad standing a few feet away, grinning from ear to ear. "Do you think I could keep *that* away from you?" Perry Hitchens shook his head, still smiling.

"Robert, where were you? Why didn't you call in? No one knew what happened to you until the spotters called in. Why didn't you let us know where you were?"

"Sweetheart," he held her in his large hands. "I was busy."

"Too busy to call me?" Instantly, she blushed at her question.

"Well, yes. Just this once. I was too busy to call you," he said, smiling at his beautiful lady. "Besides, I didn't have a phone, a radio, nor did I know you were here in the city."

"You're just making excuses!" she smiled and slid into his embrace teasing him.

"Yes. Absolutely!" They laughed and reveled in their joy of being together. "I need to file my report, and then we can go. Okay?"

"Yes." Yolanda released him and stood properly straight with her hands behind her back. "You go file that report and come right back here. Do you understand me, soldier?"

He bowed slightly from the waist. "As you wish."

Perry Hitchens stepped into stride with his son as they walked toward the command center.

"You're gonna have your hands full with that one, you know," he said, half in jest. "She's a pistol."

"Yeah, Pop, I know," Robert replied, "and I'm looking forward to the next fifty years of trying to figure her out."

The two men walked together as father and son and as friends. The deep respect between the two was their treasure. The addition of a spirited and beautiful woman vastly increased the value of their small family. They both decided it was going to be interesting and wonderful.

chapter 38

Oval Office, White House – 8:43 PM EST

"Hell of a day, Mike," President Al Makin said as he sat behind the Resolute Desk. "I don't think we need many more like this one."

"Never," Mike replied. "Or another *week* like this one."

An aide entered the Oval Office with the latest information from the West. Al Makin scanned the documents. "Mike, it looks like we still have a lot of people out there facing trouble."

For decades, United States armies had fought wars on foreign soils, but this time the fight was in the homeland. This time it was America's turn to fight back the invaders, and that was exactly what was happening. From vigilante groups organizing in their own neighborhoods, to National Guard and Reserve groups and Regular Army, Americans rose to defend their homes and families.

"People all over the country have answered the call. I hope they can maintain the strength needed to see this thing through to the end." The numbers and information on the documents before him were grim, but at the same time, encouraging. He looked up at Mike.

"Mr. President, I believe people will stir up that strength as long as it's needed. It's something in the American way. People tend to do whatever needs to be done." Mike rubbed his face with the palms of his hands and left out a breath. "And they'll probably do it faster and better than if they sit back and wait for someone in this town to fix things."

Al Makin smiled and chuckled. "We can help, but I think you're right. No one builds a house better than the man who is going to live in it."

"Is your family headed home soon?" Mike asked.

"Not for a couple of days," Makin replied. "There's something nice about being lost in the hills of West Virginia. Keeps one away from all this," he said, waving his hand around the room. "They tripled security out there since I came back to Washington, you know. Funny."

"I sometimes wonder if we shouldn't have done the same here. It may have increased the odds a bit," Mike said.

"Could be, but we'll never know," the president said as he stood. "Mike, get out of here. Go home to your wife and family. I'm sure they'll be happy to see you."

He walked around the desk toward Mike. The president of the United States extended his hand to a friend. He looked into his eyes.

"Thank you, Mike. You made a huge difference here today."

Mike's face grew hot. He hadn't considered his actions to be necessarily heroic, but he'd gone above and beyond the call. He put himself at risk for the safety of others and suffered because of it. Then again, that was just the way he was.

"Thank you, Mr. President," he said with sober gratitude. "Thank you very much."

As he walked from the West Wing toward his parking spot, Mike was struck by the stillness surrounding him. The helicopters that had brought a light brigade of Marines to the White House grounds were gone. He could pick out the Marines at the edges of the property, but just barely.

The thunder and threat of a thousand foreign soldiers was nowhere to be seen. It was as if they were never there. A gentle breeze stirred the leaves just beginning to bloom and carried a whiff of cherry blossoms. The contrast with two hours earlier was striking.

The work wasn't complete, though. The White House still buzzed with activity. The press wanted more information than national security would provide. It would take months to regain a peaceful confidence, and years to rebuild the damage done, but for Mike, this day, this week, was over. The last important requirements were to settle his family into their beds and call it a night.

Roosevelt Room, White House – 8:50 PM EST

Steve and Sam sat alone in the room. They had shuffled papers and looked at files until the room was empty. Steve could see Sam was suffering from stress and fatigue. She trembled intermittently. Her breathing was ragged. Sometimes she would drag in deep breaths, then bury her face in her fists.

He was reasonably sure it could be diagnosed if she gave someone the chance. He certainly wasn't qualified to form a diagnosis. He simply recognized the symptoms.

"How are you feeling?" he asked.

"Like I'm angry . . . and sad, about to explode, and then again, I don't really care." She looked at Steve with eyes that said it all.

"Dinner?" he offered softly.

"In a bit," a single tear streamed down her cheek. "Maybe a quart of Jack Daniels instead," she chuckled softly then hid her face. They had been down that route. It accomplished nothing and left them both feeling much worse.

"I just can't sort it out," Sam said to Steve. "Just when it all settles, and I begin to feel like its okay, something crazy happens."

"I can't stop the crazy part," Steve said, "but I want to be around anyway, whether it's crazy or not. I want to be with you, Sam."

"I know." A second tear made its run down her cheek, "But I don't know that I want to do that to you. I mean, look at me! Can you deal with this?"

"Does my vote count?" he asked.

"Of course, it does. I just don't know if it's fair to ask for that vote."

Steve watched the tough side of Sam wear away. Crumble. He ached for her. "Well, since it's my vote, I should get to cast it anyway I want, right?" He took her hand in his.

She nodded and sniffed.

"Then, I vote *Sam*, through thick and thin, come hell or high water, in sickness or in health. I vote for you, for us."

"Do you mean that?" she asked in a pinched cry. "I mean the *sickness and health* part, as in *I take you to be my* . . . you know." He did know. Tears broke and rolled down her cheeks.

"Yes. If you'll have me," Steve said. He turned her chair to face him. Sam was a mess. Her eyes were red, her nose was running, her hair was disheveled.

"Do you *really* mean that?" she said, eyes pleading.

"Absolutely." Steve pulled her close and held her as she sobbed.

"Did I just propose to you?" she asked.

"Close enough for me, Sam. Yes. I will, I do, thanks, whatever the correct response is, I'm all for it."

"Oh, good. I think I'm going to like that." She nuzzled her face against his neck and sighed deeply. Her voice turned groggy. "You know, we're going to need some help."

"Probably so, sweetheart. We've got some really great friends who have figured it out. I'm sure they'll help." She leaned heavily against him as he cradled her in his arms.

"Okay," was her only response. He knew this conversation would happen again after a couple days of rest. That was fine. The shell that protected Sam from the world had cracked. He'd made a way in. In time, she would learn she was safe. Really safe.

The Trapper Home, Washington DC – 9:02 PM EST

Mike opened the door to the kitchen and was swarmed by a tiny army in their pajamas. Sara and Robbie each grabbed a leg while Riley stretched from grandma's grasp to wrap his arms around his daddy's neck.

Robbie jumped up and down, blurting out the details of the evening. It was all lost in the noise made by his three siblings.

Mike played his part, getting sugar, wrestling with a tangle of tiny arms, hearing their accounts of the exploits of the day, and rejoicing that he was finally home. In the midst of the noise and excitement, he realized inwardly why he was willing to give everything. He was surrounded by them. He loved them.

"Okay, you wild rascals, it's time for bed," Granddad said, breaking into the turmoil and laughter. "You all got to stay up late to see your daddy, but now it's time to get some sleep."

To Mike's amazement, no one complained. Robbie and Sara bounded up the stairs knowing Granddad had a special story prepared for them. Jackson skipped along with Grandma toward the steps. Granddad took Riley from Mike. Riley looked at him drooling and buzzed a little motor-like sound with his tongue. His eyes sparkled as he slobbered on his granddad's shoulder.

Mike felt her touch before he turned to see her. Elli. She bent and kissed him while she slid into his lap. It wasn't a peck. It was one of those deep, where-have-you-been-all-my-life kisses that leave one breathless.

"Glad you're home," she said with a perfect smile.

Yes, Mike thought, *this is home*.

"Glad you're here," he said softly. He looked at her with a frankness that took even him by surprise. "I have to tell you, there were a couple of times today when I didn't know how the day might end."

"Okay, but I don't want to hear about that tonight. Catch my drift?" Her smile was disarming, but he needed to talk.

"No, I don't want to share the details either. All that can wait," Mike said searching for words to complete his thoughts. "But there was something different about today. I don't know what it was, but at times I felt invincible, like nothing could hurt me, like something was, I don't know, protecting me."

Elli turned in his lap to directly face him. The look on her face was almost comical but serious.

"Mike Trapper, you really don't get it, do you?" she said grinning.

"What am I supposed to get? What do you mean?"

"After three tours in Iraq, getting shot over there, being inches from the president when she was murdered, surrounded by deceit and spies in the White House, threatened by undercover agents at your home, jumping out of an airplane to rescue us, killing a man with your bare hands to save me, and who knows what you did *today*, and what's under those bandages," she said, looking at his arms with a scowl. "After all that, you don't get it?"

"I guess not. What am I supposed to get?" Mike felt like an idiot for not seeing what Elli was driving at.

"Mike, we pray for you *all the time!*" Elli said earnestly as she touched his cheek. "While you were overseas and I was at the folks' house, there wasn't a meal that passed, a day that went by, that we didn't desperately seek God's protection for you. Every night the kids pray that Jesus will keep you and protect you from danger. When you came home from St. Louis and the kids charged into our bed, they took your safe return as an answer to *their prayers!*"

Suddenly, Mike knew he did get it, and for too long he'd let it ride. A long-forgotten memory found its way from the shadows of his mind. A memory of a little boy asking God to make his life count for others. Mike remembered that when he had asked that from God, he had experienced the strangest feeling of approval, and gentle love.

"Yeah," he said softly. "I get it. I've kept all that on the back burner for a long time. I guess I have some past-due accounts to balance."

"Honey, you can never balance that account, but we can be thankful the account is still open."

Mike's eyes welled with tears. His mind swarmed with mental snapshots of the kids, Elli, all of them together.

"You know, I don't know how to do this," Mike admitted sheepishly.

"Don't you worry about a thing," Elli said with a broad smile. Her eyes glistened. "I can handle it."

Together, Mike and Elli slipped to their knees, and, for the first time, they prayed together.

It was the beginning.

A Note from the Author

Of course, the story in the *Oak Mountain Trilogy* is fiction. Real locations host the actions and lives of imagined characters playing an actor's role in fantasy. Yet, fiction speaks to us on many levels that allow us to experience joy, danger, heroism, or loss, without living the encounter.

This is such a story. It is a tale of the call that carries men and women beyond themselves, past their abilities and comforts, into uncertainty. The story reveals the visceral drive to preserve and protect loved ones, and the nobility required to persevere to the end.

Throughout history, peoples and nations have been called to stand against the attack of an enemy. People rise to fight destruction and, in some cases, extinction. Victory is the goal. It is not a guaranteed outcome. In the end, someone must lose. Nobility is not found in victory. Nobility is found in rising to face the onslaught.

On September 11, 2001, the United States of America faced such an attack and in a noble response rose as a nation to right the wrong, punish the aggressor, and set things "right" once again. We saw the same happen on December 7, 1941, with the attack on Pearl Harbor. An unexpected assault awoke a sleeping giant that, once roused, changed the world and altered another man's objective to dominate it.

When events of that magnitude occur, a nation is "cut to the core," laid bare for all to see. We discover what really lies within us, whether it is bravery, rage, nobility or fear. We see who and what we are.

We never see who we really are until the layers of arrogance are peeled away to reveal our core. It is then we either withdraw in fear or stand to answer the call to defend what we believe. Then, and only then, can redemption begin its work.

It is this writer's conviction that the goal and purpose in life is not attaining power or wealth, accomplishing great feats of strength or wonder, or writing the world's best novel. Rather, as individuals our purpose is to come to the revelation of who we are, what is in us, and to begin the process of pursuing a worthy goal. If the highest goal is to serve others beyond one's self, it is noble. If the call is to the character and nature of God, it is holy.

Redemption is the deliverance or liberation from oppression. It is the act of taking one's emancipation or salvation from that oppressor. When a nation bears the struggle for redemption, the effort is immense and costly in both blood and treasure. When we as men and women encounter the struggle for redemption, it costs our pride, our anger, our imaginations, and sometimes, although rarely, life itself.

We are given a free choice to pursue redemption from a self-centered life and the snares that entangle us. Unseen adversaries plot our destruction without our being aware. Political pride and religious arrogance blind us, but a path beyond the morass of confusion and deceit does exist.

That is the story in *Oak Mountain,* a tale of deception and loss. A powerful enemy engages in a plan to destroy a nation. It is the same in life. We have adversaries we must face or suffer their oppression. These spiritual foes attack suddenly and without warning, through circumstances and emotions, seeking to distract us and rip life itself from our grasp. The attacks continue without mercy, robbing us of safety and protection. *Eagle Pass* shares the narrative of that thievery. An enemy comes like a thief in the night to steal our presumed safety and relentlessly barrage us for our failures. Finally, in *Dragon's Breath,* we encounter two arenas of thought: We learn we can stand against our unseen enemy and win. We also discover the dragon we may espouse as our worst foe, is not. He may, in fact, be our salvation.

This writing is not saying that China is God, like God, or anything else, but rather to illustrate a concept. To the natural man, the enemy of his life is God. The spiritual man has his eyes open to the mystery that God, in Christ Jesus, is his Redeemer. It is the hope of this writer that, as mere men, we discover the honesty and courage required to peel off those layers of arrogance that insulate us from others, and that we learn who we are intended to be in the full purpose of His Redemption.

"The weapons we fight with are not the weapons of the world. On the contrary, they have divine power to demolish strongholds. We demolish arguments and every pretension that sets itself up against the knowledge of God, and we take captive every thought to make it obedient to Christ."
2 Corinthians 10: 4-5

Stephen T. Gerdel
February 28, 2012